Kitt
All good things

CENTRAL   c.l

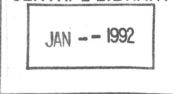
SO-AUI-618

CENTRAL LIBRARY

JAN -- 1992

OCT 17 1984

All Good Things

All Good Things

SANDRA KITT

DOUBLEDAY & COMPANY, INC.
GARDEN CITY, NEW YORK 1984

To Nana, a Gullah, who left
her own unique love and magic behind.

*All of the characters in this book
are fictitious, and any resemblance
to actual persons, living or dead,
is purely coincidental.*

Library of Congress Cataloging in Publication Data

Kitt, Sandra.
All good things.

I. Title.
PS3561.I86A78   1984   813'.54
ISBN: 0-385-19508-7

Library of Congress Catalog Card Number 84-4055
Copyright © 1984 by Sandra Kitt
All Rights Reserved
Printed in the United States of America
First Edition

All Good Things

CHAPTER ONE

By the time the car pulled to a stop in front of the boarding-house, Jacqueline felt like a limp cloth. Rivulets of moisture trickled down her neck and shoulder blades. Her curls hung in loose ringlets, some clinging damply to her forehead and neck. Although the car windows were open it still felt stifling and humid in the car, and she was glad to finally be able to get out and breathe natural air, thick and still as it was.

Jackie pushed her red-framed sunglasses onto the top of her head and opening the car door, gracefully swung her slender five-feet-seven-inch frame out to a standing position. She squinted at the lopsided numbers on the door of the green house in front of her to make sure she had the right address. Absently reaching behind her, her fingers gingerly pulled the thin fabric of her white blouse away from the wet skin it had been plastered against for hours.

Jackie briefly bent back into the car, gathering her bag, a map, and car keys. A car went past her and someone whistled appreciatively at her rather provocative stance, her incredible long legs encased in jeans.

"Hey, mama!" a fading voice shouted as the passing car moved off down the street. But Jackie ignored the voice as she stood up and slammed the car door closed.

Suddenly the door to the green house jerked open and a middle-aged woman, small in stature but very round otherwise, came out with a wide smile of welcome on her mahogany face. The smile and open countenance of the woman did much toward loosening the nervous knot in Jackie's stomach. She walked straight and tall to the front of the house, looking up at the woman on the top step. The woman spoke before Jackie could say anything.

"I know you must be Jacqueline Taylor. You're just as pretty as Gwen said you'd be! Come on in here, darlin', let me get you somethin' nice and cool to drink. I swear you picked the hottest part of the day to be travelin'!"

The rotund cheerful figure turned back to the house keeping up a steady stream of chatter. A bemused Jackie followed mutely behind her. She was immediately hit by a wave of cool air from the interior of the house, and she let out a sigh of relief. She followed the woman into a foyer and then off to the right into a large sunlit parlor that was also relatively cool.

"I was expectin' you sometime late this afternoon, but soon as I heard the car in front of the house I said to Timothy, that's her! I know that's her!" and she shook her head chuckling, her teeth flashing bright momentarily in the dark features of her face.

"It's very nice to meet you, Mrs. Curtis." Jackie extended a hand. The woman was forced to tilt her head back and look up into Jackie's face.

"You sure are tall!" Mrs. Curtis commented with a grin, taking Jackie's hand firmly. "And call me Hannah. I stopped being Mrs. Curtis when Mr. Curtis died! Go on now. Sit down and catch your breath. I'll get us some tea!" Fluttering her hands in the air she turned into a room at the back of the parlor.

Jackie stood a moment looking around the old-fashioned parlor with its threadbare oriental carpet, and the doilies on the chair arms and backs. A grandfather clock just inside the archway to the parlor rhythmically ticked. There was also a fireplace, at the moment filled with a profusion of potted plants and flowers. It gave the room a homey, comfortable fragrance and feel. Jackie walked over to a Victorian love seat in front of the parlor window and sitting down, put her bag and map on the floor. She warily removed her glasses and used the tips of her fingers to pick and fluff up the flattened curls. Jackie relaxed against the old cushions of the chair and settled into being in the old house. She was suddenly very grateful that she'd let her best friend, Gwen Owens, talk her into this arrangement of staying in a boardinghouse, rather than a sterile hotel room for a month while she completed her half of the assignment.

She brushed her damp hands down her denimed thigh, thinking how far she'd come in two years—from a New York model with steady work and bookings, with first class accommodations at the finest hotels to being a struggling photographer. Here she was in a strange city trying to finish a book with a friend and only a half promise that it would ever be published. Jackie was just thinking how much more comfortable half promises were than lightly made promises that were never kept when Hannah Curtis came back carefully balancing a tray. She slowly lowered it to a glass-topped round coffee table, and sat down next to Jackie.

"Gwen has told me so much about you," Hannah said passing a glass to Jackie, condensation making the glass cold and slippery in her hands. "She said you two met in New York and that you modeled together?"

"That's right," Jackie answered after sampling the sweetened tea. "I was studying at New York University in my freshman year when Gwen arrived. We met at a party and became friends. The first time she went for an interview at an agency she asked if I'd go along to keep her company. She was very nervous."

"She shouldn't have been. Gwen has lots of presence, and so much flair! Why, when she was a little girl she always used to say, 'Aunt Hannah, I'm gonna be famous someday!' Well, she's almost gone and done it!"

Jackie smiled ruefully. "Yes . . . she certainly has. When Gwen sets her mind to doing something, it's as good as done. I just didn't expect to be pulled along with her. It was a real surprise when the agency signed both of us."

Hannah laughed merrily, her ample bosom rocking up and down with the sound. "Just goes to show those people have good taste, darlin'. And it must have been fun wearing all those nice clothes and making so much money."

Jackie lowered her eyes, twirling the ice in her glass. Her full bottom lip pouted out slightly and she shrugged. "I suppose," she responded vaguely.

She supposed it all had been fun, getting caught up in the magic of makeup and designer clothes, being photographed by the best, being fawned over and protected by an agent, seeing her face everywhere—and earning so much money. She'd never been able to reconcile being paid what she considered outrageous sums for just being pretty and wearing clothes well. But right now she was grateful because the money she'd saved gave her time to now find out if she could really be a good photographer.

It had all been fun also, until she'd realized her insides needed as much attention as the outside was getting. She didn't want to be just pretty decoration. There was much more to her than that. And, it had all been fun until Mark. Hannah's voice broke into her thoughts.

"Despite all the fun and clothes, I always tell Gwen don't lose her bearings. Always remember to take care of herself, and always remember home. Where is home for you, darlin'?"

"I've always lived in New York with my mother. My parents divorced when I was nine. My father remarried and moved to California. I haven't seen him in about five years."

Hannah tisked in sympathy. "Don't you have any sisters or brothers?"

"No, there's just me. I always wished I had an older sister to talk to, but . . . it didn't work out that way."

Hannah sighed, shaking her head slowly, "No, darlin', sometimes it sure don't!"

"Gwen told me you were like a second mother to her."

"Lord, yes! Her mother and I were best friends. Mr. Curtis and I were never blessed with children of our own, but I never hesitated to share mothering Gwen and her older brother." She looked rather knowingly at Jackie. "And now I have another one to watch over. Gwen said that you'd been through a lot of changes lately . . . had a bit of a rough time."

Hannah's soft drawling voice trailed off as she watched Jackie, expecting her to pick up the threads of the story. But Jackie stiffened immediately, gathering her defenses around her. She wasn't ready to have casual conversation about her disastrous marriage to Mark and subsequent divorce. Nor was she willing to explain her reasons for dropping out of modeling at the very peak of her career. Deliberately misunderstanding Hannah Curtis' probing comment, Jackie forced a smile to her stiff facial features.

"Gwen exaggerates. We wanted to do this book together and we never realized it would be so much work."

Hannah pursed her lips together and nodded. "I see . . ."

"And it's hard with Gwen in New York writing the copy and me here alone to take pictures. Gwen knows Charleston—I don't!"

Distracted, Hannah chuckled softly. "That girl always did

have three or four irons in the fire at once. Tell me about your book. What's it to be on?"

Jackie finished her tea and set the empty glass on the tray, taking a cream-colored linen napkin to wipe her hands. "Well, Gwen is always talking about Charleston and how wonderful the city and people are. But she says she's always wanted to do a book on the families on and around Johns Island."

"Johns Island . . ." Hannah mused softly. "Why, that used to be a very pretty area. Lots of small farms with plenty of fruit trees and beautiful flowers. The people there have always been friendly."

"Gwen said so. But I think it's the past, the old history that fascinates her. It seems the Gullahs have a unique language dialect, and some of the cultural aspects of the blacks there are still very West African."

"Well, it's true the people are different down there, but I don't see how you're going to get a whole book out of it! And not all of it is pretty."

"I'm not necessarily looking for pretty," Jackie said carefully, struck with the thought that pretty didn't necessarily mean good, or better than. "Gwen says the Gullahs have a heritage that spans not only generations, but an ocean, and still continues."

Hannah frowned and shook her head, her brown work-roughened hands habitually patting her thighs. "I don't know much about that, but I'm sure there are people who live around there who'd be happy to talk to you. And the town library will be filled with books on it. You know, the people here are proud of Carolina history. I'm sure you'll find all you need to know about Johns Island."

"Mostly, I need to take pictures. I thought I'd drive around this afternoon and get acquainted with the layout of Charleston. Maybe drive outside of town."

"Oh there's plenty of time for that, darlin'. Now you just come with me and I'll show you your room. You probably want to shower and change your clothes."

Already she was up and moving toward the stairs and Jackie had no choice but to follow. The stairs creaked and groaned under their footsteps, and the dark wood of the banister was worn smooth and shiny by many hands over the years. Jackie could smell the faint odor of lemon oil in the wood grain. It made her smile. This house had been lived in, and used well.

Hannah opened a door onto a room at the side of the house. It was moderately lit with sun and the outside light falling on the few pieces of wood furniture covered in ecru lace and pastel cotton was like a hand-painted sepia photograph. Jackie smiled again at the pure country aura of the room, knowing that if she turned her head, there would be a double four-poster bed against the wall complete with dust ruffles and shammed covered pillows. She looked and was right.

Hannah showed her the bathroom, a large closet, and the back stairs leading down to the kitchen and dining nook. She gave Jackie keys to the house and told her this was her home for as long as she wished. She could come and go as she pleased.

Jackie retrieved her bags and camera equipment from the car and struggled with them up the stairs to her room. She dropped everything and stood in the middle of the room taking a deep breath. Now that she was totally alone, she was aware of being more tired than she'd realized. And with the exhaustion had come a melancholia. Even after two years she still had trouble keeping it at bay. She moved to the dresser, trance-like, her mind deep in thought, and gently touched the hand-crocheted runner on the top. She absently took note of the old-fashioned cut-glass tray holding a comb and brush and a jar of hand cream. Reluctantly Jackie pulled her large dark eyes up to the mirror over the dresser to look steadily into her own image.

There was a fairly tall, very slim young black woman of twenty-seven. Her curly brown hair was shorter in the front and on the sides than in the back, and accentuated most attractively her long neck and well-shaped face with its square jaw. Her teakwood skin was smooth and flawless with high cheek bones as befitted her former profession. A wide full mouth, capable of being sensuous and curved in good humor, was at the moment only petulant as it pulled down sadly at the corners. She would not have been particularly flattered by anyone's commenting on her good looks. They had served her well, to be sure, but few people had bothered to probe beneath the finished exterior and find the person she really was. She wondered now if anyone ever would. Certainly Mark had never cared.

Suddenly impatient with herself, she began to strip off her

travel-worn clothes and dug in her cases for a fresh outfit. She chose a denim skirt and a lilac cotton blouse. Gathering her things she headed for the bathroom and a much needed shower. Jackie came downstairs forty-five minutes later feeling refreshed and alert. Her tote containing her camera, film and two different lenses hung heavily over her shoulder. The aroma of ham baking with cloves filled her nostrils, and she found her way into the kitchen. Hannah was just completing the final toss to a bowl of potato salad and there was the smell of sweet gherkins and onions in the air. She smiled as Jackie walked in.

"Darlin', I thought for sure you'd fallen asleep. I wouldn't have blamed you a bit. And I never thought to ask if you were hungry."

"No, thank you. I stopped for lunch after crossing the state line."

"Well, I usually eat around six o'clock or so. I hope you don't mind early dinners."

"I don't mind. I thought I'd explore some since I still have the rest of the afternoon to get acquainted with the streets and roads. Maybe I'll take some preliminary pictures around Charleston. I'm sure Gwen is going to want some images for the book."

"Gwen said you were a photographer."

"I'm trying to be. I got fascinated with cameras from modeling. It always amazed me what a camera could capture, and then when you see the finished picture it's . . . it's so much more than you thought!" Hannah chuckled with indulgence at Jackie's enthusiasm.

"Well, darlin', I sure don't know nothin' about pictures changing. I mean, if you take a picture of a tree, it's always a tree! Right?" she said with finality.

Jackie laughed at the simplicity of Hannah's view. It would do no good to explain the feeling she got from photography to this straightforward woman in her beige house dress and calico apron. Life was very simple for Hannah Curtis. Jackie envied her that. "At any rate, I much prefer being behind the lens than in front of it. And who knows, I might become another James Van de Zee!"

Hannah squinted in puzzlement, as she opened the refrigerator to put the salad inside. "Who's that?" she asked.

"James Van de Zee is a black photographer well-known for the pictures he took of prominent black families in New York during the 1930s and '40s."

Hannah turned back to Jackie, wiping her hands on the skirt of her apron. She frowned, shaking her head. "I don't recall having heard the name, darlin'. Is he any good?"

Jackie laughed, the sound suddenly light and easy. "The Metropolitan Museum of Art in New York think so! They have a room filled with his work!" With that and a brief wave of her hand she headed toward the door. Calling over her shoulder to Hannah, she said she'd be back by five o'clock. Jackie climbed back into her compact car and briefly consulted her map. Taking a quick look out the window for oncoming traffic, she pulled the car into the lane and headed in the direction of the bridge that would take her across the Ashley River toward Meggett and Johns Island.

It was still very hot, but her shower had done much to rejuvenate her. She allowed herself to get excited once again at the prospect of having her work published in a book. Thank goodness someone had thrust a camera into her hand after she'd left Mark. Thank goodness they'd said, go use your eyes and leave your heart alone to heal. It hadn't been quite that simple. After all she had been totally dependent on Mark and had willingly allowed him to manage her career and her life.

She and Gwen had been modeling only a year when she'd met Mark Bennett. She had been only twenty-one at the time and overwhelmed by the attention he directed toward her. He was thirty, sophisticated, managing editor of a fashion magazine, and so supremely sure of his charms. Well, hadn't she fallen for it? Mark became her mentor, molding and shaping her. Her lover, initiating and leading her. Her husband, controlling and managing her—and finally her nemesis.

Perhaps she eventually would have adjusted to his high-handed way with her. Perhaps she would have learned to let him be right all the time. But there had been other women, and she would never adjust to that. Having a pretty wife was apparently not enough for Mark Bennett. He also had to have any fresh young thing that went through his office. Jackie had been devastated by the knowledge, especially when she recalled the memory of her father's affair with another woman while married to a beautiful accomplished wife. The idea that she herself might not be able to hold Mark's attention and affections made her feel less than a full woman. Being very pretty had really meant nothing at all. Then he'd accused her of being childish and insecure. Be that as it may, she didn't feel she deserved to be treated so casually.

Jackie's hands tightened on the wheel of the car, and her foot involuntarily pushed harder on the accelerator. Feelings of humiliation could still grip at her insides. But she was long past the stage of angry tears. She was never going to waste another tear on that man—not a single one.

Jackie brought the car under control and slowed her speed. She let her large doe eyes sweep over the landscape, letting herself become distracted from past memories by the variety of trees and lush spring flowers. She began to see a potential picture in the unfolding scenes around her. There were small ramshackle cottages with collapsing fences, interspersed with stately mansions behind high wrought iron gates and drooping Spanish moss and dogwood trees. Oh yes, she would get good pictures here.

Thank goodness also for the photographer from her agency who'd spotted her interest and given her her first used camera. It had been lots of hard work at first and so much to remember. But something clicked, figuratively speaking, and she was launched on a new career—and a new life. A few magazines began to pick up her pictures and soon a few were calling her regularly for her special way of photographing people, her way of seeing a building or a street. This was something unique and part of herself. She would never again give up herself so completely to anyone as she had to Mark.

On a sudden whim, Jackie pulled the car off the main highway onto a dusty road heading toward the coastline and a pond she thought she'd seen. The road bumped along, the auto wheels stirring up a dry reddish dirt into a cloud around the car. After a half mile the road ended, but in front of her car was the pond, of an odd amber-colored water. It was only after Jackie had gotten out of the car that she saw the small house barely visible through the thick growth of tall grass and trees. It was a tiny, charming little structure, more of a cottage than a full house. It was sorely in need of scraping and a fresh coat of paint. The off-center front door was a peeling green color. There was one six-paned window to the right of the door, and three to the left. A much worn deck surface constituted a walkway going from the door outward for about five yards, ending in the natural flatness of the ground. The house looked very dark and closed up, and there were no immediate signs that it was occupied. But for the time being Jackie ignored it. She walked around before finally reaching for her camera. Going in the opposite direction from the house and her car she began to shoot a roll of film, loosening up and adjusting to the land. At first she concentrated on tree and foliage groupings that seemed unique to the area, certain wildflowers and ground covering. She turned back once, pleased with the light passing over the small house hidden in the trees, and snapped several frames. She moved absently toward the edge of the pond, concentrating on the view through her eyepiece. The ground began to give way beneath her as her heels sank in the soft, over-wet earth. Regaining her balance she moved quickly back. From a more secure spot Jackie finished the film.

Fiddling with the mechanism to rewind the film, she walked blindly back to the car. The low deep voice behind her suddenly made her jump and spin around. Walking slowly toward Jackie was a man a little over six feet tall, athletically built, and very casually dressed. He looked to be about thirty-five. He wore a pair of well-worn jeans, sneakers, and a sweatshirt with long sleeves that had been cut off almost to the shoulder, exposing well-developed arm muscles. Both hands were pushed deep into the jeans pockets causing the fabric to pull taut across equally well-developed thighs. The stranger looked at Jackie earnestly from eyes almost topaz-colored in their lightness. His slow movements toward her were graceful, like a predatory animal, emitting raw masculinity. Jackie, perturbed, raised her eyes to his and realized he was talking to her.

"W . . . what?" she stammered aware of a sudden frightening increase in her pulse. She started backing up to the car somewhere behind her.

"I said, what are the pictures for?" he repeated in a natural questioning way. His eyes quickly swept over her tall frame before looking again into her face.

Jackie couldn't understand her sudden inability to talk or

function, or, for that matter, to breathe because he was so close. He didn't appear threatening, but on the one hand was the fear of being in this isolated spot with a strange man and not knowing if she was safe. On the other was a curious fascination at finding a good-looking black man casually at home in some backwoods outside of Charleston. He did not sport an Afro, modified or otherwise. His hair was cut very close to his head, and it struck her immediately that he reminded her a bit of Harry Belafonte but with a skin tone darker and richer. Jackie found her tongue and lowered her eyes, embarrassed when she realized she'd been openly staring.

"I didn't mean to trespass. I didn't know."

"I didn't say you were trespassing. I just want to know what the pictures are for?" he said, amusement laced in his voice and words. He made her feel a bit foolish, but she wasn't going to let him intimidate her.

"Just who are you anyway?" she asked. He grinned at her mockingly. Jackie backed right up to the car door.

"I could ask you the same question."

"Well, I can tell you I'm not spying and I'm not a bill collector!" She flashed a look of amused derision at the simple but dilapidated house behind him. "And I'm not from *House and Garden!*"

"I'm relieved," he murmured sarcastically, stepping closer to her.

Jackie drew the camera in front of her chest instinctively, as if to protect herself.

"I'm not going to attack or murder you for taking pictures. I just want to know what they're for," he said patiently.

"Why should I tell you?" she asked stubbornly.

"For starters, I live here."

"Oh . . ."

"For another, I don't want pictures of my house printed for a hundred million readers, *House and Garden* or whatever."

"I think I can put your worries to rest on that count!" she interrupted.

He took yet another step until there was barely two feet between them. Jackie caught her breath and looked up apprehensively into his face.

"And if that isn't enough, you didn't ask."

"I'm sorry! I said I didn't mean to trespass."

He merely repeated his question slowly and patiently, spacing the words as though talking to a child, or someone who didn't understand English. "What are the pictures for?"

"You're beginning to sound like a scratched record," Jackie said flippantly. "Don't you know anything else to ask?"

"I'll get to that in a minute. You haven't answered the last question yet." He seemed so calm, so much in control, and Jackie suspected he was inwardly laughing at her. But she was on totally unfamiliar ground in more ways than one. She backed down, letting some of the wind out of her own sails.

"I'm here to take pictures for a book I'm working on," she said evenly, looking straight into his eyes. He reached out a hand suddenly and gently took the camera out of her grasp before she could react. She made no instant move to take it back.

"Do you know what you're doing?" he asked as he finished removing the film from the camera with expert ease and then passed it to her.

"Of course I know what I'm doing!" she said with some indignation.

"I don't think so."

"What do you mean?" Jackie frowned, nonetheless curious.

"Pictures of my house and that pond aren't going to add anything to your book."

"But you don't even know what I'm looking for!"

"I know what you're not looking for and that's pictures of ponds with ancient houses on them. This is not unusual in South Carolina. What is your book supposed to cover?"

"Johns Island."

He nodded seriously. "Johns Island and its people are unusual." He gave her back the camera.

Jackie felt now as though he were taking an assessment of her and she didn't much care for the scrutiny.

"Have you been to Johns Island before?" he asked.

"No, but I . . ." Jackie admitted, then tried to explain.

"Do you know anything about the island?" He crossed his arms over his chest.

"No I don't. I . . ."

"Do you have any idea what makes it so special?" he asked persistently.

"Well, not really, but . . ." She tried again to explain.

"I didn't think you knew what you were doing," he said in conclusion.

His blunt statement made her angry, but he wasn't totally wrong, either. Jackie bit back the sharp retort sitting on her tongue. "What do you suggest?" she asked.

"You need someone to be a guide for you. Someone to show you around and save you some time. Someone who won't let you take pictures and waste film on all the wrong things." He said it all very quietly, and Jackie had the distinct feeling he was trying not to belittle her. She may have started out about this the wrong way, but he was prepared to take her project seriously.

"And just who do you have in mind as a guide?" Jackie asked, already knowing the answer.

"Me, of course," he responded blithely.

"Of course." Jackie answered in wry amusement despite herself.

He grinned at her, crinkling the corners of his eyes. He had a wonderful smile.

"I thank you for the offer but no thanks!"

"I'll even throw in a little local history."

"I can read up on that myself."

"My way is better," he coaxed.

"Why better?" She was now curious.

"Because you could never read up on what the local people could tell you. I can introduce you to some of them." He was quietly persistent and Jackie was suspicious as to his reasons for wanting to help her. "Look you'd be very safe with me. Everyone around here knows who I am."

"But I don't!" Jackie said with raised brows.

"That can be changed," he said. "My name's Eric Davidson." He held out his hand, and raised his brows in further amusement at her hesitation.

Jackie looked with slight distaste at his hands stained and streaked with paint. "I . . . I'm Jacqueline Taylor from New York."

"Hello, Jacqueline Taylor from New York. You're a long ways from home."

Jackie was aware in that moment of the capability of strength in the hand holding her own firmly, and longer than was necessary. She pulled it away. Eric Davidson put his hands back into his pockets and turned to lean back against the car very close to her. Jackie stiffened, his nearness making her nervous as she tried not to show it.

"Why Johns Island?"

"I'm sorry?" Jackie was forced to ask, coming out of her private haze.

"Why a book on Johns Island?"

"It was the idea of a friend of mine. She's always been interested in the people there. She's in New York right now, but she's writing the text and I'm taking the pictures."

He chuckled. "It's hard to write a book on Johns Island if you're in New York."

"Gwen has other commitments right now, but she'll be down in a few weeks."

"Gwen?" he questioned with a slight frown.

"That's my friend."

"In the meantime, you're on your own," he concluded.

"That's right."

"Where are you staying?"

Jackie hesitated, not wanting to give too much away about herself to a stranger. "With the friend of a friend."

"That's clear enough," he said ruefully.

Jackie began to think she wasn't at all sure she wanted this person being her guide, spending time in her company, asking questions, getting close. She thought him a little too sure of himself. Already that put her at a disadvantage. Certainly if he worked his time would be occupied every day. She was almost relieved at having found an excuse to get out of his offer. As though reading her silence and understanding the thoughts running through her mind, Eric Davidson shifted his position, turning to face her more. He looked down at Jackie and spoke seriously to her.

"I think the best thing to do, first of all, is to just ride around the county and get familiar with some of its features and landmarks. This will give you a good overview. I know some of the families, so I can arrange for you to meet and talk with some of them. But that can wait for a few days."

"Look I'm sure you're, er, too busy to be bothered with me,"

Jackie said, glancing skeptically at his soiled and paint-stained clothing.

"I'm a painter . . ." he supplied, answering the unasked question. "I just finished some work so I have a few days free."

"Well, what I plan to do first is make use of the library, and then I plan on taking my pictures."

"You'll still save a lot of time if you have help. My grandmother was born on Johns Island. I have a firsthand knowledge of the place."

Jackie looked up at him in surprise, intrigued against her will by that last bit of information. Her eyes met the odd openness of his and quickly she glanced away. There was a low rumble of a laugh from deep in his chest.

"You're not afraid of me, are you?" He smiled, teasing her.

"Of course not," she said promptly. "It's just that . . ."

"Just what?" Eric continued to smile at her mockingly.

"Well, I wouldn't know what to pay you for your time," she finished lamely.

He shrugged. "You wouldn't have to pay me anything."

Jackie looked in open disbelief and suspicion at him now, and raised her brows archly.

He laughed openly. "There's suspicion written all over your face! *Now* I believe you're from New York!"

"With good reason! One thing I've learned is that no one does anything for free! This is business, Mr. Davidson."

". . . Eric."

"*Mr.* Davidson. I insist on paying for your time."

Eric speculated for only a second, watching the mutinous transformation on her face. "Suit yourself," he agreed. "What's the salary?"

Jackie chewed on her bottom lip, deep in thought, and pulled absently on the curls in her bangs. She looked at him, as though to take his measure and decide what he was worth. But that was of no help since she kept encountering his light eyes studying her. Jackie straightened, having reached a decision.

"How's five dollars an hour?" she ventured in what she hoped was a firm voice.

Eric Davidson merely nodded, and Jackie wondered if he'd really heard what she'd said. "When do you want to start?"

"Well, I just got here today and I have some things to arrange tomorrow. But we can start the day after."

"Fine." He nodded again, removing his hands from his pockets and crossing his arms over his chest. "If it's all the same to you we'll use your car."

"Okay," Jackie said, seeing no problem in that.

"You can pick me up here day after tomorrow."

"Okay," she said again, slightly annoyed with his having taken over the arrangements.

"Let's make it early," he pushed himself away from the car allowing her to approach the door.

Jackie clamped her jaw shut.

"And don't forget your camera." He grinned.

Jackie rolled her eyes at him and turned around to the car. Eric's hand moved in front of her as he bent forward to open the door. This brought his head close to Jackie's, and a shiver went through her as they almost touched. He looked at her but said nothing as he pulled the door open and held it for her.

Glad to be able to get away, she scrambled into the front seat and immediately reached for the ignition. Her hasty climb into the car caused her skirt to gather and bunch and it rose well above her knees, giving Eric Davidson an excellent view of her long legs. He closed the door and bent down to be eye level with her.

"I wonder how many men have told you you ought to be in pictures?"

Jackie stared at him. She smirked, for she had long ago lost count. "And are you about to add yourself to the list?" Jackie asked, expecting him to say yes.

"You don't need to hear that, and I'm not so obvious. I already know you used to be a model. You move and hold yourself like one. Old habits are hard to break. And I know body types." He paused a long moment and grinned at her. "*And* you have terrific legs."

Jackie ignored his second comment. She'd heard that before, too. "There's no such thing as a body type, Mr. Davidson. And I'm a photographer."

He looked at her a moment longer, then slowly stood up, lifting his hands in a gesture of surrender. The smile, however, still played around his mouth.

"I'll see you day after tomorrow," she stated flatly as she started the car. Jackie pulled away from him and the car curved onto the dusty road once again. She never looked in her rearview mirror to see if he was still standing there. She was having enough trouble wiping the strong, virile image of him from her mind.

It was five-thirty when Jackie arrived back in Charleston, her encounter with Eric Davidson diminishing with each hunger pang that went through her. Hannah was in the dining room when she entered the house, and leaving her bags and equipment by the stairwell, Jackie went to help Hannah set the table for dinner.

"Oh, there you are, darlin'. I was just saying to Timothy I sure hope that girl didn't go and get herself lost!" She shook with a gentle laugh.

Jackie frowned, still seeing no signs of the mysterious Timothy. Was he a neighbor? Another boarder? An affectionate friend to Hannah?

"Can I help with anything?" she asked the older woman.

"If you want to help, you can just do justice to that ham I cooked this afternoon. I need to fatten you up! Shucks, girl . . . you'll never find a husband if you're all skin and bones!" As soon as the words were out of her mouth Hannah's eyes widened and she gasped at what she'd said. Jackie flinched noticeably, but forced a smile to her mouth.

"I haven't eaten since noon, so I think doing justice to your ham will be easy." But the silence from Hannah stretched on.

"I thought I'd take your advice and use the library tomorrow. And I found someone who knows the area and will show me around."

"Oh good!" Hannah breathed in relief, reacting more to the passing ill moments than she was to anything Jackie had just told her. The phone rang and Hannah went to answer, leaving Jackie to finish laying out silverware and napkins.

"Jacqueline! It's for you. It's Gwen calling all the way from New York!"

Jackie moved toward Hannah and took the outstretched phone excitedly as she sat in a cushioned chair by the phone stand. "Hi, Gwen."

"Well, I see you got there okay. Why you couldn't fly like normal people is beyond me!"

"I guess I'm not normal people. Besides, I enjoyed the drive down by myself."

"But there's so many fools out there on the road. Girl, I was worried. I told Hannah she was to take real good care of you when you got there."

"Yes, I know," Jackie said with emphasis.

"Oooops!" Gwen commented, knowing what Jackie was referring to, but not sounding particularly apologetic either. "Just concerned about you, hon."

"Thanks, Gwen. But despite popular opinion recently and in the past to the contrary, I can take care of myself."

"Okay, okay. Calm down . . . I get the message," Gwen soothed.

Jackie sighed. "I'm sorry, Gwen. I know you mean well. I've just had a very long day, that's all."

Gwen gave a throaty laugh on her end. "Welcome to South Carolina . . . and the heat! What do you think so far?"

"It's too soon to say. On the surface it's just as you said it would be. I'll give you a better report when you get here. I did find a local person to show me around. I'm paying him, of course."

"Him?" Gwen asked, suddenly alert.

"Yes. He's a painter. From the looks of him and his house he could probably use the money. He says his grandmother was born on the island."

"Is he good-looking?"

Jackie had to laugh as Gwen came right to the point as was her way. "I suppose you could say he is, but that's not the point."

"Don't be too sure, girl. You can be quietly swept off your pretty little feet and never know what hit you!"

"I don't think so. I'm planning to keep my pretty little feet on the ground!"

"Ummm. I still wish you'd get in touch with Spence. He could be just as much help."

Jackie grimaced in exasperation. "Gwen, I told you. I don't want to meet Spence right now."

"But he'd be good for you, hon! He's just the sort of man you need! He's smart, caring, knows what he's doing. . . ."

"I don't need a man. I've already had one, remember?"

Gwen sucked through her teeth in dismissal. "Mark doesn't count. He was too slick for you."

"That's one way of putting it. Anyway, it doesn't matter. I'm fine just the way I am."

"But Spence would help you forget. You'll like him, Jackie."

"You make the man sound like a sedative, Gwen!" Jackie quipped.

Gwen laughed. "He can be very effective!"

"Well, if he's such a paragon of manhood, how come you aren't after him?" Jackie could visualize her friend shrugging languidly on the other end.

"I've known him too long. He's my brother Eric's best friend and practically family. Besides, I need someone who moves as fast as I do and who likes to party. Spence likes to do things at his own pace."

Jackie grimaced again. "He sounds dull . . . and orthopedic!"

Gwen howled with laughter. "I'm going to tell him you said so! Anyway, if you change your mind I think he teaches at one of the local colleges. Give him a call."

"I'll think about it. In the meantime, you hurry and get down here!"

"I will. Oh, and listen . . ."

"Yes?"

Gwen hesitated. "I saw Mark recently."

"Did you?" Jackie questioned with detachment.

"He asked about you, wanted to know how you were doing."

"I could care less," Jackie interrupted, but despite her brave words an image of Mark appeared in her mind clearly. "Look, I gotta go. Hannah is holding dinner for me. Talk to you soon?"

Gwen sighed. "Talk to you soon, hon. 'Bye now."

Jackie hung up, pursing her lips thoughtfully as she repeated in her head Mark's asking about her. She quickly pulled herself together, pushing the thought to the back of her mind. It was not nearly as hard as it used to be. For that she was grateful.

CHAPTER TWO

The city of Charleston was clean and orderly, quiet but brisk in its functioning. The people moved much slower than in New York, but Jackie experienced no trouble in adapting. With her much-marked map clutched in her hands and a pair of comfortable sandals on her feet, she parked the car in the downtown area and proceeded to explore. She was comfortable in her wanderings, but she didn't quite fade in with the rest of the populace. Though she would have denied it, she was very noticeable, and just her carriage and gracefully thin body caused others to turn and watch her in admiration.

By chance she stumbled onto what is known as "Catfish Row" from *Porgy and Bess* fame, and she admired the narrow cobbled alley with its colonial style houses. Feeling sudden inspiration, Jackie stood centered in the alleyway and shot a few pictures toward the entrance. What she saw was the sun shining brilliantly through the archway, but the alley itself was dark and muted, patterned everywhere with red and gray brick.

She admired the intricate wrought-iron work that made up gates, fences, and gratings to windows along the streets. She loved the still working gaslights, the profusion of poinsettia greens, dogwoods, and palmettos. They grew everywhere, even surrounding the bases of lamp posts and fire hydrants. Their fragrance filled the air, and was pleasant to sniff.

Jackie happened upon a photo studio and went in to introduce herself to the owner, a short thin man with pale blond hair and very thick glasses, who watched her as she entered the store with a rather owlish expression. She explained what she was working on and what her needs were. He was cooperative and nodded as she spoke.

"Are you any good?" he twanged in the drawl that Jackie was still not used to. The question irked her. It was the second time in twenty-four hours that someone had questioned her ability.

She wondered in irritation if she looked particularly hapless, or did all young women in South Carolina get asked that question? She answered smoothly that she'd been selling her work for almost two years. He didn't seem particularly impressed.

"We get lots of picture takers around here. Pretty state, South Carolina is." He jerked a thumb to the wall behind him and for the first time Jackie noticed an arrangement of some twenty color and black and white pictures obviously of areas in the state. The pictures were pretty, postcard quality, but not outstanding. They didn't make you feel as though you could get any closer and know anything more about the subjects. Two pictures did catch her eye, however. One was a black and white picture of an old black woman. Her face was a map of life lines, the eyes still sharp and bright and filled with humor. A pipe was clamped in her mouth, and she smiled around the stem of it at the camera. The other picture showed an old farm nag with a rooster perched saucily on its hindquarters.

"If you have anything worth showing, I'd be glad to display it for you. Lots of the photographers 'round here get extra work this way. Some even get picked up by the local galleries." He peered at her, his glasses making his watery blue eyes larger than life.

"I appreciate that, but I'm not from South Carolina."

"Oh, I knew that the minute you opened your mouth. You're from up North. That don't make no difference. You got some pictures worth showing, I'll show them for you."

Jackie frowned, a thought needling at her. "What do you get out of it?" she asked. Suddenly the thin pinched lips spread into a broad grin.

"Why, all the photographers do their processing at my lab, and buy all their film and supplies from me in bulk. I also do framing."

It wasn't a bad deal. Jackie found herself purchasing ten more rolls of film and a filter. She left off the film shot the day before, requesting a contact sheet. Jackie thanked the shop owner for his offer, and promised she'd have something for him by the end of the week that he could display.

It was almost two-thirty before Jackie headed in the direction of the public library. A young man made an obvious pass at her as she walked, but she was quick to politely discourage him.

"I'm not interested," Jackie said with a small tight smile, and kept on going.

"Can't you even say hello?" the young man shouted after her. Jackie shook her head, continuing away from him.

"Not even that!" she answered without turning her head.

Noticing that the light had changed in her favor, she ran quickly to cross the street, putting distance between her and her admirer. Jackie allowed herself a chuckle at the thought that the come-on from black men in Charleston wasn't any different than in New York.

Jackie had, after starting to model, quickly gotten over the novelty of being whistled at, or approached in familiar ways. She'd been much more receptive and intrigued by the men who'd been able to have whole conversations with her without once saying how pretty she was and, did she model. Unfortunately they were few and far between. It was just as well, then, that she wasn't looking to establish a relationship, since she'd have been doomed to disappointment. Not that she didn't know an attractive man when she saw one. And immediately Eric Davidson came to mind.

Just this morning at breakfast he'd come up in the conversation with Hannah as the older woman had questioned Jackie on her plans for research.

"Well . . ." Jackie began, "I found someone to show me around Johns Island. He said his grandmother was born there. I just want to be able to have a little background before we get started."

Hannah frowned, looking at Jackie alertly. "Who is this person? Where did you meet him?"

Jackie chuckled around a piece of toast still in her mouth. She swallowed before answering. "It's okay, Hannah. I think he's safe enough."

"But who is he? Where does he live?"

Jackie explained how and where she'd met Eric Davidson, that he seemed gainfully employed and not particularly dangerous. Hannah continued to frown.

"Eric Davidson. Now why does that name sound so familiar?" Hannah looked pointedly at Jackie, and shook her head as the information she sought refused to come. "Why is he offering to do this?"

"I offered to pay. And besides, he's on home ground and I'm not," she admitted, seeing the truth and wisdom in Eric Davidson's statement of yesterday.

"Humph!" Hannah grunted. "Well if you ask me, darlin', it sounds like a case of a fly buzzing around the jam pot!" and she gently slapped her palm on the tabletop for emphasis. "And you have to be so careful these days, especially a pretty thing like you!"

Jackie nibbled thoughtfully on her toast. She'd only spent about a half hour with Eric Davidson the day before, but in her mind it was enough time for her to assess that he did not approach things in that manner—so obvious and irksome. There was a quiet underlying control to him. He was a man sure and confident in himself. It didn't strike her that he would play games to get what he wanted, or that he would tolerate games in others. Irrelevantly Jackie thought that he, no doubt, had all kinds of women dancing to his tune. Well, that was fine if one liked that sort of cloying attention.

But she reconsidered how foolish she'd been to so quickly agree to his being her guide. After all, who was this painter living in a secluded area in a house that looked less than reputable? Perhaps it was his self-assurance that she'd responded to. Or had it been something else?

It was foolish for her to try and convince herself that Eric Davidson wasn't attractive, because it had hit her at once. He hadn't been threatening, but he definitely could not be ignored. He had almost imperceptibly eliminated her objections, which admittedly had been weak to begin with. And he'd indicated he thought her idea for the book a good one which just needed direction. Unconsciously, Jackie had accepted the vote of confidence from him.

Jackie recognized another factor, and quickly put down her toast, her mind reeling at the thought, her body suddenly stiff with awareness. Her ex-husband had been very confident. He had been totally capable of brushing aside her objections, doubts, hesitancy, and fears. For a long time she'd even been happy just to let him be the one in complete command, until she realized one day she'd given up almost all control of her own life. Eric Davidson better not be entertaining any such thoughts where her book project was concerned, Jackie thought positively. But instincts told her that this was not what he wanted of her. What he did want, or expect, Jackie didn't allow herself to think about.

Jackie's mind jumped to the present as she entered the columned entrance to the Charleston main library and, locating the information desk, asked if there was a section on local history. Ignoring the small public elevator, Jackie began to climb the broad staircase to the second floor and entered a room off to her right.

The room was small and wood-paneled, and filled with books. The walls contained maps of Charleston in order of the progressive changes in the city's geography, layout, and architecture. It was a cozy room, much more like someone's private study than a public room. There was no one present, save an older, rail-thin woman sitting behind a small cluttered desk in the process of cataloging yet another book for the collection.

"Excuse me." Jackie stood uncertainly in front of the desk.

"Yes?" the woman asked vaguely, continuing to finger a number of Library of Congress cataloging cards, her brows furrowed in deep concentration.

"I'm here to do some research and . . ."

"Lord, who isn't!" the woman murmured caustically in a rich, raspy drawl. Then she blinked back to the present, suddenly remembering her position. She peered over the top of the cards in her hand at Jackie's momentarily stunned expression, and let out a sigh. "I'm sorry, my dear," the woman apologized. "I'm really suffering through this. I'm a good librarian, but I *hate* cataloging!"

Jackie smiled sympathetically.

"Now, what can I do for you?"

"Are you Mrs. Martha Jarrod?" Jackie queried.

"Yes I am. Who spilt the beans?" Mrs. Jarrod asked in a wistful tone.

Jackie laughed. "Hannah Curtis."

Mrs. Jarrod's brows immediately rose in recognition. "Oh, Hannah! Then it's perfectly okay. Hannah and I have known each other for years! What awful things has she told you about me?" the raspy voice intoned, the gray eyes narrowing in the pale fine-boned face.

"Just that you were the only person who could help me find written material on Johns Island and the people there."

"She's absolutely right!" Mrs. Jarrod nodded immodestly. Jackie laughed again, liking her.

Jackie proceeded to explain what she was looking for and asked Mrs. Jarrod for suggestions as to where else she could get information. Mrs. Jarrod pursed her lips for a thoughtful moment.

"Well now, the best thing, of course, is to talk to people who live on the island."

"I'm hoping to do that."

"You should consider getting someone local to show you around."

"I've already made arrangements with an Eric Davidson to . . ."

"Oh, Eric! Wonderful. He's the perfect choice!" Mrs. Jarrod said with smiling enthusiasm.

"Is he?" Jackie asked, intrigued.

"My goodness, yes! Some of his folks are from Johns Island. But Eric has made it his business to know about the area." Mrs. Jarrod's expression and voice grew rueful with memories. "I ought to know. He's made a pest of himself often enough when he was in high school. Always wanting to know one thing or another. Very inquisitive. Sharp as a tack, too!"

"Yes I can believe it," Jackie said thoughtfully.

Mrs. Jarrod forged right on, not hearing Jackie's response. "And he's such a lovely young man. Highly thought of around here. He's a painter, you know," she informed Jackie.

"He told me."

"And a very good one!" Mrs. Jarrod added, making Jackie frown. She didn't think it took that much effort to be a good painter. But perhaps Mrs. Jarrod was talking out of knowledge and obvious pride and affection for someone she'd known for so many formative years.

Jackie sighed. "Then I don't suppose I could do better in finding someone to help me."

Mrs. Jarrod's brows shot up, and then they came down as she gave Jackie a look that indicated she found her question strange.

"Well, I suppose you could. But why would you want to? I mean, Eric's perfect! Besides, it would do him good to squire around an attractive young woman. He tends to forget the rest of the world when he gets to working."

Jackie took in the information with a little skepticism based on her knowledge and past experience of men. If she and Mrs. Jarrod were talking about the same Eric Davidson, Jackie found it hard to believe that he was ever without female companionship. Of course, she had no intention of being a companion to him. He was hired, after all, to serve her needs . . . not the other way around.

Having disposed sufficiently of the question of who needed whom, Jackie attempted to get Mrs. Jarrod back to the subject of her research. She recommended a number of books to Jackie, and showed her where to find them on the shelf. Jackie soon found out that researching was a laborious, plodding chore. But finally she hit on an author with a lively sense of humor and style of writing that was interesting and, for the next few hours, escaped into the past history of the Carolina sea islands.

Jackie got so involved that she never heard the voices in friendly exchange at Mrs. Jarrod's desk, or the mention of her name. And it wasn't until someone took the seat opposite her, laying down several oversized picture books with a thump, that her attention was jerked away from her intense concentration. She looked up with an expression of annoyance at the interruption and into the topaz-colored, mocking gaze of Eric Davidson. She stared blankly at him for a moment, as if he were an apparition conjured up by way of her conversation earlier with Mrs. Jarrod.

"What are you doing here?" she asked flatly, and with a degree of unwarranted irritation.

"Good afternoon to you, too!" he quipped with a lopsided grin. Jackie had the grace to squirm under his teasing reminder of her poor reception.

She'd forgotten how tall he was, and even sitting down his physical presence was firm and undeniable. Eric was dressed pretty much the same as the day before, but his sweatshirt today advertised some college from which the shirt must have been obtained. It was just as paint-smeared and faded as his other. Jackie found herself surreptitiously looking at Eric as if fully seeing him for the first time. But this was not strictly true. She'd been more than aware of him the day before. He made the person of that young man earlier this afternoon seem insignificant. He made Mark seem insignificant. Jackie shook her head gently to clear it.

Eric crossed his arms over his chest and sat back in his chair, looking her appearance over thoroughly. A slow suggestive smile curved his full mouth. Jackie raised a brow and tilted her head suspiciously.

"Are you following me?"

"Not hardly. This is a public building, you know."

"It's for research!" she pointed out smugly.

Eric continued to smile, but his eyes with their peculiar lightness narrowed as they rested on her. "And don't you think I'm capable, or may have need for research myself?"

Jackie lowered her eyes and merely shrugged. She realized it was a childish thing to have said to him. She didn't know what to think. Eric Davidson had his own contradictions which confused her still. He leaned across the research table and her pile of books and papers to bring himself closer to her.

"Have you been buried here all afternoon?" he asked quietly.

"No. Only a few hours, really. I walked around Charleston after lunch, just to explore. It's a nice city."

"I agree." He grinned. "Welcome to my hometown."

Jackie found herself smiling at his overture. "It's very different than New York." She looked directly at Eric. "Except for the men. They seem to be the same everywhere."

Eric frowned. "What do you mean?"

Jackie shrugged once more. She wished now she hadn't recalled that silly incident this afternoon. She of all people should have known that it happens from time to time.

Eric continued to search her face for a meaning. "Did someone bother you?" The tone of his voice was both serious and slightly hard, and Jackie reacted with surprise in her eyes to what sounded like genuine concern.

"It . . . it was nothing. The usual catcalls. I can handle it."

There was a small silence while Jackie nervously closed one book, and opened another.

"You probably can," Eric finally responded, his deep voice still quiet. "I have no doubt the dude came off the worse for it."

Jackie was suddenly uncertain again. She didn't know if he was laughing at her, or being sarcastic. Either way, she didn't much like the insinuations. "It wasn't like that at all. Anyway, nothing much was said."

"It was obviously someone who found you very attractive. He was probably just showing appreciation."

"Well, he had an annoying way of showing it," she said contritely.

"Or maybe you were too defensive about it."

Jackie lifted cold eyes to Eric's brown pensive face. "You don't know anything about me. What do you know of my defenses?"

Her sudden indignation added an attractive liveliness to her features that Jackie was not aware of. Eric's eyes traveled from her swept-back curly hair with its wispy tendrils, to the faint flush of her soft teak-brown face. He came back to her eyes. "I know you have plenty of them. Probably more than you really need. I certainly wouldn't want to be the object of your anger. If looks could kill . . ."

Jackie held out for as long as she could, but she couldn't suppress a dry chuckle from surfacing. ". . . You never would have survived yesterday afternoon?"

"Exactly!" Eric suddenly smiled. Jackie couldn't help but notice what a truly good-looking man he was. "That's why I'm glad your loaded and ready machine gun only has caps in it after all." He said it so easily, so obviously trying not to get her angry that Jackie felt foolish for being so uppity. She relaxed in her chair and smiled a bit ruefully at him.

"A pop instead of a blast?"

He nodded, raising his brows as she finally saw the point. They both laughed softly together. Eric stood up then, slowly and gracefully, and Jackie had to tilt her head to see his face. He pushed his hands into the front pockets of his jeans. Jackie averted her eyes from the sensuous movement of his limbs. The purely physical action caused something to stir deep within her.

"In any case," Eric said now, "everyone deserves the benefit of the doubt."

Jackie looked at him, wondering about his calmly talking to her in this fashion. "And are you possibly talking about yourself, Mr. Davidson?" she questioned in a curious tight voice.

"Maybe," he said smoothly.

"Why do I feel like you're lecturing me?" Jackie asked quietly.

"No lecture. Just a little gentle advice," he said with indifference.

Jackie lowered her eyes with a small private smile. She sighed. "Not gentle or subtle. But I understand."

"Are you settled in yet?"

His sudden change of subjects silenced her while her emotions and mind switched gears. But she was grateful for the change. "I'm doing fine. I've found a lab to process my film."

"Bob McIver's lab."

She looked at him surprised. "How did you know?"

"Bob's the best in the city. And he's a nice guy to work with."

"He seems to be. I'm glad I found him." She placed her hand flat on top of an opened book. "And I thought I'd spend some time in the library this afternoon."

"So you can impress me tomorrow morning?" He smiled wickedly, his light eyes winking at her.

"No. So I'll have a better idea of what to look for in terms of documenting the people and the land," Jackie responded patiently, nonetheless piqued that he'd not been that far off the mark.

"Good idea." Eric nodded. Then he frowned at her, and pulled his bottom lip between his teeth as he stood deep in thought. "Wait a minute. I think I know of one source that should be really good."

Without any objections from Mrs. Jarrod, and with an obvious long-standing familiarity of the room, Eric disappeared behind a high-backed chair and returned several minutes later with two books. One was a kind of personal account, by the son of a former plantation owner, of the author's childhood and adolescent exploits on the sea islands, growing up among the black families there. The other book was a series of large-scaled topographic maps of the islands.

Eric spread the book open right over Jackie's papers, and leaning intimately over her shoulder he pointed out exactly what constituted the sea islands. The soft curls of her head were occasionally brushed by Eric's chest and arm as he bent forward, a long firm finger pointing out a feature on the map.

Jackie found her concentration dissolving as she became more aware of the masculine person behind her. It had been a very long time since she was as alert to a male presence as she now felt herself to be with Eric Davidson. It was provocative and startling. He finally straightened and she realized she hadn't heard most of what he'd just said.

"That should give you a good start," he was finishing.

"Thank you," Jackie murmured, now pretending to study the colorful maps.

"Well . . ." Eric said, gathering his books under a muscular arm, and glancing up at the clock over Mrs. Jarrod's desk. ". . . That was an introductory free tour. Tomorrow it'll cost you!" He grinned good-naturedly at her.

"I didn't know I was keeping you from anything important!" Jackie said caustically.

"You were. But you can make up for it another time. I'll see you tomorrow. Oh, and in the meantime, try not to slay any more innocent admirers." He winked, waved, and left the room.

"Arrogant turkey!" Jackie murmured ruefully, turning back to her work.

CHAPTER THREE

Jackie got up and prepared for the day with a sense of anticipation. She tried to tell herself that it was because she was finally getting started. She was finally going to do something positive toward her joint venture with Gwen instead of just talking about it. Not only did she check several times to make sure she had enough film and her lens and tripod, but she just as carefully checked her appearance, not quite satisfied with what she wore. She was dressed in a pair of straight-legged jeans and no fault could be found in the way they smoothly covered her legs. Her yellow top was banded at the waist for a close fit but billowed gently over her chest and ribs. It had short capped sleeves and a boat neckline.

It was a comfortable and simple outfit, but Jackie had changed her mind twice before deciding on it. In annoyance with her picky mood, she raked a comb impatiently through her curls, wondering why choosing clothes this morning had turned into a major project taking an extra half hour. Eric Davidson didn't bother about clothes, she thought fleetingly. But also she wondered for some unaccountable reason how he'd look in a sports jacket with a pale shirt opened coolly at the throat. Jackie conjured up a picture of him bare-chested. Truly shocked at the turn of her thoughts, she grabbed all her equipment and hastened down the stairs from her room before the thoughts went further.

Hannah was seated, this morning, in an old Coney Island type lounge chair under a tree in her yard. The lounger seemed so out of place in Hannah's old-fashioned surroundings. She was reading a letter, but there were also several stacks of papers at her feet in the grass.

Jackie smiled in memory of yesterday morning as she and Hannah had breakfast, and Hannah repeatedly referred to

Timothy. Unable to stand it anymore, Jackie had finally turned a confused countenance to the older woman.

"Hannah, I'm sorry if I'm being nosy, but just who is Timothy?"

"Timothy?" Hannah repeated blankly. Then something dawned in her eyes and she laughed, her body heaving all over. "Why darlin'! Timothy isn't a who. He's a what!" She went over to the screen door and opening it, gestured beyond to someone outside to come in. "Timothy, come in here! I want you to meet someone!"

Jackie waited anticlimactically, wondering still how she'd missed a third person in the house. But through the door lumbered an ancient, slightly overweight dog of indeterminate origins and color. His tongue dripped saliva and hung with the effort of climbing the single step into the house. He gave Jackie one less than curious look, and sought out his water dish next to the kitchen sink. The dog lapped a few times and then collapsed on the floor, almost sitting in his own dish. He regarded Hannah with a look that could only be described as tender.

"Jackie, this is Timothy." Hannah introduced her, and Hannah's look at her four-legged companion could easily be described in the same way.

The mystery of Timothy was now solved.

Jackie saw Timothy squeezed under the stretched-out leg-rest of the lounger. She had no idea how he'd managed to get under and could only hazard a guess as to how he'd get out.

As the screen door opened to show Jackie framed in the doorway, Hannah beamed and moved to get up. But today, Jackie was firm.

"Please don't get up!" she admonished Hannah. "I really couldn't eat breakfast. Not after that incredible gumbo last night!"

Hannah hesitated, but seeing the truth and the determination in Jackie's set features, slowly sank back down in her seat. Timothy lifted one heavy lid to expose a jaundiced eye as he looked at Jackie. But he quickly closed it again in disinterest and went back to sleep. Hannah absently bent to stroke his ear.

"Are you sure, darlin'? Now I can't have you running around in this heat with not a thing in you. How about some toast and coffee?"

"No, nothing, thanks. I may be gone most of the day. I have no idea when I'll get back," Jackie advised Hannah in an apologetic voice. She didn't want the older woman held up in her plans because she wasn't sure what she was doing. "I'll worry about dinner when the time comes."

"Well, if you insist," Hannah responded, none too sure, a frown creasing her dark face. She looked at Jackie and frowned even deeper. Wagging a finger she lectured, "Now you be careful. If you're not sure about this guide person you just bring yourself right back home. You hear?"

Jackie hid a smile. Hannah was really too much, bless her heart.

"I promise I'll be careful," Jackie said solemnly. She checked to make sure she had everything. She even thought to bring a small recorder to keep track of questions she might ask, and the answers to them. Thanks to her fruitful hours at the library yesterday, she had a basis for attacking the problem of what to cover, what to see, and what to ask. She smirked as she heaved the tote onto her shoulder, remembering Eric Davidson's statement about trying to impress him. If nothing else, even he would have to admit she was serious about her work.

Once again, she crossed the Ashley River, going against the early morning traffic as she headed out of town. The day was only partially sunny, and Jackie hoped it wouldn't interfere with her picture taking. She concentrated on remembering the turnoff from the highway that would take her to the pond again, and the house where Eric lived. For some reason apprehension swirled around her stomach muscles. This is stupid, Jackie thought to herself. She had no cause to feel uncertain about seeing the man again. In any case, there was no reason to assume she couldn't handle him if need be.

Jackie found the cutoff easily enough and slowly drove down the road, trying to avoid another cloud of red dust. Before she knew it, she was pulling the car to the same spot where she'd parked two days ago, and turning off the ignition. It was very quiet, and once again Jackie had the sensation of the house being all closed up and empty, of no one living here. And there was no immediate sign of Eric Davidson. Jackie continued to sit in the car, sure that he must have heard her drive up, and expecting him to come out of the house at any moment. But she waited and waited until she felt both foolish for just sitting, and impatient with his absence.

Sucking her teeth impatiently, Jackie tooted the car horn, the high beeping sound splitting the air shrilly and disturbing the morning quiet. A score of birds flapped away from the noise to a safer distance in a farther tree. But still there was no Eric.

When there was still no response, curiosity made Jackie push the door open and climb out of the car. Standing with her legs planted apart and her fists braced saucily on her narrow hips, she looked all around her. The sun through the trees created shafts and beams of light from which she could see steam from the ground moisture swirling up in vaporish forms. It made an intriguing picture to her photographer's eye, but her mind was too much on Eric.

Jackie walked up to the small house and knocked loudly on the door. There was only silence from within. After the second try, she twisted the door knob and was surprised when the door swung open several inches.

"Good morning," came the quiet deep voice behind her. Jackie spun around, her mouth parted in a startled sound. Eric stood regarding her with a smile on his lips, his eyes in his handsome face looking into her own. Jackie noticed at once that he was dressed in the now familiar jeans and sweatshirt, and wondered irrelevantly if he owned any other clothing.

"You are a very nervous person," he commented mocking her. "You must have a very guilty conscience."

"No, I'm not nervous! You just have an evil habit of sneaking up behind people and scaring the life out of them," Jackie answered him bluntly.

A muscle tightened unexpectedly in Eric's jaw, and Jackie saw steel in his eyes and in the look directed at her.

"And you just have an evil habit of being evil!" he responded softly.

Jackie was momentarily taken aback by this and had no immediate answer. She felt warm waves of embarrassment sweep over her. Eric relaxed and grinned at her in an obvious effort to maintain a light mood. He lifted the several bundles he carried in his arms.

"I was out getting breakfast for us." He stepped forward and past Jackie, using his shoulder to push the door open as he entered the small house.

Jackie continued to stand in amazement, staring after his broad back.

"But . . . but I don't usually eat breakfast," she protested weakly, not knowing how else to answer.

"I do," came back Eric's calm response from somewhere inside the house.

Jackie let out an exasperated helpless sigh. She turned and looked at her parked car, the thought flashing in her head that she should leave this impossible, annoying man and go on about her business. She turned at the sound behind her and found Eric filling the door frame as he held the door open for her. His eyes briefly glanced in the direction she'd been looking and back to her.

"Well . . ." he asked pointedly, "are you coming in, or are you going to run off?"

Jackie glanced at him and stiffened her back. Her square jaw lifted defiantly and she narrowed her dark brown eyes at him. But Eric only broadened his smile as he watched her display of indignation.

"You aren't the least bit threatening, Mr. Davidson. But we had an appointment—a business deal, remember? I was expecting to drive around this morning. We're wasting time!"

"I know we have a deal, but I never agreed to driving around before breakfast. And you don't start paying for my time until after we're in the car. Are you coming in?"

"You are *impossible!*" Jackie said helplessly, rolling her eyes heavenward. But she realized that there was nothing to be gained by arguing the point back and forth. She forced some calmness into her demeanor. Without fully registering her action, she looked again at her car as if in indecision.

Eric laughed at her suddenly, harshly, shaking his head. "I tell you what, I'll leave the door open. Okay?" And with that he turned back into the house.

Leaving her standing there only served to make her feel even more foolish, and sighing, Jackie slowly entered the house. She was immediately surprised to find that it was not dark and gloomy inside the tiny structure at all. A quick impression was that the walls were painted white making the room seem much larger, and there were several more windows on either side of the room, allowing for plenty of light.

By the time Jackie'd entered the house Eric had again disappeared. But there was sound and movement in a room that exited off to the right from the small living room and she assumed him to be there. Still standing uncertainly in the center of the floor, Jackie looked around the very simple but neat and cleanly furnished room. She was standing on an oval braided rag rug. There was a chocolate-brown sofa facing the fireplace, and another rag rug in front of it. There was an old lobster catch that had creatively been turned into a coffee table with a sheet of plate glass on top. A floor lamp at one end of the sofa was positioned between the sofa and an old overstuffed arm chair. There was a cane chair between two side windows against one wall. Jackie was surprised and ashamed to admit that she'd expected something much more primitive. This was far from primitive and far from what she'd considered of Eric Davidson. And it was lovely. Jackie found herself leaning thoughtfully against the sofa and looking again around the room. The hominess of it reminded her of Hannah's house.

She followed the sounds into the other room and found herself entering a narrow kitchen with a window at the end wall. Here she found Eric unpacking his bundles. There was something already boiling in a pot on the small stove, and coffee perking in another. Eric unwrapped three apparently freshly caught porgies, tomatoes, oranges, and a loaf of bread. He completely ignored Jackie's presence as he went on to clean the fish and remove the heads. Jackie watched his deft sure movements in fascination. Not looking at her he commented. "You can sit and watch me eat, or you can have some."

"No thanks," Jackie maintained, wondering if he intended to eat all of this himself.

"I work long hours, sometimes six or seven at a stretch. I need my morning nourishment!" He flashed a wide grin at her.

Eric washed and dried the fish, salted and rolled them in cornmeal to coat them.

"Can I help?" Jackie asked for want of anything else to say or do.

Eric looked at her briefly before turning his attention to the frying pan and the oil getting hot in preparation for the fish.

"You can stir that pot." His head nodded to the stove. "And there're a few oranges to squeeze for juice on the table."

Jackie gently stirred the bubbling white mixture and frowned, wondering what it was. She lowered the fire under it and the mixture simmered and thickened as some of the excess water boiled away. Eric silently produced an old-fashioned glass juicer, a bowl and knife, and left Jackie to manage on her own. She felt very odd—domestic—doing this. She liked to cook but had almost never had the opportunity to do so, either at home with her parents, or later with Mark. She would have loved to prepare meals for the two of them to be eaten quietly, slowly together while they talked. But Mark was always moving too fast for that kind of intimacy. Why was it that only with Hannah, and now here in a too narrow kitchen with Eric, did she begin to get the real meaning of the word "home"?

Jackie wondered suddenly how different a person she would have been if she'd had a mother more like Hannah Curtis and less like the business executive her own mother was. Martha Taylor was not a cold woman, just a highly motivated one with a single-minded determination that neither her husband nor daughter knew how to cope with. She stood for no nonsense, got things done, and had little patience for those who didn't. Jackie could hear in her mind the arguments that had gone on seemingly forever between her parents. Her father, a teacher of history, wanting his wife to spend more time with him and their child and less with her business commitments. Her mother, wanting her husband to be more appreciative of her and to aim higher for himself. Jackie, caught in between, confused and very lonely. Jackie had dreams and goals she wanted to follow. But she needed the trappings of a home as well, and people to share it with. She needed someone to be there and care about her. Modeling had given her an instant family, for a while. Dozens of people had worried about how much sleep she got, what she ate, whom she saw. She had lost herself in it gratefully, letting it all happen around her. And then she'd given even that up, leaving her alone once more after Mark Bennett.

Eric's kitchen was not at all conducive to two people working together, and Jackie constantly felt the brush of his arm or shoulder or back as they moved around each other. The constant physical contact awakened all her nerve ends, and she felt short of breath. Jackie began to feel the kitchen get even smaller around her. She was glad when she could finally pour the juice into a pitcher and step aside.

She could not help a small sniff at the air, now filled with the smell of coffee and lightly frying fish.

"I don't usually eat this late," Eric explained to Jackie. Her watch showed nine-fifteen. "I'm normally up and at it by six-thirty."

"My God! That's still the middle of the night!" she groaned.

"It gives me a longer day to get my work done."

"But you're not doing anything right now?"

"I just finished a lot of work. I'm taking a break for a few days before starting all over again. I want to be finished by the first or second week of May. I'm committed to another project this summer that may take me out of the state."

Somehow in the narrow kitchen a small bistro style table with two chairs was situated under the window. Jackie watched as Eric set the table with two plates, glasses, cups, and silverware.

"I didn't realize painters kept so busy," Jackie commented.

"It depends on the painter. I very often make my own work."

"Do you like painting so much? Isn't there anything else you'd rather be doing?"

Eric looked at her quizzically as he lifted the cooked fish from the pan and put it on a platter.

"What makes you think I don't do anything else?"

His voice was challenging. Feeling trapped again by her own thoughts, Jackie shrugged and absently carried the juice and coffee to the table, forcing her once more to brush past Eric who made no move this time to get out of her way.

"You just seem to have so much spare time on your hands. It just seems it could be used more constructively."

Eric stopped to lean back against a counter and stuffed his hands into his pockets, frowning at Jackie. "I am using it constructively. I'm going to be your guide for a while. Afterwards, as I said before, I do have more work to do."

He continued to silently regard her with an expression that was now closed and unreadable. He looked down at his sneakers as though considering his next words.

"I very much like the work I do. All of it."

Jackie persisted. "But haven't you ever wanted to do more. Be more?"

His cat-colored eyes searched hers. Jackie couldn't help wondering what it was he was looking for in her at that moment. A muscle worked in his jaw and his nostrils widened with some underlying emotion.

"I'm doing almost everything I want to do, and I'm everything I want to be. For the moment," he said very quietly. He added pointedly. "There's not a thing wrong with my kind of work."

In confusion, Jackie pulled on a loosely hanging curl and turned to the stove. "Should I bring this, too?" She reached for the simmering pot to cover the awkward moment.

"I'll get it," Eric said brusquely and reached over her arm with a pot holder to lift the pot from the burner. He went to the table and sat down to eat his breakfast. Jackie had the choice of either returning to the living room to wait for him, or sitting with him. Moving forward slowly, she sat down opposite him. The table did not provide a lot of room, over or under it, and their knees touched and pressed against one another. Their eyes looked up and locked for a quick breathless second before Jackie shifted to the side, bringing her legs out from under the table edge.

She again pulled nervously on a curl and missed the fleeting smile Eric gave her as he watched. He poured some of the white porridge-like substance onto his plate. He added sliced tomatoes, bread, poured juice and coffee for himself, and lifted his fork to begin. Jackie watched his plate in awe, there being not an inch of clear space left on it. She watched the white stuff with butter melting on it and couldn't bring herself to ask what it was.

"At least have some juice and coffee," Eric coaxed in his deep voice. His eyes swept over her tall, thin frame. "Believe me, it won't hurt you at all!"

Jackie grimaced at him but nonetheless poured herself some of both. She could not help being assailed by the aroma of the fish and the fresh bread, but she lifted her chin, averting her eyes to the window.

Eric chuckled, shaking his head gently in amusement as he filled his fork with food again.

"What's so funny?" Jackie asked suspiciously.

"You. You're so damned stubborn. You won't give an inch, will you?"

"I don't know what you're talking about," she maintained stubbornly, proving his point.

"I mean, you'd love to have some of this, wouldn't you? But you're determined not to relax and enjoy breakfast with me."

"We didn't agree to this."

"Okay, okay . . . so we didn't. But it won't kill you or ruin your book to spend an hour here. Here . . ." Eric said as he proceeded to put a piece of fried porgy on her plate and a serving of the porridge.

Jackie didn't stop him, annoyed with herself for wanting to taste it. But it didn't end there, and she had to steel herself for the further humiliation of having to ask him what she was eating. She put a pat of butter on it as she'd seen Eric do. She took a mouthful and found it tasty and very much like a cereal, but smoother. Having prepared herself for ridicule from Eric, Jackie put down her fork.

"This is very good. What do you call it?"

She looked straight at Eric as he lifted his eyes to her brown face in astonishment. He looked to see if she was putting him on, and knew at once that she wasn't. Evenly he replied.

"That's hominy grits you're eating. I take it you've never had it before?"

"Never," she answered honestly, not ashamed to admit there were foods and things common to his background and surroundings which she knew nothing about. She held his gaze for a minute longer and lifted her fork again. In a purely conversational tone she asked him, "Have you ever had Black and Whites?"

"No," he answered around a sip of coffee.

"Good!" Jackie said wickedly. "Now we're even."

Eric chuckled lightly, appreciating her maneuver. "Well . . . are you going to put me out of my misery and tell me what a Black and White is?"

Jackie quirked a brow. "It's a large, round, thick cake-like cookie that's frosted half vanilla and half chocolate."

"How democratic!" Eric commented. "A political cookie?"

Jackie couldn't help laughing. "You're making fun of it. But in

New York after school, my friends and I would buy them from a bake shop a block away."

They ate quietly for a few minutes, Eric automatically refilling their coffee mugs. He sat back in his chair watching Jackie as she ate. She felt very relaxed—and guilty. Her one thought right now was just trying to understand her giving in to Eric's invitation to breakfast when she'd been so firm with Hannah Curtis earlier. Eric stretched out a long leg and forcing a hand into his pants pocket extracted a slightly crushed pack of cigarettes.

"Mind if I smoke?" he asked. Jackie shook her head as he leaned to the side and struck a match on the burner of the stove. He lit the end and inhaled deeply, then exhaled while the smoke curled up and back into his nostril, flaring it wide.

Jackie watched him over the rim of her coffee cup, finding his motions oddly masculine. Almost seductive in the way his jaw tensed when he inhaled, the way his wide mouth formed a soft circle when he exhaled. The way his strong large fingers held the cigarette. She felt mesmerized. Her lips parted with the additional thought of whether these same hands could also hold gently, caress softly.

Her dark eyes looked up into his and the silence was filled with a tension that seemed to get more taut with each passing second. Eric's voice came soft and low, ending her lassitude, his words a shock of double meaning.

"How long has it been?"

Jackie wasn't sure she'd heard him right as her body lost its relaxed pose and was once again alert. "What do you mean, how long has it been?"

"Since your divorce."

Jackie slowly put the cup down and hoped that her hands weren't noticeably shaking. "How do you know I was married?"

He squinted against the smoke from his cigarette. "It's just a guess. You seem too protective of yourself, too cautious around men."

Jackie looked into the half-filled coffee cup. "That doesn't mean I was married."

"But I'm right, aren't I?" Eric said tilting his head to the side.

"It was a long time ago . . . and it's none of your business," she said tightly.

"Does it still hurt? Was it that bad?" he asked softly.

"What makes you think so?" she asked breathlessly, keeping her eyes lowered.

"You're very angry right now and very uptight."

"I'm not angry," Jackie said, but she was frowning, twisting the cup around in one spot on the tabletop.

"Yes you are," Eric contradicted in a low tone.

Jackie got up suddenly from the table. "Really, Mr. Davidson. Why are you constantly treating me as if I was a child?" she said in agitation.

"I'm not. I'm trying to talk to you one grown-up to another. How else do I get to know you?" he asked reasonably.

"I don't want you to get to know me. And I certainly don't want to talk to you about . . . about my past. People who've known me a lot longer than you know when to back off and just leave me alone!"

"Is that how you're used to being treated? Has everyone been handling you with kid gloves, like porcelain that can easily break? Afraid to get you upset? Pampering you? Protecting you? Letting you keep all that stuff bottled up inside? Didn't it ever occur to you or anyone else that all those pent up emotions were going to explode some day?" He spoke evenly.

His audacity was unbearable, but Jackie fought back the urge to yell and rant at him for his interference. "You're lecturing me again, Mr. Davidson. You seem to enjoy trying to humiliate me and make me feel foolish."

"You do a pretty good job of that all by yourself!" He grinned back at her, using that same controlled, maddeningly soft tone.

Jackie did no thinking at all as she next found the open palm of her hand in motion as it reached out to strike Eric. But he was quicker and he was none too gentle as his fingers gripped her wrist firmly. Jackie gasped and they glared at each other in the silence that followed.

"Sit down," Eric commanded quietly and did not release her wrist until she'd obeyed. ". . . And stop acting like a spoiled brat!"

Jackie absently rubbed the spot where he'd held her, her features still mutinous and stormy, her breathing rapid with mixed emotions.

"And relax," he advised tersely. "You're probably right. It's none of my business. Feel better now?"

But Jackie did, indeed, feel foolish and childish now. She was used to her friends putting up with her defenses and understanding them. It was a new experience having someone, a virtual stranger, tell her she had far too many. With slightly shaking hands Jackie lifted her cup and drank deeply from it, not even flinching when the hot liquid scalded her mouth. "I . . . I'm sorry," she whispered in a slightly shaky voice. Even supposing that Eric's interference had been intolerable, she knew that she had reacted childishly. Eric watched her struggling forlornly with the embarrassing moment, and recognized that it was never easy to apologize. His features softened.

"So am I," he offered, and Jackie looked up in surprise at the gentleness of his voice. There was no mocking either in his tone or in his catlike eyes, and she knew he was sincere. She relaxed at once, and as if offering further peace, Eric silently poured still more coffee into their cups as Jackie let out a deep emotional sigh.

"You're right. I was married. It ended because we were more different than I'd first realized. We never should have married."

Eric silently lit another cigarette. "We all make mistakes," he said softly.

Jackie chuckled dryly. "This was a real doosie!" she quipped.

Eric exhaled smoke into the air. "Do you still love him?"

"No!" Jackie responded emphatically, shaking her head. "But there was a lot of . . . of anger. And it was hard getting over that."

Eric looked her over knowingly. "I think there are still things that make you very angry."

Jackie didn't respond to that observation. She'd already said more than enough that was highly personal.

"Why did you stop modeling?" Eric asked, changing subjects on her.

Jackie shrugged. "It was all so . . . so superficial after a while. As long as I stayed slim and attractive, that's all anyone wanted to know about me. I needed something more than that."

Eric lowered his eyes to the table, thoughtfully tapping the ash off the end of his cigarette into an ashtray. "And I suppose your husband didn't fulfill that something more?"

Jackie couldn't begin to find words to answer that, and only let out a skeptical, low, humorless laugh.

Eric silently offered her a cigarette, but she refused. Jackie finished her coffee and Eric his cigarette. Exhaling one last time he stood up and began to clear the table. The only sound was that of the porcelain plates and the silverware hitting against each other.

With an effort, Jackie took a deep breath and sat up straight. "It's getting very late. Thank you for breakfast, but I'd like to get started now." The business Jackie was back in control.

Eric said nothing as he stacked dishes in the sink and ran hot water on them.

"Do you want me to wash those?" she offered hesitantly.

"I'm just going to leave them to soak the grease off. I can do them this afternoon." He turned to lean against the counter as he dried his hands on a towel.

"Besides, I'm not in the habit of inviting women to eat with me and then expecting them to clean up!"

Jackie wondered in annoyance how many women there had been, exactly. He looked with amusement at her, and under his smiling eyes she allowed herself to relax again, but only a little. With an exaggerated flourish Eric waved her to the door.

"The tour begins through here."

Jackie preceded him from the kitchen and back to the living room where the front door still stood open. Once outside, Jackie took in a deep lungful of fresh air. She was glad to be out of the close confines of his house. Eric locked the door and followed Jackie to the car.

"I'll drive," he said, and opened the door to get in. Jackie was surprised but offered no objections as she simply walked around to the passenger side.

She felt odd being in the passive position in her own car, but she found she didn't mind Eric's handling of the vehicle. She could see he drove well and knew what he was doing. Jackie stole a glance at his profile, and watched his brows slightly drawn in concentration, his jaw tensing. The sun occasionally touched on his brown skin, making it look cinnamon with reddish undertones. As if feeling her eyes on him, Eric looked quickly at her and back to the road.

"You really got burned at me."

"What?" Jackie questioned.

"For jumping into your business," he reminded her ruefully.

"Oh. That. As I said before it was a long time ago. It's over now."

"Are you sure?" Eric frowned.

"I'm sure," she answered firmly, effectively putting an end to the subject. At least for the time being.

Eric was an excellent guide. He was patient with her frequent demands to stop the car while she got out to examine the land, or to shoot farms and farmers, to explain the dialect. Unlike the mocking attitude he'd sometimes taken with her since they'd met, his narrative about the sea islands was loose, entertaining, and laced with amusing history and stories. But Jackie had her guard up still, keeping her distance and maintaining an aloofness. The easier, more relaxed, and more congenial Eric became, the more Jackie struggled to establish a stiff, remote position. She didn't want him to be likable.

Eric did not seem to notice as he regaled her with information about Johns Island, James Island, and Wadmalaw, all near Charleston. Edisto was forty miles to the south and he said they'd drive there another day, and on another to cover Port Royal, St. Helena, and Hilton Head near the mouth of the Savannah.

They drove to the very edge of the Carolina coast, looking out over an endless Atlantic. Eric leaned against the door of the car smoking and watched as Jackie once again set up to take pictures. Finally he came up to her, took her by the wrist, and pulled her away from the camera and tripod.

"You're making me tired just watching you," he responded in answer to her surprised exclamation. "Just sit down for a while. The picture will still be there." He sat down on a boulder, leaving room for her to perch next to him. Jackie gave in reluctantly, as Eric took out and lit another cigarette. He looked away from her, over the water and the land.

"Do you like it here? It's very beautiful."

"Yes, it is." Jackie agreed to his comment but ignored the question. She scuffed the toe of her canvas shoe restlessly in the pebbly ground.

"Why are the people around here considered to be so different? Why would Gwen be so interested?" Jackie found herself asking Eric.

"Well, first of all it's the black people of the islands that spark the most interest. Mostly it's their way of speaking. It's a unique mixture of English as the southern blacks speak it with the idioms, special adjectives, mixed with a lingering African intonation. The words come out sounding very different, a language all its own."

"Hasn't it ever changed?"

Eric shrugged. "I guess now it's changing. People don't stay on the island all their lives anymore. They leave for larger cities and a different life."

"What about their Gullah dialect? Can you still hear it?"

"Oh yeah. It's very musical—lilting. Very much like the West Indian dialect. Sometimes hard to follow, and if the speaker is excited or mad, almost impossible to understand unless you're used to hearing it. My grandmother never learned any other way of talking. I used to sit with my mouth hanging open as a kid, just listening to Nana go on and on about one thing or another. She had an opinion on everything."

"Yes! You did say your grandmother was born around here. Do you think I could talk to her someday? Do you think she'd mind having her picture taken?"

Eric turned to regard her. He squinted against the afternoon sun and she couldn't see his eyes, but there was an odd expression on his face. Partly surprise, Jackie guessed. But maybe also disappointment.

"She wouldn't have minded at all. But unfortunately for all of us, my grandmother died more than three years ago," Eric informed her quietly.

Jackie felt suddenly stricken. "Oh. I'm very sorry."

Eric smiled. "Don't be. How were you supposed to know."

Jackie shook her head helplessly. "I just got so caught up in what I'm doing, I didn't think . . . I never thought . . ."

"You're right." Eric nodded, not unkindly. "But that's how things get done sometimes. Nana was a fabulous old lady. She used to smoke a pipe and that used to knock me out! To see my grandmother smoking! She loved baseball and used to sit bent over the radio on her porch all summer long listening and smoking. And man could that lady cook! She used to make things even my mother never learned how to cook, but I loved her sweet potato pie best." Eric shook his head smiling in sweet reminiscence.

Jackie watched and listened, surprised by this other Eric Davidson. This one was more than the virile strong man whose presence disturbed her against her will and made itself felt. This was not the antagonist of this morning or the arrogant person lecturing her. This was a man who'd once been a small boy with a grandmother who was magical to him, and whom he obviously adored. This was a man with rich memories and a lively past who was so much more than she thought, and more than she wanted to know. Jackie wondered for the first time what kind of family he was from. Who were his parents, his sisters and brothers? What was he like as a very young man? Why wasn't he married? Or was he?

She frowned and fidgeted with her new thoughts. It was not her business to know. She was not sitting here on the edge of the United States waiting to find out. Jackie felt the tips of Eric's fingers touch her bare arm and she jumped, her eyes flying wide to his.

"I'm sorry you couldn't have met her. She was really something else! And she would have liked you!"

"Why?" Jackie asked in honest curiosity.

A smile began to grow on Eric's handsome face. "She just would have. She would want to have 'She-She talk' with you and probably tell you 'Un lick da' gal good-fashion.' " Eric spoke in a cadence Jackie had not heard before and couldn't begin to decipher.

Eric laughed in his deep voice at the expression on her face. Jackie started to speak but Eric shook his head and stood up.

"Sorry. The translation for that is another day. Finish your pictures before the light goes." And he casually strolled back to the car leaving Jackie to feel in great doubt as to whether she really knew Eric Davidson at all.

Jackie finished her pictures as Eric advised, but she wasn't sure she was pleased with the results. She felt impatient with her camera and her abilities. Stepping back away from the equipment she looked around again, slowly registering everything in her mind. She finally gave up. It would not help her or the book to force a picture where none existed. She'd lost her concentration, was momentarily distracted. In her mind was an image of Eric Davidson sitting cross-legged in front of a grand-mother with a pipe in her mouth, listening to the music of her voice and words.

She looked over her shoulder at him to find him still leaning against the car, his strong arms crossed over his chest, one hand holding a cigarette. His head was turned away from her as he watched a small fishing craft off the coast. His expression was completely relaxed, completely off guard, and Jackie was re-sponsive to what she saw. She took the camera off the tripod and replacing her wide-angle lens with the telephoto, shot what she saw of Eric through her lens.

Jackie finished the film and felt she'd done enough for one day. She gathered her equipment and Eric came to help her load it into the small car.

"Did you get what you wanted?" he asked.

Jackie looked at him hard for a second before answering. "I don't know." She sighed. "I think I got some good stuff here, but . . ."

Eric waited, opening the car door for her.

"I love photography, but sometimes I see things better with my own eyes. And what I see with my eyes I can't always put on film," she tried to explain.

Eric nodded. "I know what you mean. Sometimes you use your eyes from the insides out—with feelings. Or sometimes through windows on the past. That's hard to capture on film. That's why I like painting. I get to use my eyes all the time."

His last comment confused Jackie and she just stared at him. Eric, misunderstanding her expression, added mysteriously. "You just keep looking. You'll eventually see what you really want to see all the time."

CHAPTER FOUR

That afternoon set the pattern for the next four days of exploration. Each day Eric would drive the compact car to another part
of the sea islands, explain its characteristics, and then step back
while Jackie felt her way around the unfamiliar people and language and landscape to hunt out those images she wanted to
capture on film. For the most part Eric watched her silently,
offering few suggestions, but was patient and helpful when she
needed it. She was always aware of his tall dark presence.

The second morning Jackie arrived to pick up Eric she found
breakfast already made, but on not so grand a scale as the first
time. There was no protest or show of impatience from her this
time, and she was surprised at how easily she was persuaded to
take a seat at the absurdly small bistro table and share eggs and
ham, and more of the white hominy grits. As she ate, Jackie
wondered how many other women Eric Davidson had made
breakfast for in his narrow kitchen. How many had he acted as
guide for on the coast of South Carolina? How many had he
loved—or made love to?

Jackie's fork dropped to the floor, startling her out of her daydream. Eric quickly retrieved it and gave her a clean one. She
accepted it, eyes lowered, cheeks tinged with embarrassment.
She found herself taking fugitive glances at him, at his hands
and his mouth, feeling her breath catch in her chest for no good
reason. Feeling her body abandon itself to lethargy at odd, unex-
plainable moments, and finally explaining it all away to South
Carolina late spring heat. He continued to wear the sweatshirt
and jeans and Jackie continued to think of him as a much
younger man than he actually must have been.

A weekend appeared out of nowhere and Eric had to remind
her that on the seventh day, even she had to rest. And besides,
he had plans for the next few days. Jackie experienced the contradiction of being glad for the break away from him, hoping

the time would wash away her odd dreamy state, but also not knowing what to do with herself for two days.

The only moments of total antagonism that remained between them came at Jackie's insistence on paying Eric at the end of each day for his time touring her around. The more Jackie insisted, the tighter and more obstinate he became until she threatened to end the whole arrangement. He'd ended up giving in, calling her Boss Lady in a none too flattering way, and left the car, slamming the door harder than was necessary. It didn't fail to leave Jackie feeling let down and confused, but at least she felt she was the one in control.

She grew to admire and love the different places that made up the sea islands. And although the research would end in the story of Johns Island, Edisto Island became her favorite. It was there that her senses were most aware and alert to colors and smells. It was there that gave her her most creative challenges in picture taking.

Edisto was the last of the islands Eric had brought her to, and the one she insisted on coming back to a second time. There she photographed sections of farms somewhat run into the ground, but the land and lopsided shacks belonging to no one else but these gentle, good-humored people who worked them. The lilting dialect was confusing to understand, but pure music in its other qualities. It was late on Friday afternoon when she and Eric worked their way back to one spot close to the coastline waters, which left the land sandy in some places, swampy in others.

By herself as she usually did, Jackie set up her tripod and camera, snapping pictures until her mind's eye zeroed in on the one she really wanted. Eric was somewhere behind her, leaning a shoulder against a tree as he smoked and quietly watched.

"That's going to make a lousy picture," he said evenly behind her.

Jackie tried to ignore him, his few criticisms having the ability to make her feel inadequate. It was hard for her to give him credit for having a good eye for composition, even better than her own. She wanted to feel that there was some one thing she did better all on her own. Stubbornly she kept her back turned and continued to set the camera where she wanted. She never heard Eric move, but suddenly there was a gentle grip on both her shoulders as he tried to pull her back from the camera, and she instinctively resisted.

"What are you doing?" she asked irritably, only aware of his hands which seemed to burn through her cotton blouse to her skin beneath. She was so conscious and sensitive suddenly to his presence, the touch of his hands. His strength all seemed to follow along his arms and into his hands and fingertips. For an inexplicable moment she knew the desire to let those hands pull her back against his broad hard chest. She felt tired enough to give in.

"I want you to just stand here and look. What are you taking a picture of?" Eric let go of her shoulders and came to stand next to her. Slowly Jackie let out the breath she was holding. She frowned, looking across the almost flat landscape, trying to regain her concentration. There was a mud pond, and a shack off to her left.

"I want to get this as a panorama. I think . . ."

"You think? Why? What are you trying to show?"

Jackie hesitated. She hadn't thought. She couldn't remember. She'd lost her train of ideas when Eric had touched her. Vaguely, she rubbed her temples with the tips of her fingers, trying to gather her senses. What did she want the picture to say? That in this lonely isolated spot of land people had none-theless lived, raised families and food, and thrived for genera-tions.

"I want to show life here. Right in this empty place."

"Okay. How can you show life here just shooting a pond with some scattered trees?"

Again he put his hands on her shoulders and again an odd shock of electricity ran through her. He turned her to her left.

"Now look this way. What do you see?"

Jackie let her eyes roam over everything in front of her. There was a line of low hanging moss. The ground around it was somewhat steamy, but being carefully picked over by a bunch of scrawny hens and roosters. A dog lay limply, half supported by the remaining stump of a long ago cut tree, its ears twitching sporadically to dislodge the flies annoying it.

The shack in the shadowed background stood ancient and on the ratty edge of total collapse, its open door yawning into a black interior. There was a clothesline, barely visible from the other side of the house, with freshly washed clothes. And there was a basket of ripened red tomatoes sitting on a pail turned bottom side up, right next to the door.

Jackie's overworked, tired eyes took it all in and suddenly picked up the brilliant red of the tomatoes and the bright-colored fabric on the clothesline against the gray bleached boards of the house. She got her camera, set it up once again. Behind her, Eric softly suggested playing with the exposure time to emphasize different aspects of the frame.

This one scene led Jackie to do a whole series until she noticed the sun beginning to move farther west, and no longer giving her the light she needed. She began then to dismantle her equipment and pack it away in her camera bag. They were some distance from the parked car and had to make two trips to reload everything.

Eric turned from putting the camera bag in the trunk of the car to see Jackie moving toward him through the narrow curving avenue of trees. Her tripod was held awkwardly under one arm, and two cameras hung over the other arm, and lens cases in her hand. The ground was a tangled web of vines and weeds. Jackie's toe caught well under one and her next step sent her flying forward and down, her arms and hands instinctively dropping their burden as she reached out to break the fall.

Jackie heard someone shout her name, or at least she thought she did. It might have been her own voice let out in an involuntary groan of pain as her knees and elbows made hard jarring contact with the ground. She lay, momentarily stunned. Then Eric was hunkered down beside her, grabbing her shoulders to turn her back against his chest and pull her into a sitting position.

"Hey! Are you all right?" Eric asked urgently in his deep voice.

Jackie had her bottom lip between her teeth, and she mutely nodded yes.

"Are you sure?" Eric persisted, his hands moving slowly and gently down her arms, squeezing and testing for injuries. Moving down to her thighs to straighten out her bent legs from under her.

She lay back against the warm, hard comfort of Eric's chest, in the semicircle of his arms. The curls on her head brushed under his chin and against his throat. He touched her knee and moved the hand up her thigh again. Jackie moaned, and closed her eyes tight not wanting to cry.

"Damn it! You are hurt!" he said angrily. He reached under Jackie's arms, his long fingers pressed against the round curve of her breasts. Eric moved to one knee and one foot on the ground, and slowly pulled Jackie to her feet.

She felt dizzy, but it was not from the fall she'd just taken. She swayed with the fear of the one she might take right into Eric's arms. Feeling her breath come raggedly between her teeth, she firmly pushed his hands away.

"Stop it," she managed to get out. The words were said in a shaky voice, making her sound agitated and confused.

Eric looked at her hard for a second, his expression concerned. Jackie jerked her eyes away from his and swayed again.

"This is not the time to get touchy!" he said in exasperation. "I think you really hurt yourself." He took her gently by the arms, his topaz eyes sweeping over her in some knowledgeable way, looking for bruises and cuts.

Jackie had mud all over her tan jeans, and twigs and leaves stuck everywhere, some even managing to cling to the curls of her hair. She twisted one arm free from Eric's grasp and rubbed the elbow that had hit the ground the hardest. It was sore and tender to the touch.

Eric pulled leaves and debris from her clothing, his hands gentle, brushing over her hips and lower back, her breasts and shoulders. She began to tremble.

"Don't faint on me now!" Eric softly teased, but Jackie never heard him. This was the closest she'd ever been to Eric physically and she was alarmed at the devastating effect it had on her system.

His shirt hinted of oil and paint, of turpentine, linen and gesso. There was tobacco permeated into the fabric, and all over he smelled like a man. It was intoxicating and heady, so unlike the cologned Mark. She slowly inhaled, wanting it to fill her senses, to get drunk on it and let it obliterate her past.

Jackie's eyes seemed glued to the movement of a pulse in his throat. Eric slowly pulled her closer until she rested, unresisting, on the incredible firm surface of his chest. She could feel his strong heart beat against her own rapidly rising and falling chest. Jackie felt a feathery brush of lips against her temple.

"Jackie, are you okay?" he whispered.

She was far from being okay. "Please . . . don't," she whispered, and moved to pull back. Eric held her fast.

"I'm not going to hurt you," he said impatiently, softly.

"Then just what are you doing? Administering first aid or kindness? Do I look so needy?" she implored looking up into his face. Jackie began to sink into the depths of his eyes. His brown skin with the laugh lines and deep furrows on either side of his mouth looked warm. At the moment a muscle in his jaw worked tensely with some unnamed emotion and energy. She wanted to reach out and smooth it down, but of course didn't.

It was not mercy that was reflected in Eric's eyes. She couldn't gather herself enough to identify the look he now gave her. It was new to her, unfamiliar.

"Kindness is not exactly what I had in mind," he whispered in a voice gone husky and caressing.

Eric bent his head to Jackie's, tilting his to accommodate his wide mouth to the surface of hers. The touch was tentative, exploring, gentle, but nonetheless Jackie felt her knees begin to give way and she let her body be supported by the strength of his. Ending the exploration, Eric's lips parted to make a complete claim to Jackie's, and hers parted in complete acquiescence. His arms closed further around her back and somewhere in her flustered mind she was grateful, knowing that otherwise she wasn't sure she could stand on her own.

It did not occur to Jackie immediately that she was being rather cooperative, or that she was enjoying this embrace. It was gentle and she was susceptible to that. She was being drawn into a warm vortex of feeling as she fully experienced the taste of Eric's mouth on hers. It would be so easy to just let go, give in to the consuming sensations he created. But suddenly, in alarm, she forced her head to the side and away, trying to catch her breath. How could she have thought this man was not dangerous. He was a hazard to every part of her. Her nerves, her senses, her emotions—her body, as it betrayed her and responded to his touch and nearness.

"Eric, please," she said in a strangled voice and tried to push him away.

Reluctantly, he let some space develop between them as he slid his large hands to her waist and provocatively up to her rib cage. Her stomach muscles knotted.

"Please Eric, what?" he asked.

"Please stop," she answered seriously.

Eric considered her for a moment, and letting out a sigh, stepped back and released her. "Your ex really did a number on you, didn't he? Now, at least you do know how to say my name. I guess that's a start. Is that what it takes? You getting hurt, me kissing you?"

"We're not going to start anything. I was . . . was just upset, that's all," she muttered.

"Yes, you were. But now you're recovered, is that it?"

"Yes! That's it," she said, but still not in control of her senses.

Eric shook his head in wry amusement. "Damn! You're going to go kicking and screaming all the way, aren't you? Even if it's something you want, or that's good for you."

"You couldn't possibly know what I want . . . or what's good for me!" she muttered. Jackie brushed her hands impatiently back and forth over her head and shook it to dislodge the remaining soil. She made the attempt on her pants next, but it was hopeless. They needed washing. Eric walked past her and retrieved her tripod and cameras.

"Oh, no! My cameras!" she wailed, rushing over to take them from Eric.

"I think they're okay. The cases were on." He bent to pick up the lens cases.

"They seem okay." She frowned, twisting them this way and that, testing the buttons, and knobs. Satisfied, she sighed, and again closed the cases around the camera bodies.

Eric stood speculating, his eyes on her, one hand on his hip.

"Look, I think you've had it for today. Let's get this stuff put away. I'm taking you back."

She started to protest and quickly gave it up. She was tired, and sore all over, and she looked a mess. Eric moved to open the car door, and limping slightly, Jackie followed. Eric came back to her side and with an arm around her narrow waist, helped her back to the car and into the front seat. Her legs still dangling sideways out the door, Eric removed her canvas shoes to find one ankle swollen and red. Jackie winced when he touched it.

"Sorry." He muttered an apology as he continued to probe the tender area.

"It's not fractured, but you shouldn't plan on going dancing tonight."

"Oh hell! I'd hoped to get out tomorrow."

"Forget tomorrow. You should rest that leg. Besides, I couldn't take you around."

"Oh . . ." she murmured, vaguely disappointed.

"I have plans for the weekend. You could use two days' rest yourself."

Eric had begun to absently, gently, massage her ankle and Jackie felt a warm lethargy attack the rest of her leg.

"My leg feels better, thank you," she said breathlessly and pulled it out of his grasp.

Eric shot her a speculative look, the muscles twisting tightly in his jaw, before he got up, closed the door on her, and came around to the driver's side.

It was almost dark now, and a multitude of unfamiliar night sounds broke through the still air. Jackie was now thankful for Eric's driving leaving her free to relax. She closed her eyes warily, and rested her head back against the headrest. With her eyes closed she was conscious of the remaining tingling sensation of Eric's mouth on hers. She resisted the temptation to touch her lips with her fingertips. She had not ever been kissed like that by Mark. Mark's kisses had been too sure. Taking quick, hard possession of her and forcing her to his will. They had been demanding. With his kisses Mark had invaded her being. She never participated in them. She had been controlled and victimized by them. But more disturbing than any of this was the realization that Mark's kisses had never left her weak-kneed as Eric's brief touch had done.

Jackie squirmed, blaming her agitated state on her ungraceful fall to the ground, and the fact that she was probably still shaken up.

"Are you sure you're okay?" Eric asked suddenly.

"Yes," Jackie answered simply, too weak to say more.

"Are you in pain?"

Yes. "No," came the monosyllabic answer.

"You'll be home soon," he assured her, taking her relative silence as a sign of how uncomfortable she was, his voice sympathetic.

Jackie was forced to give him her address and he nodded silently, indicating he knew where that was. She was happier than she'd admit to when the car pulled up in front of the green wood-frame house. Jackie opened the door before Eric had a chance to come around to her side and assist her. She lifted her feet to swing them out of the car and she suddenly exclaimed.

"Oh, no!" she groaned. "My shoes! Where are my shoes!" She searched around under her seat, but knew she wouldn't find them.

"Oh Christ!" Eric murmured. "I'm sorry. It's my fault. I must have left them on the ground next to the car back on Edisto."

Jackie collapsed back in her seat in defeat. Complete exhaustion swept over her all at once. She wanted to give up, go to bed, hide, and sleep for a week.

"I hope you have another pair," Eric said, and although his face was perfectly straight, his mouth quivered in amusement.

"That's not funny!" Jackie said tersely.

"Come on." He smiled. "I'll help you to the door."

"Any more of your help is likely to get me killed!" she mumbled, standing up without his assistance and promptly wincing upon taking the first barefoot step.

"Not unless you succeed first," Eric said sarcastically as he bent and placed an arm under her knees and lifted her into his arms and against his chest. Jackie was forced to put her arms about his neck or risk rolling out of his hold and onto the ground. She'd had enough of picking herself up off the ground for one day, and held on tightly.

Eric was amused, and a deep chuckle rumbled in his chest. She could feel it against her side. Jackie realized in irritation that Eric was enjoying her predicament of being dependent on him.

The door to the green house pulled open and out came Hannah, her hands raised in supplication.

"Lord have mercy! What happened darlin'?" she asked, greatly upset.

"It's okay, Hannah," Jackie soothed over her shoulder as Eric carried her effortlessly up the steps and past the door that stood open.

Hannah hurried ahead of Eric, indicating the love seat in the front parlor. He gently set Jackie down, and stood back with his hands on his hips as Hannah tisked over Jackie.

"Lord, child. What happened? Did you have an accident?" and she looked suspiciously at Eric who smiled at her, immediately melting Hannah's reserves.

"No. No, not really, I . . . I just tripped and fell. I think I twisted my ankle."

"But where are your shoes?" Hannah asked in confusion.

Jackie looked helplessly at Eric, who looked down at his toes to hide his smile. He didn't seem at all inclined to make the situation easier.

"Well, you see . . ." Jackie began.

"I'm Eric Davidson." Eric chose that moment to become involved. Jackie and Hannah looked up at his tall form, and a smile of pure pleasure lit Hannah's dark face. She reached out to take Eric's offered hand.

"How do you do," Hannah cooed so sweetly that Jackie's eyes flew open and she rolled her eyes to the ceiling.

"I'm Hannah Curtis. Won't you sit down?"

"No thank you. It's late and I have to get going. I believe, er, Miss *Taylor,*" he emphasized, "left them behind when we took them off to examine the injury."

"Are you the young man who's Jackie's guide?" Hannah asked guilelessly.

"Yes, I am," Eric admitted, quirking a brow at Jackie briefly.

"How lovely!" Hannah gushed. Jackie thought she would die.

"Yes, isn't it?" Eric agreed blandly. He began to back toward the door, his eyes on Jackie now. "Stay off that foot. Soak it in Epsom salts if you have any. I'll stop by Monday to see how you're doing. No expeditions, okay?"

"It's not necessary for you to come by. . . ." Jackie began.

"Why darlin'! I think it's very nice of Mr. Davidson. Of course he can stop by if he wants!" Hannah said. Then she frowned at him. "But if you got here this evening in Jackie's car, how will you get home?"

"Don't worry. I'll get there."

"Are you sure you won't stay a while?" Hannah implored

sweetly. "We'd love to have you to dinner with us, wouldn't we Jackie?"

Eric looked at Jackie and she could only stare back at him. "Some other time, maybe," Eric said to Hannah, letting Jackie off the hook.

"Maybe Monday, if you stop by," Hannah encouraged.

"Thank you. Nice to have met you, Mrs. Curtis."

"Hannah, please."

"Hannah." He nodded once more to Jackie and left, the door closing softly behind him.

"Why, what a very nice young man!" Hannah said in surprise.

Jackie closed her eyes and groaned.

Hannah never gave Jackie's swollen ankle any time to be a nuisance or to continue to hurt. After Jackie had limped upstairs to her room, she stripped off her stained and wrinkled clothing and ran a bath. Later, sitting on the edge of her bed, light robe wrapped around her, she allowed Hannah to soak the foot, rub some strange-smelling ointment into the tender skin, and bring her dinner on a tray. She sat on the bed eating, while Hannah carried on a mostly one-sided conversation about Eric Davidson.

Jackie herself had many thoughts about the Eric Davidson she thought she knew, but she wasn't prepared to discuss them with anyone yet. Eventually Hannah, taking Jackie's silence as an indication of pain and fatigue, removed the dinner tray and said an early goodnight to her young houseguest.

But it was not to be an early night for Jackie. She was left in the quiet of her room with two ideas to ponder. One was the overwhelming effect she'd experienced by Eric's light kiss. It had only lasted a few seconds, but even now as she thought of it, she felt it again on her mouth. She also felt an odd swirling of feeling deep in her stomach and she grabbed at it as though in pain. She had felt surrounded by Eric, but in a gentle protective sense. Not like the imprisonment she'd eventually come to know with Mark where concern for her and her wants was not the controlling factor.

The second idea was that maybe Eric was not all that he seemed to be. He'd been so easy with her, although she was a bit susceptible at the time and tired. But Hannah was not a person

to be easily fooled or easily swayed. Eric had charmed her almost instantly, winning her completely to him. It had annoyed
Jackie that he would step into her small domain, temporary as it
was, and sweep into the center of attention as though he be-
longed there.

Yes, he had a certain raw masculine vitality that no doubt
appealed to many women, no matter what the age. But yes, too,
there seemed to be much, much more. First of all, where her
project was concerned, Eric took her very seriously, and was
helpful and cooperative. In those moments they were as equals,
as she came to trust more and more his views and opinions
about how best to work.

Jackie remembered her excursion into the Charleston Library
a week ago, and Martha Jarrod's glowing commentary on Eric.
And then Hannah's easy acceptance of him. Surely, both of
these people couldn't be wrong. But then if not, what did that
make her opinion of him? He was personable, and he had an
easy way about him, a subtle sense of humor. There was really
nothing at all to object to in Eric Davidson—except the way he
made her feel inside when he got too close to her.

Jackie was not altogether happy with the thought. It made her
very uncomfortable and very unsure. She had so misjudged
Mark and her relationship with him that she wasn't sure she
could trust any of her senses where Eric Davidson was concerned. There was still a questioning apprehension she had with
him that left her confused and defensive.

Mark Bennett had not mistreated her, but he'd been indifferent. With a sense of heightened surprise and anticipation, Jackie
suspected that Eric would be anything but indifferent. What
would he offer her? And could she let down her guard long
enough to deal with it?

For the dozenth time Jackie beat her pillow into a more comfortable position, hoping for sleep to overtake her and wipe out
the questions and fears, and leave her in peace. But this she was
not able to do until her own emotional exhaustion matched the
physical one. Only then did she finally fall asleep.

Saturday dawned sunny as usual, and the thought of spending
it all indoors was too much for Jackie to bear. Her foot was
much better and she only felt a little discomfort when her full

weight was placed on it. When she saw it would not hurt too much she became restless.

"Darlin', I really think you should not walk on that foot. It could be weak and you'll twist it all over again!" Hannah advised.

Jackie let out a long sigh of some impatience and stared moodily into her coffee.

"Why, I said to Timothy, thank goodness that nice Mr. Davidson was there with you." As if in agreement, Timothy's tail thumped on the kitchen floor from somewhere under the table, followed by a grunt and a snort. Jackie had to smile.

"Hannah, I promise you it doesn't hurt. It's just a little stiff."

"See! I told you so!"

"Anyway, I don't plan to do any walking. I thought I'd go into the photo lab and drop off some film and pick up some things I left at the beginning of the week."

Hannah crossed her arms over her ample bosom and eyed Jackie stubbornly.

"Umph!" she commented, still not giving in. "I just can't agree with you, darlin'. Why, even Mr. Davidson said you should stay put for at least one day!"

That did it. Something clicked inside Jackie like a trigger. She was not about to have Eric Davidson dictate her life.

"Well, Mr. Davidson doesn't know how my ankle feels, and it's my ankle!"

Hannah looked questioningly at Jackie's vehemence, but finally sighed, shaking her head, and threw up her hands in surrender.

"Well, if you insist, I can't make you stay." Hannah said as she got up and headed toward the backyard and her garden. "I just hope you don't make it worse. It won't do to cut off your nose just to spite your face!"

Hannah's sage comment and the soft closing of the screen door left Jackie alone and in a little doubt of her own good sense. But nevertheless she got her exposed rolls of film, got into the compact car, and drove across town to Bob McIver's shop. He greeted her and questioned her on how the picture taking was going for her book. Jackie told him as she took a magnifying glass to examine the negatives and contact sheet from the film taken the day of her arrival.

The last three frames were of the house and pond where Eric lived, and for the first time she noticed a strange shape in the corner of two scenes. It was much too small for her to make out clearly, no matter how she squinted or manipulated the glass.

"Is something wrong?" Bob asked, leaning his blond head over the sheet.

"No," Jackie murmured, trying to keep her hand steady. "I just think there's something in this picture I hadn't noticed before."

"Ummm," Bob answered, taking the glass from her and bending over the sheet even further until his nose was actually against the paper. "Well, I can't make it out either. But why don't you enlarge it so you can see it better?"

Jackie looked at him.

Bob waved to a door next to the entrance behind his counter. "You do know how to use an enlarger, and develop your own images don't you?"

"Yes, of course."

"Good. You'll find everything you need through that door."

Still Jackie hesitated.

"It's okay." Bob answered her doubtful look. "I let professional photographers use part of the studio and charge them by the hour. It's your hour. Either you know what you're doing or you don't! I can always print 'em for you."

Jackie flashed him a sudden grateful smile, lighting up her whole face. "I never expected to be able to do this! I thought I'd have to wait until I got back to New York before I saw any work by my own hands!"

Bob chuckled. "No need to wait 'til then. We're progressive down here," he said with great humor. "Learnt how to do some things quite a while ago. Got hot and cold running water, too."

Jackie's mouth dropped open. Bob McIver looked up at her with his round magnified eyes and suddenly started laughing.

"Just teasing," he assured her. "I know exactly what you meant."

Jackie let out a long, relieved sigh and smiled again.

"You know," Bob began, looking at her seriously. "You sure would make one terrific model. You're tall and pretty . . . why waste your time working so hard to take good pictures when you can be paid to have them taken of you?"

Jackie didn't take offense at the question, but she didn't know how to explain simply about her past experience.

"Modeling isn't all it's cracked up to be," she answered ruefully. "Photography makes me feel that there really is something I have talent for."

Bob clicked his tongue and shook his head, going back to restocking a film case on the wall. "Too bad . . ." he murmured.

Jackie picked up her negatives and contact sheet and went into the back room lab. The faint smell of photographic chemicals with their distinct sharpness widened her nostrils. She turned on the safety light to locate paper, chemicals, trays, timer, water, and drying rack. Setting up everything the way she would in her makeshift darkroom at home in New York, she proceeded to lose track of time.

From the first roll of film she experimented with a number of frames, either enlarging the whole image or parts of it until she soon had a number of prints to be dried. She again examined the peculiar object in the corner of the last few frames, and curiosity winning out, chose to just enlarge that one corner enough to see what the object was.

Jackie did a test exposure on a scrap of print paper and leaned over it anxiously as the image blurred and formed under the development chemicals. She frowned, still, until finally she recognized the form of Eric Davidson. He was obviously somewhere behind the house, but Jackie had enlarged the image too much to get details, and the picture before her was grainy. Eric stood with one hand in his pocket, looking off to his left over the pond, as though he'd been standing there for some time looking at one spot. The right hand was lost somewhere out of sight of the frame.

Seeing this image reminded Jackie of her other rolls of film. She retrieved them from her bag and began to develop them one by one. Afterward, she printed a contact sheet for each, and started making enlargements of a number of images. Some of these included pictures of Eric she'd taken during the week against the background of the sea islands. He had not been aware of any of the pictures as she took them, and even as she printed and looked them over now, she wasn't sure why she had done it. The pictures were good. But they also frightened her.

Whatever it was she was looking for and found in these captured pictures of Eric Davidson, sent a shiver through her.

Jackie finished her work and cleaned up the studio, leaving with the chemicals still clinging to her hands.

"Well, how did you make out? Let's see the results."

Before Jackie could object, Bob had snatched the pile of prints from her hands and laid them spread out over the counter to examine each one. Jackie was suddenly very grateful for the instinct which had made her put all the pictures of Eric away first in her tote bag. She found herself anxious to hear Bob's opinion. She stood silently as Bob pursed his mouth and made little sounds deep in his throat, fingering and adjusting his large glasses over his weak blue eyes.

"Well . . ." he said, putting several aside almost at once, "I can tell these are the first that you took." But he never said if they were good or not. "Ummmm. These are pretty good," and he put together a second pile. This left seven or eight that he spent more time over, nodding his head.

"Yes. These are excellent. Now I think you could develop this one a bit more so there's more contrast. It's a bit too gray right in here."

Jackie looked over his shoulder where his index finger pointed, and agreed with him. It was apparent to her that Bob McIver, despite his bad eyes, knew a thing or two about a good picture. He made one or two other suggestions. Some Jackie agreed with and some she didn't.

"If you're willing to leave these four with me, I'll display them for you."

"Are you serious?"

"Well, you're a serious photographer, aren't you?" he asked peering at her.

Jackie nodded.

"Fine. I'll put these four up. If no one picks them up in the next two weeks, you can have them back."

Jackie opened her mouth to speak but was interrupted as Bob answered her unasked question.

"But if they sell, I'll take ten percent—agent's fee!" He grinned.

Having stood for several hours in the studio, her sore ankle began to throb. She was more than happy to gather the rest of her work and start back to the house.

Reluctantly seeing the wisdom of both Hannah's and Eric's advice to stay off her leg, Jackie remained in the house on Sunday afternoon. Hannah left her early to attend church services, wearing a bright flowered dress and a wide-brimmed straw hat which made her seem even wider, but complemented her round mahogany face.

Timothy kept Jackie company in the yard as she read the local Sunday papers. But she couldn't keep her mind on them, and feeling restless got her camera and shot pictures of the indolent Timothy as he snoozed under the lounge chair. As if sensing that he was momentarily the center of attraction, Timothy rolled his fat body onto his back, trying unsuccessfully to look like a playful puppy. His paws collapsed as all four bent limply skyward and his tongue lolled from his mouth. Jackie laughed at his antics. This was the most movement she'd ever seen from him.

When Hannah got back from church with her absurdly wide hat on, Jackie embarrassed her by taking her picture several times before she could turn and run into the house, waving her hands in dismay.

"You shouldn't waste your film on an old lady like me! Go and find something pretty to photograph."

"Hannah, you are going to make a *very* pretty picture." Jackie smiled in reassurance at her. But nonetheless, Hannah scoffed and quickly put on her ever present apron and took refuge behind her kitchen counter.

"How's your foot today?"

"Oh, much better," Jackie answered, wiggling her toes and rotating her ankle in demonstration.

"I sure hope that Eric Davidson stops by tomorrow," Hannah remarked innocently, beginning to wash and strip a head of cabbage.

"What on earth for?" Jackie asked in surprise.

"Well, I just think it would be nice if he came to see how you were doing and maybe have dinner with us. I think he was really concerned about you, darlin'."

"I wouldn't call it concern," Jackie muttered ruefully, remembering well the way he'd held and kissed her.

"Still it would do you good to just sit for a spell and keep him company. You can't take pictures all the time," Hannah lectured reasonably.

Jackie shifted uneasily on her chair, pulling nervously on the loose curls at her neck. Keeping Eric company during the week when she was busy fulfilling a job was one thing. Keeping him company in the close quarters of the parlor or dining room was quite another. His nearness had a tantalizing effect on her which she did not fully understand yet. And she wasn't at all sure if she was ready and willing to do so.

"I think I'll make chicken fricassee and dumplings. He sure looks like he'd have a hearty appetite." Hannah chuckled, her body heaving in mirth.

"I don't think you have to go to so much trouble, Hannah," Jackie said.

"Lord, child, it's no trouble. Cookin' is one of the things I do best!"

And with that she continued to verbalize her dinner menu for the next night. Jackie offered to help and Hannah put her to work preparing scalloped potatoes and a salad for their Sunday meal. Jackie mixed dough for rolls and set the table for the two of them.

"I didn't know you could cook!" Hannah mumbled around a mouthful of the sampled hot roll.

Jackie shrugged. "I guess people think if you're attractive you don't have to know much else. But I like to cook. I just never have a chance to do any."

Hannah tisked. "Darlin', I never thought to ask if you'd want to prepare dinner yourself for your young man."

"Hannah, really! Eric Davidson is not my young man. I'm just hiring him to show me around Charleston."

"Umph!" Hannah responded as she reached into the refrigerator for a stick of butter, ignoring Jackie's negations.

There was a silence between the two women, Hannah stirring a pot on the stove, Jackie absently setting out napkins while her mind wondered in fantasy. She did not deny to herself that she would have enjoyed the intimacy of cooking for two. Making a special meal for someone who was special. She wandered into the kitchen to keep Hannah company.

"When I was married," Jackie began tentatively, softly,

"Mark and I never seemed to be home long enough for meals together. Sometimes I'd go into the kitchen and cook up all this food, pretending I was making it for a lot of people."

Hannah listened intently as Jackie talked about her marriage, aware that she was doing so for the first time of her own accord.

"But I'd have to give it all away to neighbors or else watch it spoil. I like to cook. It's just not much fun doing it for myself alone."

Hannah sighed, shaking her head lamentingly over the foolishness of the young. Marriage had obviously gotten a lot more complicated than when she was a young woman making a home for herself and Alvin Curtis, her husband.

Jackie munched absently on a carrot, frowning at some inner thought. Hannah moved around her kitchen humming a church hymn from the morning's service.

"Hannah?"

"Yes, darlin'."

"What should we have for dessert?"

Hannah chuckled. "We haven't had dinner yet! You must be hungry. I think there's some ice cream, or we could . . ."

"No. I mean, what about tomorrow?"

Hannah turned and looked in surprise at Jackie. "Well, darlin', what would you like to have?" she asked.

Jackie twirled the carrot stem between her fingers. "I don't suppose there's time to make a sweet potato pie, is there?"

A slow smile spread over Hannah's face until she beamed, her teeth flashing bright in her face.

CHAPTER FIVE

The overhead chandelier hung low enough over the dining table to cast shadows over the faces of the three people seated for dinner. One face was animated and lively, all emotions clearly displayed. The other two were more uncertain, each changing as it was viewed by the other.

Hannah had seated them for dinner so that Jackie found herself opposite Eric, and unable to avoid his open gaze, the sparkling light in his eyes, or the shape of his mouth as he ate and talked. He did justice to Hannah's chicken and dumplings, eating with the hearty appetite she said he'd have, and thereby complimenting the cook. During dinner he directed most of his conversation and questions to Hannah, occasionally including Jackie with a smile or a look, but clearly Hannah was the object of his considerable charm this evening.

Jackie half listened as she watched him furtively from under her lashes, or over the rim of a glass. He was so at ease, so obviously comfortable that she found herself unaccountably put out with him. There was so much command about him, such confidence and sense of self that Jackie knew he'd be immediately comfortable no matter where he was.

Right now, this only served to make Jackie wonder at his willingness to be her guide, let her boss him and pay him for the time. All her suspicions were aroused as she wondered who was Eric Davidson, really?

When he'd come into the house just a few hours earlier, he was dressed almost as she'd gotten used to seeing him. He wore jeans, although they were designer jeans which accentuated the firm muscled columns of his legs, and his sweatshirt, pushed up along his forearms, was a rust color, spotlessly clean, without paint or oil stains. Replacing the sneakers were brown loafers of a soft kid leather.

Jackie had just finished setting the table and placing a pitcher of ice water on it when the bell rang. Despite her calm of the afternoon Jackie felt a moment of uncertainty as she went to answer the door. When she opened it, Eric was standing there with his hands on his hips, looking decidedly imposing.

"Good evening," he said evenly, nodding slightly to her.

"Good evening, Mr. Davidson," she said deliberately, opening the door wider for him to pass through. Eric bent and picked up a bag sitting at his feet. He followed her inside and they turned to face one another, drawing deep breaths as if they were about to do verbal battle. But before a word could be spoken, Hannah came in from the kitchen, an apron covered with printed red strawberries over her light blue dinner dress.

"Oh, Mr. Davidson!" she exclaimed, clapping her hands over her breasts. "I'm so glad you could make it this evening!"

"It was nice of you to invite me." Eric answered in such a way that it was perfectly clear the invitation had been from her and not Jackie. Jackie only gave him an indifferent look.

"I'll call you Hannah," Eric continued, "If you'll call me Eric."

Hannah giggled in an uncharacteristic way, surprising Jackie, who'd never seen her so flighty.

"Now darlin'," Hannah said, taking hold of one of Jackie's and Eric's arms. "You take Eric into the parlor and sit for a spell while I finish dinner. It should be ready shortly."

Jackie pulled back, not wanting to be left alone suddenly with Eric. "Oh, Hannah. Let me help you."

But Hannah was firm. "I won't hear of you leaving your company all alone! Now go on! I'll bring out some lemonade for you two." And giving them each a gentle push into the parlor, went off to the kitchen once more.

Jackie sighed inwardly, and slowly looked up into Eric's face, which grinned openly at her.

"Better luck next time," he quipped.

Jackie gave him a dark look and sat on the love seat which she immediately saw as a mistake, as Eric promptly sat down next to her. His exposed forearm rubbed against hers with an incredible heat, making her jump as though she'd been burned. She absently rubbed her skin.

"How's the ankle?" Eric asked seriously.

"It's fine, thank you," Jackie answered, not meeting his eyes, but knowing he was watching her carefully. "You know you really didn't have to check up on me. It was only a slight twist, and all I had to do was let it rest, which I did on Saturday."

"Liar," he interrupted softly.

Jackie's eyes flew to his in astonishment. "What did you say?"

"I said, liar. You were at Bob McIver's on Saturday working in the lab."

"What were you doing? Following me just to make sure I stayed put?" she asked in annoyance.

Eric ignored her display of anger. "Bob also does some framing. I took some things into him late Saturday afternoon. He told me all about you. Showed me your work. Told me he thought you were really talented."

Jackie looked down at her hands, her suspicion now so uncalled for. His calm completely defeated her, and she constantly found herself responding in defensive anger. She wished she could feel more sure of him.

"I agreed with him," Eric ended softly.

Jackie lifted her chin, and looked at Eric as he continued to scrutinize her. She forgot she was staring for the moment and Eric didn't seem to mind. Jackie's mind gathered around a new thought. This was not a man to be treated lightly. Nor could he be dumped into the same general category as a Mark Bennett. Even she had to admit there was no comparison here. She was also struck with the embarrassing awareness that perhaps she'd been treating Eric Davidson just a bit too superficially. That was a mistake, because she recognized not having liked it very much when it was happening to her.

"What were you having framed by Bob McIver?" Jackie asked suddenly, completely away from her other thoughts.

Eric raised a brow in surprise at the question and then smiled almost as if in appreciation of the fact that she was asking about something concerning just him.

"I left a few paintings for him to frame."

Jackie frowned. "Paintings?"

"Of course," Eric said, his amusement growing at the confused expression on her face.

"Are . . . are they yours? I mean, did you paint them?"

"Yes, I did."

"But I thought you said you were a . . . a painter!"

Eric patiently nodded, his mouth quirking at the corners.

"But you're a *real* painter!" Jackie concluded brilliantly.

Eric laughed deep in his throat, his eyes enjoying the look of dumbfoundedness on her pretty brown face. Eric raised a hand and gently brushed the back of two fingers over her smooth cheek.

"What other kind of painter is there?" he asked, putting her on the spot.

Jackie flushed, and dropped her eyes. "Oh God. I . . . I'm a little ashamed. I was thinking"—she stopped and shrugged—"that you were a house painter or something."

The two fingers slid down along her jaw and under her chin to raise her face to his. "Is there anything wrong with being just a house painter?" Eric asked softly, looking seriously into her eyes, searching for an honest answer from her.

Jackie met his probing gaze fully, and knew in that instant it didn't matter to her what Eric was.

"No, nothing," she whispered breathlessly.

"Then don't worry about what you thought. It's only what you think now that's important."

She was slipping again, into the depths of his eyes.

Hannah came back in carrying a tray. Eric sprang up to take it out of her hands and place it on a small table she indicated.

"Now you two just enjoy yourselves."

Eric reached for the bag at his feet. "I brought a small gift for you."

"Oh darlin'. Now that wasn't necessary."

Eric pulled out a small square straw basket and handed it to Hannah. She frowned in concentration as she pulled the green bow loose. Inside the basket were flower bulbs and seeds. It was the simplest of gifts, but a thoughtful one, since Hannah so loved to garden. Jackie wondered how he'd known to bring just this kind of thing.

"Why, thank you, Eric. That was really very sweet of you," Hannah said with feeling. "How did you know I had a garden?"

"By the flowers I saw planted in the fireplace the last time I was here. I was sure you'd be a person who loved to see things grow."

"Well I sure do! And I'm going to wrap these in a moist towel until I can put them in the ground first thing tomorrow morning." And she walked away looking very pleased.

Again there was a silence. Nervously Jackie picked up a frosted glass of lemonade and began to sip. "I'm sorry there's nothing stronger to drink," she commented.

"This is fine," Eric said, also taking a sip from his glass.

"It was nice of you to remember Hannah with a gift," she said awkwardly.

"Oh I remembered you, too." Eric smiled. While Jackie protested in embarrassment he reached once more into the bag and came out with a pair of very soiled canvas shoes.

Jackie looked at them in total confusion for a moment before recognizing them as the ones left on Edisto several days earlier. She suddenly started laughing, shaking her head in amusement.

"Your slippers, My Lady. They're not glass, but . . ."

"That's okay. I'm no Cinderella!"

Eric sighed dramatically. "Then I guess I'm no Prince Charming. Too bad."

Jackie looked at him, unable to tell, once again, if he was teasing or not. He was concentrating on finishing his glass of lemonade.

"You don't look the sort of person to believe in fables," she commented ruefully.

Eric turned to look at her, his eyes thoughtful as he considered his answer to her. He half smiled, deepening the furrow on one side of his mouth. "Let's just say I believe in happy endings."

An unwanted image of Mark appeared in Jackie's mind. She said in a flat voice, "Things don't always end that way."

Eric nodded in rueful agreement. "You're right. Sometimes they don't. But it is also said it's better the second time around."

"What is?"

"Love."

Jackie chuckled cynically. "There are no second chances in fairy tales."

"I wasn't talking about fairy tales." Eric said low to her with meaning. She turned her head to look at him, at the evening light reflected in his eyes, at his firm mouth and jaw. She felt as if Eric was silently conveying some message to her, and if she wasn't being so cautious with him still, she'd understand. They sat quietly in the dark of the unlit parlor, in a silence that was emotionally charged, and which slowly enveloped them.

Jackie had not fully recovered from that floating sensation when Hannah called them in to dinner, and so she was very quiet throughout the meal. Now as she sat contemplating Eric opposite her, so thoroughly at ease and obviously enjoying himself, she wondered at the man he was deep down inside of the one she saw. Eric took that exact moment to look at her, and found her gaze one of puzzlement and fascination. He surprised her by smiling and winking at her.

"Well, I suppose everyone's ready for dessert," Hannah said, making to rise from the table.

"You just sit here," Jackie admonished firmly, gently pushing Hannah back into her chair. "I'll get dessert. You sit and talk to, er, Mr. Davidson."

"Oh don't be so stuffy, Jackie! He's a friend, after all. Call him Eric."

"Yes, please do," Eric encouraged smoothly before ignoring her and turning back to Hannah.

Jackie went into the kitchen and sliced three portions of the warm pie, putting them on dessert plates. She then poured three cups of coffee and made two trips to bring it all to the dinner table. Hannah was chuckling in delight at something Eric had said, no doubt flattering her, Jackie thought. But nonetheless she felt left out of the fun. Eric only glanced at her briefly before turning back to Hannah. Jackie felt piqued. Well, at least one of them was thoroughly enjoying the evening.

"Tell me about your family, Eric," Hannah boldly asked as she put a generous helping of sugar into her coffee.

Eric wiped some pie crumbs from his mouth with a napkin and cleared his palate with a gulp of coffee before answering. Jackie found herself listening somewhat in anticipation.

"Well, there's my mom and dad. He's retired now, and they live in Wilmington, Delaware."

"What is your father retired from?" Hannah asked.

Eric frowned and hesitated for a second. "My dad was a painter, too," he said rather reluctantly. "My mother taught high school math."

"Oh how lovely! Jackie's father was a teacher, too!"

Eric looked at her. "Then we have something in common," he

said to her. "I have a sister a few years younger than myself. She's married with two little girls and there's another baby on the way. She and her family are here in Charleston."

"And you never married?" Hannah persisted innocently, but Jackie looked at her in suspicion, wondering at all these personal questions to Eric.

Eric shrugged and raised a brow in a sheepish expression. "I never found the time or the right person."

Hannah tisked. "Now that's a shame. A big handsome man like you!"

Jackie was wishing the floor would open up and let her drop through, or that she'd miraculously become invisible. But Eric only laughed good-naturedly.

"Not everyone will agree with you, Hannah." He looked at his now empty plate. "Ah . . . do you suppose I could have another slice of that pie?"

"Oh of course, darlin'! I'm so glad Jackie thought of it for dessert." And this time before Jackie could escape to the kitchen, Hannah was on her feet with Eric's plate and headed back to the kitchen. Eric swung his handsome face toward Jackie, his eyes thoughtful, before they filled with a smile. He didn't say anything, for which Jackie was momentarily grateful, but his look was suddenly very complacent, confusing her all the more.

Dinner was finished at last and Jackie cleared the table, carting the empty dishes to the kitchen as Hannah and Eric continued to talk. She realized at some point as she scraped and stacked that she really was enjoying the job. She had an odd feeling of being useful and needed that had never come with any other function she'd performed so far. Certainly not as a model, nor yet as a photographer. She felt at home.

Jackie began to run a soapy pan of water for the dishes to soak, and to put away leftover food. Timothy, sprawled against the door to the backyard, watched her for a moment before succumbing to his dream world. Even having ancient Timothy, silent and morose for company, made her feel secure.

She was halfway through the washing when someone came through the door behind her. Looking over her shoulder, she was surprised to see Eric coming casually into the room, looking around, his hands pushed flat into his pants pockets. He had a habit of doing that which Jackie saw as a nervous movement, or perhaps not knowing what to do with his hands. But she couldn't imagine what he had to be nervous about.

He came to stand so close behind her, breathing over her shoulder, that if she leaned back the tiniest bit she would have been against his chest. A plate slipped out of her soapy hands and back into the water, splashing her and the counter.

"Careful," Eric said low in amusement. "That's an expensive way of eliminating dirty dishes!"

Jackie ignored his comment even as a shiver went through her from his nearness. She hastily rinsed the plate and placed it in the drain rack. Taking a moistened sponge she turned to wipe the counter and stove top, putting distance between her and Eric. He turned to lean back against the edge of the sink, watching her.

"Would you like some help?"

"No thank you." She looked at him slyly. "I'm not in the habit of inviting men to dinner and then expecting them to help clean up."

He quirked a brow, conceding the point. "Except that Hannah was the one who was kind enough to invite me."

She shrugged. "I'm almost done anyway. Where is Hannah?"

"She said she was going to retire for the night. But it sounded suspiciously like letting 'the young folks' have some time to themselves."

Jackie grimaced. "Hannah's sweet and old-fashioned."

"There's nothing wrong with old-fashioned," Eric countered, as he allowed himself to be pushed away from the sink so that Jackie could squeeze out her sponge. "I'm a bit old-fashioned myself." Eric confessed.

"Oh, and she asked if you'd make sure that Timothy was inside before locking the yard door."

"I guess I'd better let him out for a while," she said as she swung open the door for the great beast, and he obligingly got up and lumbered out into the darkened yard. This left Jackie truly alone with Eric, and she felt a degree of control slipping away from her.

She picked nervously at the sponge in her hand, shredding pieces of it, refusing to meet Eric's gaze, knowing full well that he stood watching her every move. She walked quickly past him and back to the sink, looking almost in desperation for something else to occupy her hands and mind.

"Dinner was very nice," Eric said, taking up his position again next to the sink, his arms crossed over his hard chest. Jackie scrubbed vigorously at a determined spot in the sink, the movement sending her curly hair into feathery motion.

"I'm glad you enjoyed it, but as you yourself said, it was all Hannah's idea."

"Yes . . . but dessert was yours. I liked that best," his voice said caressingly.

Jackie scrubbed even harder. Suddenly, Eric began to chuckle deep in his throat. Strong brown fingers reached out for her wrist and taking hold, gently turned her to face him.

"Jackie, you're scrubbing a hole in the porcelain!" he teased. With his other hand Eric took the sponge out of her hand and dropped it into the sink. Jackie's mouth flew open about to express outrage, but nothing came out as she found herself looking into Eric's eyes. Everything about him seemed so close, larger than life.

With a minimum of movements and effort, Eric moved Jackie in front of him, his one hand, wet from the sponge, damp and cool on her arm. She was forced to step over one outstretched leg braced against the floor, to avoid tripping. Then Eric's large hands settled on her waist, and Jackie felt her breathing go shallow. She put her hands on his, as if to move them, or stay them, or push them away. But Eric quickly captured them, sensing the start of a struggle. His chuckling stopped and Eric looked into her eyes, looked at her chest rising and falling in agitation under her black cotton top. His eyes moved back up to her mouth, parted and moist. Before she could voice a protest he slowly pulled her toward him against his hard chest, and settled his mouth on hers.

The kiss was caressingly tender, coaxing a response from her against her will. With her acquiescence, Eric deepened the kiss, forcing her mouth open further. The kiss began to have an instant drugging effect on Jackie. This was the second time he'd kissed her and the second time she was aware of a gentle exploration of her mouth, whirling her mind, and shattering her senses. Eric's mouth teased at hers, melting her. He moved to the corner of her mouth, and in a foggy state Jackie tilted her head back away from him. But it only allowed Eric to transfer his kiss to her chin. One large hand slid up from her waist to her head to forcibly tilt her back to him. She was unconscious of her encouraging movement that made it easy for him to capture her mouth again.

Eric's arms closed more securely around her, the contact was potently enticing, and a wave of pure pleasure swept all through her. Her arms slowly worked their way to his chest, just to meet and cross behind his neck. Some low sound of satisfaction escaped her. Jackie lost herself for wild moments, letting the delight take over, feeling as if she was drowning in it. She was ashamed to admit it felt very good to be held this way. Eric's obvious masculinity just served to make her more acutely aware of her own femininity and its needs.

Slowly she pulled her hands down and placed them on Eric's chest as though to steady herself, and with a tremendous effort pushed against him until their mouths separated. She had to suppress a gasp for air, willing herself to swallow the moan rising in her throat.

Eric pulled back, searching her face, his breathing deep and ragged. His hands, gently massaging her waist and hips, pulled the lower part of her body back tightly against his own. To Eric her face seemed closed and without emotion, but it was a total contradiction to the rampant feelings inside her which she now hid so well.

Jackie pulled away and went back to the sink as though nothing had happened, but she only stood there, too bemused to remember what she'd been doing before. Behind her Eric let out a long deep sigh.

"Whatever it was your ex said to you, you believed every word."

Jackie felt the blood rush to her face in embarrassment. That this virile man, almost a stranger, should know so much, should understand so much was beyond her. She didn't want to be cold; she just felt safer that way.

"I don't know what you're talking about," she said in a tight, dry voice. Eric turned away and Jackie could hear him taking out a pack of cigarettes. She heard the match being lit and soon the long exhalation of air.

"Oh yes you do," he said softly, positively. "And you may be stubborn, but you're not indifferent."

The truth of that struck her forcibly. God, she certainly knew that, but he had no right to tell her so with such arrogance. She was having enough trouble allowing herself the natural pleasure of just being in his company. "You think all I have to do is fall into your open arms, allow you to make love to me, and all my problems will miraculously vanish!" Jackie said incredulously.

"Not all at once . . . but sooner or later," he mocked, unruffled by her outburst. "You just don't want to admit that you enjoyed it. Or that I might be right."

Jackie turned away from him, but Eric grabbed her by the shoulders and forcibly turned her back to face him. He held her fast, the lit cigarette still burning in one hand. His look was serious now, all amusement and teasing gone. He was intent, almost hard. He wasn't going to allow her to ignore him.

"Somewhere after your divorce you decided that attack was the best form of defense. The only problem with that tactic is you're attacking for all the wrong reasons, and all the wrong people. All right! So maybe your ex was some kind of royal creep. Not everyone is going to be like him. And whatever it was he said to you . . . did to you, you don't have to take as law or God's truth. He could have been all wrong!"

"Let me go, Eric," she said breathlessly, her voice unsteady. Eric held fast, shaking her once.

"Why do you only call me Eric when you're angry? Are you angry at *me* . . . or with yourself?"

"You're not making any sense," she said, twisting in his hold. He let her go.

"Or maybe I'm making too much sense! Why are you so angry?" Eric looked at her puzzled, as she hugged her arms where he'd held her tightly. Jackie looked uncertainly at him, but she was trembling. A light brightened in Eric's eyes.

"No! No, I take that back. Maybe you are angry. But you're also scared!"

Jackie turned her back to him.

"Why, Jackie?" he asked. "Are you really so afraid to care again because you might be hurt again?"

"I'm not afraid, because it's not going to happen again. Once was quite enough."

Eric chuckled, shaking his head sadly. "I suppose you just won't allow it, eh?"

"No, I won't."

"And what are you going to do with all those other feelings?" Eric asked softly, coming close behind her again. He threw his half-finished cigarette into the sink and gently slipped his hands around her waist, pulling her back against his chest. Jackie resisted as another telltale shiver went shooting through her. But Eric held her firm.

"What other feelings?" she asked in a shaky voice.

Eric kissed her dark shiny curls, brought his lips down to her ear, nuzzling the soft skin. Her knees weakened. He moved farther down to the side of her neck sending a sensuous tension through her. "The ones that say hold me," he whispered seductively, his warm breath and mouth playing havoc with her nerve ends.

Jackie's eyes closed against this new assault.

"The ones that say touch me." He nibbled at a lobe, his arms holding her tight across her stomach. "The ones that say be kind."

Jackie stiffened at once and Eric felt it. He didn't try to hold her when she pulled away this time.

"I don't want to talk about it anymore," she said in a tired voice.

Eric watched her, not without compassion. "It's not just going to go away, Jackie. And it's not going to get better until you do."

Hearing a thud against the yard door which made her jump guiltily, Jackie turned to let Timothy back into the kitchen. He waddled to his water dish and collapsed on the floor. Jackie locked the door in the deep silence of the room, as Eric turned away in frustration, running a hand over the crinkled cap of his close haircut. He let out a deep sigh and turned back to her.

"I'd like some more coffee if you don't mind," he requested tightly.

Jackie hesitated, wanting to tell him there was no more so there'd be no excuse for him to stay longer. But the coffee maker very clearly showed almost a full pot. Silently she plugged it in to reheat, and set out fresh coffee cups, feeling the need for the strong brew herself.

While she prepared the coffee Eric lit another cigarette, smoking it quietly at the kitchen table, seemingly deep in thought, but occasionally glancing her way. Finally she poured the coffee. She would have remained standing except that Eric looked at her impatiently and, slightly more subdued, she sat opposite him.

From Eric's point of view, she looked as though she wanted to be rid of him. There was no way for Eric to be sure that he'd read her correctly earlier or for him to know that her countenance of stiffness and withdrawal was only a facade to protect herself from his acute observations. Jackie wasn't ready to do without them. She had nothing firm yet with which to replace them. There were new tentative, unexplored reactions physically to Eric, and she suspected that there were also feelings behind them. But she needed time to find out. Time to make the change.

"Jackie?" he called her name softly.

She looked at him warily. Eric hesitated, his eyes scanning her face for some real insight into her state of mind. "Now don't go getting your back up like a hellcat, but"—he spread his hands—"why did your ex leave you? What caused the divorce?" he asked in genuine curiosity.

Jackie stared at him a long moment, in a combination of surprise and irritation. Surprise that he would ask so boldly, that he'd want to know. But irritation because she suddenly wanted to tell him so he'd know how wrong he was about her, and maybe stop judging her. Jackie put her cup down, and wrapped her hands around the warm bowl of it, trying to let the sudden gripping tenseness out of her body. She frowned into the black liquid and slowly began to shake her head. Eric was about to protest her unwillingness to talk when she finally spoke.

"Mark didn't leave me. I left him," she stated very simply. Eric waited but she said no more as the entire episode of her marriage flashed movie-like through her mind. She remembered the first time she suspected him of infidelity and the first time she knew for sure. The first time she confronted him with it and his denial, and the first time he said, yes it's true. A knot began to form in Jackie's stomach. She concentrated on the deep black liquid in front of her as though it would hypnotize her and send away the bad memories in an instant.

Finally, she let out a sigh, sipping the coffee. It was a nice, strong jolt to her system.

"I take it you didn't want him or he didn't want you anymore. . . ." Eric asked carefully, still not sure if she'd flare up at him.

"Oh, he wanted me all right. I was very good for Mark. But he wanted his girlfriends as well. All of them. And he told me so."

Eric's knuckles strained and lost color under the tightened grip he had on his cup. But his face did not change expression. It was neither pity nor concern nor anger, outwardly. It was simply intent and alert. Jackie found it easier to talk as she went along.

"I was a very visible model in New York for more than a year. My face was everywhere. It meant a lot of work and money for my agency, and for Mark's magazine. So, to ensure that he'd always be the first to benefit, he married me," she said with a touch of irony at Mark's deviousness. "It was the best, the cheapest insurance he could buy." Jackie got a faraway wistful look in her eyes as the visual memories persisted in her mind.

"Funny . . . Mark never said, 'I love you.' It was, 'We'll be good together, Baby.' He was sharp and fast and very sure of himself. I was impressed. And I was very young. But I found out there were other women. Lots of them. So"—she shrugged—"I left him."

"And you gave up modeling as well at the same time?"

She grinned ruefully. "Models generally have very short careers anyway. There's always a prettier, younger face than yours. But I truly became interested in photography because of it. It was the first time I paid attention to a camera and what it could do. It was like a new toy. I grabbed it and ran off to play all by myself. And I . . . I needed to change everything."

"Even yourself, I suppose?"

"Myself most of all. I could never be, never do what I did before. And if I was going to change and be a different person, this time I wanted to be what *I* wanted to be."

Eric contemplated her with a frown and leaned forward to rest his elbows on the table. "What is it, exactly, that you want to be?"

Jackie lifted her brows at him. "Independent," she answered meeting his eyes.

"Completely?"

"Yes," she answered, but she hesitated.

"Not needing anyone for anything? Not anything?" he asked softly in a deep probing voice while his eyes held hers.

Jackie chose not to answer, but instead shifted her eyes away impatiently.

"That's foolish," Eric stated sternly. "And even you should realize that. If you don't now, you soon will."

Jackie looked at him and gave a short laugh. "You sound so sure."

"I'm reasonably sure," Eric corrected.

Jackie couldn't help laughing in real amusement. "And there speaks a man of experience! Have you been married and divorced so that you know what it's like?"

Eric shook his head, drinking from his coffee. "No. I've never been married."

"Why?" Jackie wanted to know, feeling there was much more than what he'd told Hannah at dinner.

"Some people don't, you know," he teased, but she was not to be put off. Eric shrugged. "It just never happened. I was busy for a whole lot of years learning to paint. I needed all my own time. But, I haven't ruled marriage out." And his warm eyes flicked caressingly over her. "As a matter of fact, I'm sure I will marry someday."

"Anyone special in mind?" she asked with more than just idle curiosity.

Eric looked at her a moment and shrugged again, looking away. "Maybe . . ."

Jackie felt a liquid warmth flood her suddenly as she had an image of handsome Eric Davidson telling some beautiful young lady that he loved her and wanted to marry her. Jackie felt elation, and a pain and anticipation. It was very akin to jealousy, which she couldn't understand.

"Anyway . . . end of story," she murmured.

Eric was so still and quiet, Jackie smiled at him a bit cynically. "What, no more lectures, Mr. Davidson?"

He looked quickly at her, very alert, an odd expression in his eyes. He almost stiffened and it made Jackie momentarily curious, but he visibly relaxed and quirked a brow and the corner of his mouth. "No more lectures," he responded. Eric crushed out his cigarette and drained his coffee. His brow furrowed in thought. Jackie took the empty cups to the sink.

"And, not end of story," he said as he got up from the table, pushing his hands into his pockets. "Just the beginning of another one. A good one for you this time. My grandmother used to say, 'All good things in their time.' "

Jackie turned to face him. "Perhaps your grandmother was right. I hope so," she responded sincerely.

Eric smiled at her warmly. "Grandmothers usually are. They're very wise that way."

All her tenseness had left her, and her anger. She felt drained, exhausted, sad, and pensive. But also, purged and freer than she'd felt in a long time. She looked into Eric's eyes and wondered what he was thinking. But he gave nothing away as he faced her. She had a sudden desire to feel his hands holding her again, and just as quickly the thought was gone, replaced with a wariness that caused him to frown at her. Eric moved slowly toward her, his eyes searching hers. He whispered her name and reached out for her. Timothy let out a low, distinct growl that could not be mistaken for anything but a warning. Both Eric and Jackie looked down at him in surprise. His large heavy head was lifted and he peered at Eric.

Eric laughed in real amusement, but nonetheless, stepped back. "You sure pack some heavy-duty armor, Jacqueline Taylor."

"Timothy thinks I need protection," Jackie said ruefully, flattered by the animal's sudden watchdog attitude over her.

"If anyone needs protection it's me!" he responded caustically. Jackie made no resistance at all this time, as Eric stepped closer to her and softly kissed her. Jackie allowed herself the pleasure of it, enjoying the gentleness of his touch.

Timothy's untimely interruption, as unwelcomed as it was, at least served to break some of the tension. She felt more comfortable, and smiled somewhat shyly at Eric. He answered her smile, and reached to tuck an errant curl behind her ear. Then he reached for her hand and taking it firmly, pulled her around in front of himself in the direction of the front door. "Come on and walk me to the door," he said.

Jackie moved willingly ahead of him and Eric released her hand. They reached the front door, and suddenly she didn't know what to expect of him. They stood facing each other. Eric sighed and placed his hands around the cool slim column of her neck, peering intently at her.

"Tomorrow we take up the tour again. We'll begin talking to some people I know around here. You can record them if you like. I'm sure they won't mind."

"That would be nice," she answered in a vague, dreamy voice. "I was always sorry I never recorded my grandmother. She was so unique."

"She must have been," Jackie responded, but Eric didn't ask her why she thought so. He looked as though he wanted to come closer, or do something. Maybe say something. Finally, he just shook his head.

"I think your ex must have been totally out of his mind," Eric said bewildered.

Jackie was very surprised by his comment and could only stare at him.

"Goodnight, Boss Lady. Don't be late tomorrow," he said, running the tips of two fingers down her smooth cheek. And then he was quietly gone.

CHAPTER SIX

Their daily trips became more specific, and Jackie finally narrowed them to Johns Island, finally meeting the people that Eric knew there. There were still farms here, with yards abundant with fruit trees and flowers like dogwood, azaleas, and magnolia. It was like being in a small-scale paradise. The rural black families were unpretentious and friendly, warming to them immediately.

Jackie was practically adopted by one family, the Harrises, who seemed to view her, on the one hand, as a young person deprived of the joys of being part of a big, boisterous family, which was true, but on the other hand, holding her somewhat in awe for her obvious sophistication and presence.

When Jackie and Eric arrived, day after day for more than a week, Lotte Harris would immediately run and gather curious neighbors to meet the odd young woman, and to have them sit and smile shyly at her, answering questions, and occasionally asking a few of their own. They told wonderful stories and Jackie sat in rapt attention, absently picking at and eating boiled salted peanuts, unaware of Eric's eyes watching and enjoying her reactions to all she heard and saw.

Lotte Harris had never been off Johns Island, but she told a colorful story of the first time her husband, Fred, left for several weeks to find temporary work to help the family through a bad crop year.

"Fred wuz goin' drive far a man de place dey startin' to dig far a ditch. En I tek de chillun to cousin May's, dey stay dar far week time. . . ."

It seems that while Fred and the kids were gone, Lotte spent three full days making jam, preserves, and chutney to sell locally. She'd also put together three tufted patchwork quilts from scrap material.

Jackie was enchanted when Lotte Harris gave her a jar filled with pear chutney to take away with her one afternoon. And as they moved through the small kitchen filled with its numerous unusual odors, Jackie finally asked Mrs. Harris to explain the meaning of the words Eric had said to her weeks before in the Gullah dialect. At first Mrs. Harris didn't seem to understand Jackie's efforts, but then her furrowed brow cleared and she laughed shyly, shaking her head.

"Go te Eric, see kin he tell." She smiled. And Jackie did just that, reminding him that he'd promised to tell her.

Eric hesitated, looking almost embarrassed by the answer he'd have to give and making Jackie all the more suspicious.

"Eric!" Jackie pleaded. He looked at her, and pulled a loose curl on her forehead.

"It means, you're very pretty," he responded.

Jackie stood looking at him for long minutes. To have Eric tell her this which had long ago lost its meaning, suddenly made her feel exposed—and special. Jackie returned his smile happily.

Sometimes she'd forget what she was there for, and get caught up in the ritual of just visiting. Eric would sit talking quietly back and forth with his friends, smoking in a lazy fashion while keeping half an eye out for Jackie's progress. The women, all much shorter and stouter than herself, exclaimed and wondered at her thinness and height. They invited her cheerfully into their cramped kitchens to sit hospitably and sample the day's preparation of foods. She tasted the local things she'd only heard about from Gwen, but had never had before. Neck bones, rice with black-eyed peas, red rice with shrimps, butt meat cooked with green collards, and a sweet flat pan bread called "Potato Poon." Everyone, even Eric, would laugh at her expression upon finding out at times the strange and different things she ate.

Jackie was pleased at what she'd been able to gather in just a few weeks and felt much more optimistic about the book and its publication possibilities. She talked to Gwen excitedly on the phone one evening, telling her what she'd been up to and how well the research was going.

"Well, it sounds like there won't be a thing for me to do when I get down there!" Gwen quipped.

"Oh yes there is. You're doing all the writing, remember? Don't back out on me now!"

Gwen laughed.

"I mean, I'm taking some great pictures, but I don't think it's enough to carry a book. You have to tell the readers something!"

"Man! You're really caught up in this, aren't you?"

Jackie stopped to consider. Yes, it had been very exciting gathering her information so far. It wasn't just stuff picked up here and there in a reference book, or from city records. She had been places, spoken to people, heard them. It had all come very much alive for her. And she couldn't have done half as much without Eric. He had been right after all.

"Jackie? Are you still there?"

Jackie blinked and dropped back into the present.

"Sorry, Gwen. I was thinking about your comment. This project does mean a lot to me. I think I've done a good job, and I think the book's a great idea."

"Well, I guess I've left you on your own enough, hon. Besides, it sounds like you're getting used to the place."

"It's funny"—Jackie frowned—"I feel like I've lived here for a long time."

"It must be the heat! Don't go getting carried away. You're a New York girl and it's where you belong! That is, unless you found something down south to keep you there." Gwen hinted broadly.

"What do you mean by that?"

"Carolina has some very fine men, honey. Don't tell me you haven't met even one that's made you sit up and take notice?"

Jackie had an instant image of Eric as he'd appeared at dinner more than two weeks ago, virile, handsome, and casually dressed. The rust color of his shirt did warm shadowy things to his rich brown skin and pale eyes. His presence did disturbing things to her. A muscle tensed in her stomach at the memory of his holding her. She evaded Gwen's question with an indirect answer.

"I haven't had time to date anyone, if that's what you mean."

Gwen sighed. "Girl, let me tell you something. You're taking this book too seriously. All work and no play makes Jackie a *tired* and dull girl!"

Jackie laughed.

". . . And I'll bet you haven't given a thought to reaching Spence?"

"Nope. Not a one!" Jackie confirmed cheerfully.

"What am I going to do with you?" Gwen clicked her teeth.

"You don't have to do a thing with me but help me finish this book."

"Okay, okay. I just wanted you to know I'll probably get down there some time next week. I'm doing a shooting in Washington, D.C., for a fall catalog, and then I'm all yours."

"Hannah's been asking for you. I hope you're better at fighting her than I am. She'd determined to put weight on me and I think she did it!"

"Honey, I wouldn't be a bit surprised. Just enjoy it. I certainly will when I get there. I could use some real home cookin' for a change, and nobody cooks better than Hannah."

Gwen promised to see her soon and the conversation ended.

Jackie was used to the routine of picking up Eric in the morning and spending her days under his subtle guidance. While she spoke to a farmer and family, he might wander off somewhere and just as quietly return when she was ready to leave. He'd been right about the people on Edisto and Johns Island knowing him and they eagerly engaged in their patois with him.

He continued to mock her, but with it was also a quiet, thoughtful watching of her and her movements. They continued to spar verbally, but she'd somewhere along the line grown comfortable enough with him to stop taking everything so seriously, or too personally. She remembered his biting comment about her attacking in self-defense and knew that was not the image she wanted to present to people. But even as she began to unbend a little, something about Eric became more reticent.

At first, Jackie wasn't sure that it was happening. His cat eyes would still watch her and sweep over her slender feminine form in a way that brought burning heat to her cheeks. He'd still help her carry her equipment and offer suggestions as to her work, but at other times he seemed barely patient with her, bristling under some unnamed tension or thought. He made her curious, but she never mentioned it to him. She wondered sometimes if perhaps he was bored with the whole arrangement, or tired of squiring her around. The thought was upsetting.

One thing that did not change was the effect he had on her with his physical nearness. He'd sometimes take her hand firmly, holding it as he helped her over swampy ground, or fallen trees or rocky coastline boulders. Sometimes he'd run a hand along her arm or shoulder in a caress and give it a gentle squeeze as he explained or pointed out things to her. Or there were times when he'd give her a brief, almost affectionate kiss. She accepted them. Sometimes she couldn't remember what he'd said, her physical response for the moment in more control than her mental one. Her caution with Eric was dissolving as she came to know him better. There was an aura of command and masculinity about him that was powerful, and not to be ignored. He did not pressure her, although she recognized that he enjoyed kissing her, and perhaps even thought of doing more, but it was as if he sensed in her a need for time. It was getting to be easier and more comfortable to be with him. But she was also becoming too aware of him physically, and that disturbed her most of all.

Only once since he'd visited her for dinner at Hannah's did he draw her into an embrace that hinted at being more than just affection, and she was unnerved to recognize her ready anticipation of it. It had been a lazy morning of visiting with one family, the Harrises. Mrs. Harris had insisted that Jackie and Eric take some freshly baked apple cake filled with apple butter, some cold boiled shrimp with a tart red sauce, and cans of beer. They were lent a basket to put everything in, and it seemed sensible to stop somewhere and enjoy it. Eric drove the car inland a way, where it was cooler in the shelter of trees. Jackie had been concerned that they would waste too much time over lunch, but Eric pretended he hadn't heard her objections. However, the objection was only halfhearted; she was more aware that a quiet lunch would put them in too intimate a situation again.

Eric climbed with agility over the rough earth, heading deep into the woods, with Jackie behind him. He finally stopped, but so suddenly that Jackie plowed right into his back, and he quickly reached out a strong arm to steady her. Using a blanket from the trunk of the car, Eric spread it out, and began to empty the basket, obviously intent on enjoying the occasion. Jackie stood in uncertainty watching him before she finally lowered herself next to him.

"Come on! Relax!" Eric chided her. "Your film will still be good if you shoot it two hours from now." He opened the containers with the shrimp and the sauce and sampled one.

"Ummmm! These are good! Here, try one." Eric dipped a shrimp into the sauce and passed it to Jackie. She reached for it but Eric held it away, indicating she was just to open her mouth. She hesitated, but finally tilted her head back, showing the slim column of her throat. Eric watched appreciatively for a moment before placing the shrimp in her mouth. Jackie nibbled while Eric opened the beer cans.

Jackie dipped her own shrimp after that, enjoying the cold bite of the meat. They ate in silence, Eric comfortably licking the remaining sauce from his fingers, Jackie following suit. She could not remember ever having done anything like this before. She puzzled over the idea.

"Do you realize this is my very first picnic?" she said simply.

Eric looked at her in wonder, not quite knowing if she was serious or not.

"Is it?" Eric asked easily, watching her.

She shrugged. "I don't think I've ever done this before."

Eric leaned back until his body was supported on a bent elbow. "Poor Jacqueline Taylor from New York. Did you have a deprived childhood?" he quipped, but it touched a raw nerve in her and she stiffened.

"I had a normal childhood. Both my parents worked. . . ."

"So did mine, and there were lots of picnics. And fishing and ball games, and . . ." Eric stopped his listing as he saw a shadow cross Jackie's pretty face. "What did you do as a kid?" he asked.

Jackie began to unwrap the apple cake nervously, giving herself something to do with her hands. "I went to camp during the summers. Sometimes I'd spent it with my grandparents. But they're all gone now."

"What about your parents? Sisters and brothers."

Jackie shook her head. "I'm an only child."

Eric frowned. "Tell me about your parents. What do they do? Where are they now?"

Jackie told him as she sliced the cake, putting generous heaps of it on napkins. Her childhood was perhaps not as carefree as his had been, but she wanted him to understand why. She explained about her teacher father and her executive mother.

"And who do you take after?" Eric asked in teasing curiosity as he pinched off fingerfuls of the cake and carried them to his mouth. Jackie thought for a moment.

"Both of them, I guess. I want to do things, accomplish things. That's my mother's influence. But I also want to . . ." Jackie stopped dead as she realized what she was about to confess. Eric waited for her to continue.

"Go on," he prompted.

Jackie smiled ruefully and shook her head. "I was going to say . . ." But she couldn't think of a thing to improvise with, and she couldn't bring herself to say what was really on her mind. A silence fell as Eric finished his cake and looked at her.

"It doesn't really matter. My life is very busy right now."

"And are you enjoying it?" he asked.

It was such an odd question. "Yes. Of course."

"But?"

"No buts." She shrugged.

"And are you now and have you always been the real Jacqueline Taylor?"

"You're talking foolishness," she said uneasily. "This is beginning to sound like an inquisition!" She was starting to feel exposed and open before Eric's questioning. Apprehension took hold of her—not of danger, but of being very vulnerable. Jackie began to inwardly withdraw.

Eric sat up, crossing his long legs Indian fashion, his eyes never leaving her face. "I bet I can tell you who you are, Jacqueline Taylor, better than you can," he said, trying to keep her from running from him again.

"Don't be so conceited," she said in an uncertain voice, avoiding his eye.

"I'm just convinced. And you are, I think, confused."

"I don't want to hear this," Jackie said, beginning to gather the remains of their lunch into the basket.

"Afraid?" he asked softly.

"No . . ." she answered, but she didn't sound very convincing.

"Then it won't hurt to listen to a little guessing unless you think I'll hit the nail on the head."

Jackie let out a deep sigh of exasperation. "Okay, Mr. Davidson—talk."

There was a moment's hesitation on Eric's part, and a speculative expression crossed his face. As she called him Mr. again, he perhaps recognized that it was her own mechanism for putting safe space between them, but he'd thought they'd overcome that need by now. Eric took a deep breath and began to talk.

"Okay. You are the only child of professional parents who raised you professionally. You had all the necessary trappings of a childhood—good schools, summers at camp, lots of freedom. You were independent very early and very self-sufficient." Eric talked, not missing a beat, talking with a kind of knowledge and assurance that Jackie found fascinating in spite of herself. But she allowed no emotion to show and sat listening with an expression of mild interest.

"You learned that it was important to move, to have some goal in mind, to do something with your life." His eyes flickered over her in a removed appraisal of her physical assets. "You're very attractive, so you modeled for a while because it was easy. Then, you gave it up."

"Because?" Jackie asked.

Eric frowned, squinting at her and shaking his head slowly. "I'm not altogether sure yet. But it'll come to me."

"Go on."

He leaned back until his back was supported by the trunk of a tree. He watched her with an odd look in his eyes as he took the time to light a cigarette. He stretched out one leg and bent the other at the knee so that he could rest his arm over it, dangling the lit cigarette from his long fingers. He exhaled. His voice dropped, and he said carefully,

"Enter, your ex. He charms you, flatters you, gives you lots of attention. He breaks down your resistance and weds you. Now you have someone who needs you. But it turns out to be for all the wrong reasons. Exit Jackie.

"So you've given up being what other people want you to be, and start being yourself. Or what you think is really yourself. You find you have a talent and liking for photography, so it's now yours to do with what you will. But also . . ." Eric's voice got even softer, less staccato, more caressing as he and Jackie stared at one another.

". . . There's a basic need for real affection, warm friends around you, caring family. You have a hell of a lot of love to give, Jacqueline Taylor. And no one to give it to."

Their eyes held for a moment longer before Jackie moved. She stood up, brushing crumbs from her clothing, exercising super-human efforts to keep her hands and voice steady. She bent over the basket to fold away napkins, her vision blurring against her will, waves of emotions lapping over her, threatening to sub-merge her.

"Well?" Eric asked in his deep, controlled voice. "How did I do?"

How could he expect her to answer that? Jackie allowed her-self a swallow and blinked rapidly. When she looked at Eric, her deep brown eyes were sparkling and shimmering, but her look never wavered from his.

"It was interesting," she said, neither confirming nor denying its validity. "Shall I do you now?" she asked.

Eric's eyes narrowed at her and his generous mouth com-pressed in impatience.

"No!" He flicked the cigarette stub away into the forest and came quickly to his feet, his movements graceful and effortless. "Because you'd be totally wrong!" he said in annoyance.

"Just like you're wrong about me!" she lied sweetly, quaking nevertheless. "You can be so pompous!"

"And you can be so self-righteous!" His voice had gotten dan-gerously low.

That hurt. Jackie wasn't expecting it and she went cold. She spoke very low so that her voice wouldn't quiver and give her away to a now angry Eric who looked like he wanted to strangle her. "If you think of me that way, then why do you bother coming with me every day?"

A nerve stood out cordlike in Eric's neck. He jammed his hands into his pockets and turned away from her. He cursed under his breath. "You're the one that keeps reminding me that this is only a job."

"That's right! And nothing else."

He turned back to her. "You really know how to try a man's patience," he murmured threateningly. "Come on. Let's get this cleared up so we can go!"

"Fine with me!" Jackie muttered, bending to put everything else into the basket, while Eric shook out the blanket rather violently and folded it.

But very quickly, the silence began to depress Jackie and she began to feel an overwhelming loneliness assail her. Now that her anger had been assuaged, she couldn't bear it if they drove all the way back to Charleston in stony silence.

"Thank you for lunch," she ventured gruffly.

"Thank the Harrises," Eric said disagreeably. "They provided the lunch." He picked up the basket. "Are you ready?" and not waiting for an answer started back to the parked car. Jackie had to rush to keep up with him, and he never once looked back to see if she was there. He had already put everything into the trunk of the car when Jackie reached him.

She was hot and out of breath, and felt contrite and a little sorry for herself. And she was much too tired to be angry with him anymore.

Eric turned to look at her with a baleful expression, but Jackie watched as slowly his body relaxed and all the stiff alert muscles in him smoothed out. She thought for a moment that he would take up the argument. But a barely perceivable smile lifted the corner of his mouth as he slowly approached her, his hands on his narrow hips. Something seemed to be amusing him. She was amazed at how quickly his anger could vanish.

All the anger and frustration drained out of Jackie as she admired his tall, well-formed, handsome presence. She didn't want to fight Eric. That's not what she wanted from him. Her eyes were drawn to his mouth and she almost felt it against her own. Jackie felt alarm, not understanding what was happening to her, and not fully understanding this melting that took place inside of her every time his gaze softened on her.

Eric might have been reading her mind. Everything suddenly happened in slow motion, as Eric's hand reached out to her and he captured her chin in his fingers. Jackie watched hypnotized as his mouth lowered. His image got closer and blurred and she closed her eyes, waiting, not moving. Next she felt the feathery touch of Eric's mouth on the corner of her own, and his tongue flicked out to brush back and forth over the velvet skin.

There was an instant, frightening rise of desire in her, but Eric was pulling away. His thumb smoothed over the spot his tongue had touched.

His eyes were mysterious, almost yellow in the sunlight, and they burned hot into hers. "You had apple butter on your face," he whispered softly, and it was like a caress.

"I would have wiped it away," Jackie whispered back, still mesmerized.

Eric smiled gently, shaking his head. "Eh eh. And spoil my fun?"

"All little girls on picnics get dirty faces," she said irrelevantly.

Eric's eyes moved from viewing her mouth up to her eyes and back to her mouth again. "This was your first picnic, so you're allowed." His thumb moved over the spot again. His voice dropped even lower, almost inaudible. "And you are no little girl."

His head bent again, as both hands cupped her face and his lips pressed tentatively. Jackie responded, opening her mouth just as tentatively. Their lips brushed lightly and separated. They explored once more, Jackie feeling Eric's warm breath mixing with her own. She put her hands up to clasp his wrist, as his hands continued to hold her face. But then the teasing playfulness ended. Eric, sensing her acquiescence, settled his mouth on hers in a thorough and complete kiss. Jackie's heart pounded and she moved toward him, but the way he held her didn't allow for them to touch elsewhere, and she wanted them to. The kiss was tender and slow and therefore even more devastating in its effect than if he'd been urgent and demanding.

Jackie felt a now familiar dizziness overtaking her, the effect of Eric's touching her. She could feel the tensely held muscles in his arms, could feel the slight tremor of his body that matched her own. It made everything suddenly very different. This was no caress of casual sexual attraction. This touch demonstrated a deeper need and desire even in its simplicity and gentleness. A breath caught in Jackie's chest as in a haze of dreamy feelings she tried to understand if it was her need or Eric's.

He pulled slowly back from her, his breathing shallow and ragged, his lids lowered over his eyes, hiding his expression. But there was no mistaking his true feelings as his fingers massaged her cheeks, and his thumb slid over her lips, only to be replaced by his once more. Still, he didn't bring her into his arms, deliberately holding her off for reasons Jackie couldn't begin to guess at.

Eric suddenly turned away from her. Jackie had to reach out to touch the car for balance. She felt as though she'd been holding her breath for hours. Eric let out a deep sigh and pulled open the car door.

"Come on!" he said in a brusque voice that surprised her. "Let's get out of here!" Without waiting for her to get into the car he went around to the driver's side.

Jackie felt confused and angry. She wanted to tell him she was sorry for spoiling their picnic. But his sudden withdrawal made her feel as though she'd thrown herself on him. Eric scratched his fingers in irritation through his close-cropped hair as he drove.

"They're predicting rain for tomorrow, so I suggest we put a hold on your research," he said coldly, businesslike.

Jackie stiffened, the warm, lethargic state of just minutes ago all gone. "Okay," she agreed in what she hoped was a steady voice.

"I've been putting off some things that have to get done, so I'll need tomorrow anyway."

She didn't respond, feeling a grim despair drop over her. Was he put off by her responding? What on earth was the matter now?

"I think we should do something different the next time I see you," he said in decision, eyes on the road ahead of him. Jackie waited for him to continue. "There's a park you should see while you're here. It's a very important part of Charleston."

Jackie shrugged. "Fine with me," she answered. And not another word was spoken until they pulled up beside Eric's cozy, dilapidated house. He said a quick, brief goodbye to her and headed toward his door, Jackie watched for a moment longer, perplexed by his change in moods. She turned the car toward the city, never questioning that the day had been cut inexplicably short.

Jackie never for a moment doubted Eric, and true to his words, it rained the next day. The dreary, humid day only added to her already heightened sense of expectation. She felt restless and moody and managed to convince herself that it was all due to being stuck indoors. She'd gotten used to leaving the house early in the morning and spending the day with Eric in the generous Carolina sunshine. She felt impatient now with anything else.

The absence from Eric, even for a day, also brought into sharp focus how used she'd gotten to being with him. Alone now, Jackie reflected on the things he'd said about her on the day of their brief picnic. The truth of his words had been very hard to deal with because so much of it was unresolved from her adolescence and her relationship to her parents. No one had ever pinpointed it so clearly before. Jackie understood that at least Eric was paying more attention to her, and was therefore more attuned to all her inner workings. This immediately gave him points not only over Mark, but all those people from her modeling days who never got to know her better than they did.

Feeling very impatient also with herself, she prepared to once more drive in to the lab in Charleston, and spend the day lost in the darkroom. Hannah sensed an uneasiness about Jackie and she frowned over it. She had learned in the few weeks Jackie had been with her that it did not always help to question her directly. But Hannah was concerned about her, and watched Jackie's fidgeting around the house in helpless perplexity. She could fuss over her, feed her, be a friend, and mother her. But if Jackie was troubled in her heart, Hannah knew she'd have to work it out alone.

Absently saying goodbye to Hannah, Jackie drove into Charleston in a driving rain that made her wish belatedly that she'd stayed home, occupying her time listening to tapes she'd recorded earlier in the week, or curling up with a fat paperback.

She scrambled from the car into Bob's shop and he didn't seem particularly surprised to see her. They talked briefly over the progress of her book. He told her she'd picked the perfect day to spend in the lab. But Jackie didn't mention it was purely therapeutic today. She would much rather have spent the time outdoors with Eric. Nothing else she did seemed to be half as exciting as the time spent with him. He could be arrogant and sarcastic and totally exasperating. But he was also challenging, and stimulating in more ways than one.

As she moved to go off to the darkroom, Bob stopped her.

"Don't you want to know what happened to your pictures?"

"What pictures?"

"The ones I displayed for you the last time you were in!"

"Oh! I'd forgotten." She turned back to the counter. "What happened with them?"

"Well, I sold two."

"Fantastic!" Jackie exclaimed, diverted and overjoyed.

Having her work picked up so readily in a market other than New York, where she was known, was gratifying. It reinforced her feelings of being a true professional photographer capable of making a decent living at her trade.

"I hope you have more prints for me today."

"I don't know, Bob. These are really intended for the book. Now that I think about it, I probably shouldn't have sold those first two!"

"Oh, I think it will be okay. The buyer said they were for display in his office."

"Who is he?"

"Well, he . . . he teaches out at the university." Bob seemed to hesitate. "But he's also interested in a possible exhibition of your work."

"Bob! Are you serious?"

"Of course. It's just a little local gallery, but he said he'd speak to the manager. Just think of all the great prepublication publicity you'll get for your book! Why, someone might even suggest you do another!"

"But why would a stranger bother?"

"He said he was impressed with the way you see things."

Jackie got caught up in the fantasy. It would be wonderful if she could do another book. Bob interrupted her daydreams.

"In the meantime, you have work to do. Show me your current work before you leave here today. If the show comes off, I'll need ten good pieces from you."

"When will the show be?"

"He's aiming for three to four weeks. The semester at the university will be over then and he'll be less busy."

My research will also be over. The thought came to Jackie in a depressing jolt. She nodded to Bob and went on to the lab. The work was even better this week and she was more than pleased with her results. There were quite a number of images of Eric and she was aghast at how many she'd actually taken. But the images showed him in all the ways she'd gotten used to seeing him. The only things she had not captured were his occasional show of impatience or anger with her, and his very potent sensuality. But what she had was important to her. She'd be finished soon in South Carolina and on her way back to New York. She readily admitted that her relationship with Eric would be a welcome memory.

Jackie busied herself even more to block out the thought. Bob examined once again her finished work and promptly picked out about fifteen possible pictures. Jackie was pleased that he'd chosen one of Hannah in her Sunday straw hat, and yet another of her as she leaned over the fence in her yard to talk to a neighbor. Jackie had done a good job of capturing the friendship and affection of the two women even as they were separated physically by the white picket fence.

Again, she was careful to put away all her pictures of Eric, and when Bob questioned her about them, she told him they were just some ruined shots she would discard. He gave her the money received from the sale of the first prints and teased her that this could be the start of a profitable partnership. Jackie laughed, shaking her head, reminding him it would be the shortest partnership on record since her stay in Charleston was drawing to a close. The comment prompted another wave of depression, and leaving Bob still bent over her black and white prints, she ducked into the rain once more toward her car.

Jackie thought seriously that night of the work that remained for her to do on the book. Yes, Gwen would come down and they'd go over the tapes and photos, and she'd begin to write the text. But for the time being, Jackie's immediate involvement would be over. It was not this, however, which bothered her, or tensed her stomach with dread. It was the very real possibility of not seeing Eric again. Only now, as that reality hit her, could she admit to other feelings she had for him.

She paced her room well into the night, struggling with her feelings. It was pure foolishness to deny her attraction to him. It had been there from the very first time. He had only to approach her and she reacted strongly. She'd fought it for so many weeks she'd almost come to believe that he really did irritate her more than anything else. But it was much more than that.

Eric had treated her kindly, even as she'd fought needing that. Even when she deliberately edged him into anger, he handled it better than she would have expected, and, she thought ruefully now, better than she sometimes deserved. Jackie rested her forehead against the smooth wooden bedpost as if to still her thoughts.

"No . . ." she moaned in denial as she recalled his sensuous kisses and gentle caressing of her body. She wanted—needed—more than kindness from him. But she had been so taciturn, so defensive that she was sure she'd put him off for good. Certainly the way they'd separated the afternoon before did not speak well for the relationship, whatever was left of it.

Mark had treated her like a valuable commodity, an investment that had to be protected and guarded. Eric treated her like a person, like a woman.

For the first time in a very long time since her divorce, Jackie cried herself to sleep. It came to her now as she contemplated leaving South Carolina, in a kind of horrific clarity, that she had never truly loved Mark. And she was coming to recognize feelings for Eric Davidson she'd never felt for anyone before. Eric's calling the next morning, therefore, to cancel the day because it was again raining, brought her to another state of anguish. The conversation was short and succinct. No teasing, no special remarks. Just, I'll see you tomorrow.

But the rain finally stopped and the new day came and Eric did show up. It took all of Jackie's control to present to him the aloof person he'd come to know. She wanted nothing else to show through to him. But it was hard.

Hannah invited him in for coffee and served him rolls which Jackie had made earlier in the week. He sampled one, raising his brows in surprise.

"You can cook, too? I'm impressed," he teased, winking at her, allowing Jackie to relax with him and smile in return.

He seemed in no great hurry to leave, and calmly sat talking to Hannah while he smoked a cigarette. Jackie found it hard to participate in the conversation, suddenly aware of his physical presence and aura in the house as well as her feelings for him.

"Where are you two off to today?" Hannah questioned as she forced yet another roll on Eric.

"I thought we'd go to Cypress Gardens today," Eric replied around a mouthful of the soft sweet bread. "Ummm! These are right on the money!" he said with enthusiasm.

Hannah giggled. "You should take the rest with you. As a

matter of fact, Jackie, why not fix lunch for you two to take for the day. You can stop somewhere and have a real picnic!"

Jackie caught Eric's eye and he smiled knowingly at her. "That's a very good idea, Hannah," she readily agreed, and began to rummage through the refrigerator. She came up with cold pieces of chicken, potato salad, rolls, jam, and oranges. The thought of spending time with Eric in this fashion was frankly very appealing.

Everything was piled into the tote normally used for her equipment. Taking the weighty bag from her hands, Eric headed for the door. Jackie picked up her camera but Eric quickly relieved her of it, and passed it back to Hannah.

"What did you do that for?" Jackie asked bewildered. Eric took her hand, pulling her out the door.

"This is not a work day. This is a relax-and-enjoy-your-stay-in-Charleston day. The guide service today is free of charge. I want you to use your eyes, not your camera!"

Hannah waved them off. They stopped once to purchase a bottle of wine to have with their picnic. Jackie felt absurdly happy, and wondered at the difference forty-eight hours could make in a person. She was easy and comfortable with Eric. They were able to tease and banter, staying away from any subject that would start an argument.

They started out with Eric explaining that the gardens closed yearly on May 1, and he thought it appropriate that she should visit before it did. Cypress Gardens was the most unusual of all the major parks in Charleston because it was a swamp, although a picturesque one. It was a profusion of tall cypress trees and waterways, lined with azaleas and camellias. They took a boat ride alone through the watery passages under delicate Japanese bridges, seeing their image in the inky water. The flowers consisted of dogwoods, lavender wisteria, and poinsettias. It was near one of these exquisite bridges that they stopped to have their lunch, enjoying the warm air and the fragrance from the well-tended landscape around them.

For a time after they ate, Eric lay with his head in her lap. It was intimate and peaceful. She was tempted to brush her fingers over and through his hair, but couldn't bring herself to take such a liberty. It seemed too personal a touch, too possessive.

They finally got up to continue their wandering through the

park. Eric caught her quickly to him as he kissed her caressingly, making her senses pound with the gentle seductive movement. Hesitating at first, Jackie put her arms up to his shoulders. As if it was an invitation he couldn't refuse, Eric momentarily deepened the caress but then released her, both of them more than a little shaken by the brief contact.

"Thank you for the picnic," Eric said in a significant low voice.

"You're welcome," she murmured.

". . . And for the day," Eric continued.

Jackie smiled at him, watching the merriment in his eyes.

He leaned to kiss her forehead. "And for your company." That was the nicest thank-you of all.

Toward the later afternoon it became clear that it would rain again. They had just enough time to follow several more paths through the park, Eric holding her hand to lead her, before they headed back to the car. It began to rain finally on the road back to Hannah's.

Jackie sighed in complete contentment. "The flowers were wonderful," she said to Eric.

"I expect you to remember all the different varieties. You're going to be tested!" he teased.

Jackie laughed. "Oh yeah? What do I get if I name them all?"

Eric looked at her with a wicked grin. "I'll think of something!"

"I bet you will!" she responded caustically, smiling happily at him all the same.

It had been a wonderful day for Jackie, and she hoped that Eric had enjoyed it as much as she did. By its end, she had allowed herself to relax completely. But she quickly became alert to Eric's silence and lack of response to her further attempts at conversation. He seemed to be deep in thought. He walked her up the steps to the house and passed her the empty picnic basket.

"I'm sure it will be okay if you stayed with us for dinner," Jackie ventured awkwardly. She leaned back against the door, looking at him as he stood tall and compelling in front of her against the background gray sky.

Eric's eyes swept over her bright red halter blouse, over the white skirt she wore with it, to her eyes. He reached out and gently tugged at a curl hanging over her ear. "Is that an invitation?" he asked in a low, husky voice, leaning forward to brace a hand over her head against the door, bringing his head within inches of hers.

"If you like," she admitted, her senses filling with the smell of his shirt and his skin.

"I like . . ." Eric whispered, now running the back of his knuckles along her determined jawline. He bent to give her a brief kiss.

". . . But I can't."

Jackie wasn't sure she'd heard him, until he stood up straight and took a step back from her, effectively breaking the spell which had descended upon her.

"My time has run out." Eric sighed with a lopsided grin.

"Your time? What do you mean?" she asked puzzled.

"I told you I would have work to finish and could only take a few days off to help you. Well, I cheated. It's been almost three weeks and the work still has to be done."

"Oh," Jackie responded, trying not to sound disappointed. "I'm sorry. I wasn't aware I was taking up so much of your time," she said stiffly.

Eric noticed the immediate change in her and sighed in impatience. "Cut it out, Jackie. You were doing no such thing."

"You're right," Jackie interrupted, in full command again. "You were being paid for your time and services."

Eric stared at her, an ominous cloud taking over his features. "Oh hell!" he snapped. "Did it never occur to you that I might have spent all that time with you, payment or not, because I wanted to?"

"No, it never did," she answered softly, brought up short by his confession. "Unless you were being *kind* again," she said flatly, goading him further.

Eric suddenly slammed his fist against the frame of the door with such violence in his moment of frustration that Jackie jumped, frightened by his reaction.

"Dammit!" he fairly shouted. "One thing your folks neglected to do was take a switch to your behind every now and then!"

"Are you threatening me?" she asked, standing defiantly in front of him.

Eric looked at her stonily for a long moment, and let out an exhausted sigh. He shook his head, a short humorless laugh escaping him. He ran a hand over his tired eyes. "If I thought it would do any good, I'd have done it weeks ago!" Eric looked at her again, and suddenly stepped forward, taking hold of her arms.

"Jackie . . ." he began in an almost pleading voice, searching her face for a sign of softening and understanding, "I don't want to postpone the touring. But I have to. For just a few days!"

Jackie remained limp in his hold, wanting to collapse against his chest and plead for herself for just a few days, wanting to be near him, needing to trust him, but holding herself back, nonetheless. Her eyes softened for a moment on his, and Eric, seeing the question there, stroked her arms hopefully.

"I understand, Eric," she whispered, opening the door.

Jackie smiled wanly. "I'm sure I have most of the information I need, anyway. Gwen can help me with the rest when she gets here."

"Jackie . . ." he tried again.

"Thank you for your time," she said hurriedly. "Goodbye." And she firmly closed the door, leaning against it because she was suddenly shaking so much. She waited until she heard Eric start slowly back down the stairs. Jackie's eyes closed and she felt both defeated and ashamed. She knew she'd been totally unreasonable with Eric.

"Is that you, darlin'?" came Hannah's voice from the parlor.

"Yes, Hannah," she answered in a voice not quite her own. She moved into the doorway slowly and stopped.

"Isn't this a nice surprise?" Hannah piped uncertainly.

"Hey, girl!" Gwen's throaty voice reached her and she came forward to kiss Jackie on the cheek.

But Jackie could not move or answer as she saw Mark Bennett sitting on the love seat.

CHAPTER SEVEN

Jackie would never remember what was said in those first ten minutes as she stood almost paralyzed in the doorway to the parlor. Gwen's tall fashionably dressed frame unfurled itself from the love seat and she sauntered over to place a tentative kiss on Jackie's cold cheek. She left behind a moist lip-glossed print, and surrounded Jackie in a veil of some very expensive perfume. Gwen gave a welcome to which Jackie knew she must have responded, but her insides and emotions were in a double turmoil as she riveted her eyes to Mark.

He remained seated, watching her with a negligent expression on his face as though it was the most natural thing in the world for him to be sitting in Hannah's parlor in a quaint country home in South Carolina. He had that same cool, controlled, slightly haughty look that had left her feeling unsure and foolish when she'd first met him.

"I hope you're at least happy to see me!" Gwen laughed nervously in a whisper, as her eyes flitted back and forth between the lanky languishing form of Mark Bennett and the very rigid form of her friend. Jackie ignored her as she looked with wary curiosity at Mark.

"What are you doing here?"

Only then did he deem it necessary to come to his full height and move toward her. Instinctively Jackie stiffened as she watched his movements warily. He was as handsomely turned out as ever. Brown trousers impeccably creased, shoes shiny and smooth, shirt spotless and casually opened at the throat, its collar lying over that of the cream linen jacket which snugly fitted his thin shoulders. There was a gold chain around his neck and another matching it on his right wrist.

Jackie reasoned that there was nothing different about Mark from what she remembered except for one thing. He now wore a thick well-trimmed mustache over his lip, effectively hiding the cynical curling of his mouth that he'd shown so often to Jackie in the past. Looking at him now, she realized she was almost indifferent to him. But there seemed to be no getting him completely out of her life. Right on the tail end of an unhappy and stiff goodbye to Eric which left her feeling sorry, came Mark, adding to the list, suspicion.

She'd had enough of having her senses assaulted and confused for one day. She had no idea what Mark Bennett was doing here or what he wanted. But she knew caution was in order.

"What are you doing here?" Jackie repeated, ignoring Gwen still, and only peripherally aware of Hannah's confused and agitated state. A lazy familiar smile curved Mark's full lips.

"It's nice to see you, too," he said softly, and in a rather insolent manner looked her up and down. "You're looking fine," he said with sarcasm. Jackie knew full well that he was referring to her rather pedestrian outfit. It was not the height of fashion and certainly not what Mark was used to seeing her in. The halter top was definitely summer casual and her white skirt was a little wrinkled and grass-stained from the park and her recent outing.

Jackie started to comment when Gwen spoke up.

"Look, hon. I don't know if this was a good idea or not, but he insisted on seeing you," Gwen said apologetically.

"You can believe her." Mark came to Gwen's rescue. "I really didn't give her much of a chance."

"I can well believe that!" Jackie answered caustically.

"And she did warn me that you would not be pleased to see me."

"You should have listened to her; she was right."

"You haven't even heard why I'm here, yet. You did ask, you know." And he smiled wickedly at her.

Jackie let her brows rise. She tilted her head and let out a silent long breath. She turned for the first time to Gwen and gave her a halfhearted smile.

"I'm sure it wasn't your fault, Gwen. He can be very charming and persuasive when he wants."

"Thank you!" Mark acknowledged, not at all put out by the questionable compliment. He stepped a foot closer to Jackie and slid one jeweled hand into his pants pocket.

Jackie was immediately aware that the smooth innocent gesture was not at all like Eric's, which showed more leashed and controlled emotions, tautening his muscles and sinew, making him seem like some tamed magnificent animal.

"Anger becomes you!" Mark said with a low laugh.

"I'm not angry, Mark. Only suspicious," Jackie corrected evenly.

Mark shrugged. "You take things too seriously."

"I suppose you're now going to tell me it was wrong to try and take my marriage seriously?" she said, incredulous.

"Oh Lordy . . ." Gwen groaned under her breath, lowering her head and shielding her eyes with her hands, as if she really didn't want to be a witness to this confrontation. Hannah finally stood up and came to put a gentle soft hand on Jackie's arm. Jackie jumped, but the movement brought her sharply back to her immediate surroundings, and she turned to smile at Hannah.

"I'm sorry, darlin'," Hannah said in real concern.

Jackie squeezed her hand. "It's all right. I'm sure you weren't aware he'd show up with Gwen."

"No, I surely wasn't! But I couldn't very well send him away when he said he came to see you. He said . . . I thought . . ."

"I know, I know." Jackie took a deep breath and frowned. She was determined to make the best of an awkward situation, and also determined to get rid of Mark as soon as she could.

"I invited your, er, I mean, Mr. Bennett to stay for dinner," Hannah continued, still uncertain.

"Well, we wouldn't want to send him away on an empty stomach, would we?"

Mark reached to a side table in the parlor to pick up a glass of something cold. He raised the glass in a silent salute as if conceding that the battle had just begun, if indeed it had ever really ended. Jackie turned away from him.

"I think I'll change my clothes. I'll be down in a few minutes."

"I'll come, too!" Gwen offered quickly, following the straight-backed Jackie up the stairs.

It was not until they were in Jackie's room with the door closed that Jackie threw her things on the bed and turned to a Gwen standing unsure near the door.

"Gwen . . ." Jackie began tiredly. "How could you bring him here?"

"I told you I didn't bring him, hon. He insisted on coming, and frankly, there was no way I could stop him!"

"What does he want?" Jackie asked suspiciously.

Gwen shrugged, going over to sit on the edge of Jackie's bed, crossing her elegant brown legs at the knee. "He said he had something to discuss with you. Some sort of business deal."

"Mark's business deals make me nervous!" Jackie murmured ruefully, pulling off her clothing and putting on a robe. She reached for her usual jeans and a pale yellow blouse, but stopped in her motions. She recalled Mark's snide reference to her outfit downstairs, and decided that the occasion warranted something a little more pulled together. She put on a slim black silk summer dress with spaghetti straps, and low-heeled red sandals. For the first time since she arrived in Charleston, she applied makeup, but not as elaborate or as much as Gwen, who would never dream of being seen in public without her full model's regalia. Next Jackie brushed her soft curls into a small curly knot, and stuck colorful hair prongs into it to hold it in place. All the while she and Gwen kept up a running conversation.

"It was mean of me to leave Hannah down there with him by herself," Jackie said, applying a touch of warm apricot blusher to her cheeks.

Gwen only laughed shortly, drawing air sharply between her teeth. "Honey, I wouldn't worry about Hannah. She won't hesitate to put Mark in his place if she has to! But she was confused when she opened the door and found both of us standing there. Child, if you thought you were annoyed, you should have seen the look she gave me on the sly! She's very protective of you."

"Serves you right!" Jackie laughed without the least bit of sympathy. "I should send *you* down there to deal with him!"

"But you won't. Besides, he doesn't want to see me. He wants to see you! And how can you pass up a chance to show him you don't need him anymore?"

"He's a fool if he doesn't know that already."

"Or just arrogant and overly confident. He probably thinks you've been pining away in these backwoods over him."

Jackie stopped her hand in its application of her lipstick and watched the slightly parted surface as she easily conjured up an image of Eric's warm generous mouth curved in a smile just before he kissed her. "I've hardly been pining away," she said in a vague voice.

"I told him you and I were doing a book together about the Gullah people on Johns Island. He thought it was pretty funny. He sees us as very pretty clothes racks, and nothing more!"

"Well, who cares what he thinks anyway," Jackie said indifferently.

"You do," Gwen said very softly behind her. Jackie's eyes caught Gwen's reflection in the vanity mirror.

"Why do you say that?"

Gwen flipped a hand in Jackie's direction. "Why bother dressing up for him, then? Because you want to show him you know how to pull it all together when you want to. And wasn't it you who said that underneath all that makeup and silk there's a real live person?"

Jackie frowned. Gwen was right.

"And despite some very good reasons for wanting to see him gone, his being here has you curious as hell to find out what he wants."

Jackie sat thoughtfully on her vanity chair.

"*And* on top of all of that," Gwen said, warming to her analysis, "he probably wants to try and get you back!"

Jackie chuckled then. "Now you are crazy! Mark can have anyone he wants and usually does. He doesn't want me."

"Maybe. But you're the only one to ever walk out on him."

"The way I see it, that makes me a lot smarter than his other —women!"

"Isn't that the truth! Still, Mark has a real ego, and whether you know it or not, you managed to punch a few holes in it."

Jackie laughed briefly without humor. "If I remember anything about Mark's ego, I'd say safely that he'll survive!"

"You really don't hold any love for him, do you?"

Jackie frowned and looked at her concerned friend. "Gwen, the truth is, I'm not sure if I ever did. And I'm much happier without him."

"In any case, I just think you should be careful. Mark *can* be vindictive! I wouldn't want to get on his bad side." Gwen chuckled.

Jackie put down the lipstick and stood up. "Well, I've been on the bad side, Gwen. There isn't anything he can do to hurt me that he hasn't already done!" Jackie had a sudden thought.

"My God! Hannah didn't . . . she *couldn't* invite him to stay here. Did she?"

"Are you kidding? Besides, Mark would never stay among the peasants, child. No, he's staying at one of those swank downtown hotels in Charleston."

Jackie was relieved. She looked around. "Well, I guess we'd better go rescue Hannah."

Gwen laughed, getting up and followed Jackie to the door. "It's my guess that Mark is the one who needs to be saved! Hannah don't take no foolishness in her house!"

And it proved to be true. Mark was sadly out of place in Hannah's house and she didn't bother to make apologies. Hannah quickly summed up the situation between Mark Bennett and Jackie, and allied herself even more protectively on Jackie's side. She was the epitome of Southern hospitality as the phrase had so often been used but her usual warmth and natural vivaciousness were held in check. At first Jackie felt almost guilty, feeling that maybe she'd unjustly prejudiced Hannah against Mark. But the thought lasted only a moment. It was clear after a while that Mark's own sense of self-importance and his own snobbery did much toward making up Hannah's mind for her.

Hannah saw Mark for what he was. Very worldly and sophisticated and well beyond her sphere. But that didn't make him better than she, and she resented his condescension, veiled though it was. Humph! Hannah thought in indignation. Her Jackie deserved much better, already drawing mental comparisons between Mark Bennett and Eric Davidson.

Jackie found herself unconsciously doing the very same thing. But the result was she became pensive and withdrawn during the simple meal, not making any tremendous effort to take part in the conversation. Her mind wandered to other things. In retrospect, Jackie realized that she'd treated Eric as though he was some shiftless, irresponsible person. Her stomach tensed with the full weight of her unfairness toward him. And worse yet, how could she have expected him to take her seriously when she hadn't treated him in kind? She belatedly recognized that Eric had been sensitive, aware, helpful, and at times extraordinarily gentle with her. She cursed herself for being eight different kinds of a fool for being too wrapped up in protecting herself to see Eric for what he was. A wonderful person, and a strong man. Unfortunately, the revelations may have come too late. And Mark's presence only served to reinforce them for her.

Jackie shifted uncomfortably in her chair, the drone of the other quiet voices at the table not quite reaching her consciousness. She wondered in something close to real pain if she'd ever see Eric Davidson again.

Hannah suddenly got up and went off to get coffee. There followed a small tight silence as the three young adults at the table fought for a common ground to communicate. Finally it was Jackie who relieved the tension by turning to Gwen.

"So, what's been happening in New York?" she asked.

Gwen shrugged her thin shoulders. "Same old thing. The usual people are getting a lot of cover layouts, although there are a few new faces this year. And it's the usual hustle to get an assignment, and then fighting with the agency over your fee. Sometimes I think you were the only smart one, getting out when you did."

Jackie shook her head. "I don't miss it at all, believe me. It's too easy to forget who you are. And then soon, other people forget as well."

A short laugh came from Mark seated to Jackie's right. "You mean to say you don't miss the money, the attention, the chance to buy great designer clothes?"

Jackie looked at him blankly for a moment, and said flatly, "There isn't anything about that part of my life that I miss."

Mark raised a brow and smiled smoothly at her. "Come on, Jackie. What happened to that wide-eyed girl who was so excited about having her picture seen in my magazine?"

An image of that youthful naivete came to Jackie. Her brows quirked at Mark. "The girl grew up into an adult. The fantasy was put to rest."

"Has it been?" Mark asked.

Were all of her ghosts gone?

A wicked grin spread over Mark's smooth brown features as he clearly saw doubt in her eyes, and he pounced on it. "Maybe not."

Hannah came with the coffee and set it down on the table. "If you'll excuse me I'll clear the table and do my dishes," she said formally. Simultaneously Gwen and Jackie protested her doing the work and volunteered to do it for her.

"No. You haven't seen one another in a while, and there must be lots to talk about." She looked significantly at Jackie with a look that said, "Now don't you let him browbeat you, Jacqueline Taylor!"

Belatedly Mark thanked Hannah for dinner, but she didn't soften toward him at all, having already made up her mind about him. Jackie caught the stiff exchange and actually felt sorry for him. She was remembering the smiling, giggling Hannah who fussed over and catered to Eric and sat talking to him unconsciously for several hours. The thought and memory caused a muscle to knot in Jackie's stomach. If only she could talk to Eric and apologize.

Gwen, Mark, and Jackie sat drinking their coffee trying to maintain a reasonable atmosphere, but it was a real effort. Finally, Jackie could take no more of the fencing.

"Okay, Mark. Just what are you doing here in South Carolina? What do you want?"

His deep brown eyes moved over her, assessing her, but in his look there was also something else. It made Jackie nervous. "I'm down here on business."

"But what are you doing *here?* Don't tell me it's a coincidence that you're here at Hannah's. Gwen said you followed her . . ."

"That's it! I'm going to the kitchen. Whether she knows it or not Hannah's going to need help with all those dishes!" Gwen's tall thin body sashayed down the hallway.

Jackie turned back to Mark ready to continue with her questions. She encountered a seductive look on Mark's face that was so unexpected she couldn't speak and could only stare at him fascinated.

"It's been a long time, baby," he crooned low.

That instantly brought Jackie back to reality. "Cut it out, Mark."

"There's never been anyone like you."

Jackie laughed knowingly. "You're right about that! There have been many more than me!"

"I've missed you, you know."

"That's your problem," she said with total disinterest, somewhat surprised despite herself by his confession of missing her. She wondered how serious he was.

"But you could help me with my problem."

Jackie's chin rose alertly. "You're crazy! If you think for one moment that I . . ."

"Don't be so sure. I might make you an offer you can't refuse!" He was laughing at her now, sure of himself as he'd always been. The sound grated on her nerve ends. Too often in the past Mark had been right about things.

"I doubt it. But let's hear what the offer is first," she said reasonably.

"It was really Gwen's idea."

"Gwen's?"

"Only she's not aware of it. She told me you two were planning on doing a book on the Gullah people."

"Yeah, and she told me what you thought of the idea."

"At first, yes. But I got to thinking. Everyone's working on their fall and winter layouts. There's lots of plaids and wools and earth browns this year—real country colors. I'm talking to the South Carolina Department of Commerce about doing the whole shooting for the September issue of my magazine in and around Charleston. Some of the major department stores and boutiques are picking up the theme. You know, the North goes South—that sort of thing."

Jackie listened. Mark knew his business, knew the fashion industry. He always did have a sense of flare and theatrics where clothes was concerned, and knew how to transmit that to a consumer public. Jackie had to admit the idea was very appealing.

"I thought to bring down all my models, photographers, stylist, the works, right here to Charleston. I'd shoot in the parks, the academy, some old plantations."

"So what does all of this have to do with me? Gwen said you had a business deal to offer," she asked, still confused.

"She's right. I figure we could help each other. How would you like to make a comeback?"

"Are you serious?" she said, surprised.

"How would you like to be my star model? I'd feature you, bring back your face to the public. You know people haven't forgotten you. Baby, you were *it* a few years ago, you can easily be again."

"No," Jackie said firmly, sitting back in her chair.

"There'd be a lot of money involved, of course."

"The money isn't important."

"And we could highlight you in the New York campaign."

"I said no!" Jackie emphasized. Mark finally stopped talking long enough to look at her and the determined set of her jaw. There came a genuine note of surprise in his voice.

"I think you *have* changed."

"It's about time you noticed. I'm not the least interested in ever modeling again."

"What are you going to do with the rest of your life? Hide behind a camera?"

"I'm getting to be a good photographer. I've already proven I can sell my work. It's too early to tell yet about the rest of my life."

"Baby, you can do better."

Jackie frowned at him, getting up from the table. "Stop calling me baby!" she said in irritation, hugging herself and walking slowly into the parlor from the dining room. Mark followed. Jackie turned on a lamp and turned to face him.

"I don't want to model again, Mark. So there's the end to your offer. I'm sorry you wasted your time."

"I'm not through yet."

"What else is there?"

"What about your book?"

She looked in confusion at him. He had her full attention again.

"What about my book?"

Mark smiled at her and casually strolled to the love seat and sat down. He crossed his legs and laid a long arm along the back of the seat. He didn't answer right away, but looked at her now with an unmistakable look of desire in his eyes. He stripped her naked before him with his look and unconsciously Jackie hugged herself closer. There was nothing sensuous in Mark's perusal of her. It was blatantly sexual and laced with a tension which Jackie found disturbing.

"Come sit next to me, baby," he commanded.

But Jackie ignored him and turned her back to him to block out his compelling demand. This was how it used to be, with one noticeable difference. She wasn't going to be so easily swayed by Mark anymore. Behind her, he laughed at her stubbornness.

"Okay. Be like that," he mused. "But I'm not finished yet." Jackie knew full well he meant it in more ways than one.

"You said something about my book. I want to know what you meant."

"Only that, if you'd agree to model for my layout it would mean great publicity for the book, for the people down here, for you as the photographer and Gwen as the writer."

Slowly Jackie turned to look at Mark. The magnitude of the offer suddenly hit her full force and its possibilities were awesome. She recognized that he now held her fascinated. Mark smiled at her knowingly, and slowly Jackie moved forward and sat next to him on the love seat.

"That's better," he whispered.

"Go on," Jackie said in a strange hypnotized voice.

Mark casually reached out a hand and ran the tips of his bony fingers in a light touch from Jackie's neck to the round end of her shoulder, pulling the strap of her dress off and down. Jackie angrily twitched away, sucking her teeth at him in annoyance. Mark laughed but took his hand away.

"The book can tie in nicely with the whole theme around South Carolina. We'll photograph the models—and you—with the people here."

"But Gwen hasn't even begun to write the text yet, and we're not absolutely sure that anyone will publish it."

"So . . . you are interested," Mark said triumphantly. Jackie ignored him.

"Look at it this way. After all the hype about it connects with the fashion layouts, you'll have no trouble finding a publisher who wants to jump on the bandwagon. I may even know one or two."

That final enticement shook Jackie and she found she was almost seriously considering it. Almost. She searched Mark's handsome face and tried to see what else he had in mind. He was never magnanimous without an ultimate goal in mind. Jackie squinted at him, trying to remember all his little tricks and manipulations. Although he certainly stood to benefit nicely from the whole venture, she felt there was something more. There had to be! What he suggested sounded too good to be true.

Jackie also had to now ask herself if she was truly willing to sacrifice her hard-won independence from Mark to begin a business arrangement with him. She knew that she could handle Mark now in a business deal, and she'd been a good model. If that was all that was required of her, then it would be easy. But she knew Mark too well for it to be that easy.

"It's an interesting idea," she commented in an even voice. Mark only smiled benignly at her and delicately fingered his rich mustache. He was very complacent, as though he'd just won an important point.

"But tell me, just what do you get out of this—really?" she queried.

Mark's eyes grew hooded and warm. She was not expecting his response, and when he finally uttered it, she was totally unprepared.

"You," came the unbelievable reply.

Jackie just stared at him, holding her breath. She couldn't have heard him correctly. But there was no mistaking that self-assured smirk on his face. He was very serious. Just when she had gathered her senses and indignation enough to say something, Gwen swept back into the room.

"Well, you haven't come to blows, so I guess it was okay to leave you two alone!"

Jackie responded by getting up and pacing the floor nervously, so incredulous at his suggestion she was momentarily without speech. Mark said nothing either, as Gwen looked from one to the other. She shrugged.

"Well . . . maybe not!" Gwen said good-naturedly and sat gracefully in a high-backed chair.

"We've had our little talk," Jackie said, her voice tightly controlled. "Mark was just leaving."

"You haven't answered my question yet."

"It wasn't a question. It was a proposition! And the answer is no! What did you think it would be?"

Mark rose from the love seat and carefully shrugged his shoulders and pulled the lapels of his jacket to smooth its already flawless lines. "I'd hoped it would be that the book means a lot to you, and you'd like to see it printed."

"It will be, and without your help."

"What are you two talking about? What's this about the book?" Gwen interrupted, now curious.

"It . . . it's nothing, Gwen. Mark just had this absurd idea."

"Gwen might not think so."

"I don't want to hear any more," Jackie said, her impatience with him beginning to show.

"Well, I do!" piped up Gwen. Jackie sent her a quelling look.

"We'll talk about it later," Jackie said to her friend.

"That's a good idea," Mark said blandly. "Why don't we talk about it later. I have to fly up to Greensboro for several days. When I get back you can give me your answer."

"You already have my answer," Jackie said. A class-A headache was starting to knock against the inside walls of her temples.

"We'll talk again," Mark countered confidently. "I'll call you when I get back."

He walked toward the door and Jackie made no move to accompany him. It was left up to Gwen to be courteous and say goodbye. She came back and slumped against the door frame.

"Whew! What was that all about? It was so tense in here you could have cut it with a knife!"

"Some business deal," Jackie said scathingly, rubbing absently at her temples. "It was more like blackmail if you ask me!"

"Jackie, what are you mumbling about?"

But Jackie couldn't answer. Between Mark and Eric she was worn out to the bone with a myriad of emotions. Her head was pounding so hard she thought for sure it would roll off her shoulders.

"Not now, Gwen. I'm tired. Tell Hannah I wasn't feeling well. I'm going to bed."

"Hey, girl," Gwen asked in a soft concerned voice, slowly following Jackie to the staircase, "are you all right?"

Jackie opened her mouth to speak and knew she was perilously close to tears. She swallowed and forced herself to face Gwen and gave her a weak smile.

"I want a bath. And I want to go to sleep. We'll talk tomorrow. Okay?" She didn't wait for an answer, but went upstairs. The tears began to spill down her cheeks long before she ever reached her room. Her head was hurting, and so was her pride—and her heart. She felt all over like one big walking hurt.

It was several days before Gwen ever had a real chance to talk to Jackie because it was several days before Jackie lost that haunted look and her raw emotions were under control. The morning after Mark's visit Jackie automatically got out of bed in preparation for another day with Eric out on the road. She was half out of the bed before she remembered that she wouldn't see him today, or tomorrow, and possibly not ever again. With a groan of pure misery Jackie collapsed back on her bed and dissolved in a fit of tears, wearing herself out and falling once again to sleep.

She had a dream in which she was in Bob McIver's lab developing picture after picture of Eric Davidson. There came a knock on the lab door. "Can I come in yet?" came the voice on the other side of the door. "No!" Jackie frantically yelled. "Not yet! I'm exposing some print paper." But the door opened and all the prints of Eric faded back to plain white paper. Jackie moaned and turned over as the door opened wider and the lab filled with light.

"Jackie?" Her name was called. "Are you awake?"

Jackie blinked tearfully at the ruined images and looked up at her intruder. She opened her eyes against the light and saw Hannah standing anxiously in the doorway.

"Are you feeling better, darlin'?" Hannah asked, moving slowly to the bed, clutching her hands together in concern.

Jackie took a second to realize she was no longer dreaming. She rubbed the heel of her hand across her eye.

"Oh . . . Hannah. Yes, I guess so."

"Gwen told me you weren't feeling good and I was worried." She came over to the bed and peered with a searching frown over Jackie's sleep- and tear-ravished face. She pulled her stout little figure upright and crossed her arms over her chest.

"Umph! If that Mark Bennett's been bothering you, you just tell Hannah and I'll see to it he don't come here anymore, husband or no husband!"

Despite her anguish Jackie laughed. She swung her legs out of the bed and reached for her robe. "*Ex*-husband," she emphasized. "I wouldn't worry about Mark," she said, ruffling up her much flattened curls. "He's the least of my troubles."

Hannah started to follow her around the room. "Then what is

the problem? Are you unhappy here? Have you and Gwen argued?" Hannah suddenly gasped with some sixth sense and put a chubby hand up to rest against her cheek.

"Oh darlin'! Did you and Eric have a fight?" She tisked, shaking her head sadly.

Immediately the memory of her unfairness to Eric welled up as embarrassment. She turned clouded eyes to Hannah.

"We didn't fight, exactly, but . . . oh, Hannah! I was so awful to him!"

Hannah tisked again. "My poor baby!" she croaked softly, stroking Jackie's arm. At that moment, Jackie would have liked nothing better than to crawl into Hannah's ample lap, bury her head, and cry all over again. Instead she shook her head and began rummaging for jeans and a top. She managed a strained chuckle.

"Your poor baby has been an absolute idiot!"

"Now don't go saying stuff like that about yourself, 'cause it's not so! You've just been a bit confused is all. You just need time."

Hannah patted Jackie's arm again in comfort and headed for the door.

"And if Eric Davidson is half the man I think he is, he'll see it too!"

Jackie shook her head wryly. "You can't believe how patient he's been, Hannah. I don't want him to think poorly of me."

"Now you stop worrying about it. Everything will work out. You'll see."

Jackie looked at the older woman. "I hope you're right."

Hannah started to chuckle to herself. "Now I'd better go wake Gwen. That girl will sleep the day away if I don't get her up! Now hurry and dress and I'll make lunch."

"Lunch!" Jackie exclaimed in disbelief.

Hannah's chuckle turned into genuine laughter as she closed the door behind her. "Darlin', it's way after twelve noon. And if you don't hurry your first meal will be dinner!"

Jackie was downstairs tossing a large green salad and sprinkling croutons when Gwen emerged in the kitchen. Every strand of her gently curled Afro was in place, makeup even and carefully applied. Her tan slacks and tangerine top were color coordinated with her shoes and neck scarf.

"Gwen, do you have a date this afternoon?" Jackie mused as she stood with her hands on her hips regarding her friend.

"No. Why?" Gwen asked puzzled.

"Well, then, you've really outdone yourself for lunch! I can't wait to see what you change into for dinner!"

A soft amused chuckle came from Hannah, whose back was turned to the two young women. Gwen sucked her teeth, smiling good-naturedly.

"Well, you never know who might show up. I used to live here, remember? I left a lot of heartbroken boyfriends, girl!" she said smugly. Then her eyes stretched wide, her arms opened, and she screeched.

"Timothy!"

Jackie looked at the meticulously dressed Gwen in total amazement as she knelt and threw her arms around the neck of the lethargic animal.

"Oh, Timmy, baby!" Gwen gushed, while Jackie watched dumbfounded.

Timothy, who as far as Jackie knew never moved if he didn't have to, set his tail to a furious thumping against the floor in pure delight. Jackie laughed at the sight. Gwen gave her the most absurdly childish grin.

"Timmy and I go back a long time. He used to keep all my boyfriends in line when I visited Hannah."

"I think I know what you mean," Jackie commented ruefully, remembering Timothy's growl at Eric when he came to dinner.

"Timmy's a love!" Gwen continued scratching him behind his ear, and was rewarded with a wet lick.

After Gwen's exuberant greeting of Timothy, she and Jackie sat down to lunch, and Hannah wandered off to dig around in her yard. The two young women spent a leisurely afternoon bringing each other up to date on the latest news, and no further mention was made of Mark and his visit of the night before. They spent some hours going over the pictures Jackie had taken during the month she'd been in South Carolina, Jackie remembering warmly all the places Eric had taken her to. But she made no mention of him to Gwen.

In a way Jackie was grateful for the reprieve. Gwen's natural vivaciousness did not allow for moping, and they passed a pleasant afternoon. In the latter part of the day they persuaded Hannah to dress in one of her Sunday best, and they took her out to dinner. It was a happy evening that added to everyone's spirit.

The next morning Jackie again woke expecting to pick up her usual routine, then remembered it was not to be. She and Gwen drove into town, instead, to the library and worked on an outline for the book. They worded a proposal to be sent to a number of publishers. Then, Gwen began the awesome task of putting to paper what she wanted to say about the Gullah people that made them so special. She soon got involved in her note taking, and Jackie got restless. Promising to pick Gwen up at the library when it closed, Jackie drove over to Bob McIver's shop.

A few more of her prints had been sold, and Bob was pretty sure the exhibit would come off. The prospect excited Jackie. She escaped quickly into the darkroom where she developed film and made prints. Bob finally had to knock on the door to let her know the shop was closing.

For the next two days she and Gwen drove into town to the library to work on the format of the book. They listened to the tapes over and over until Gwen had a firm grip on what she wanted to write. Once she began, that left Jackie with nothing to do. She couldn't help thinking of Eric and wondering what he was up to, even going so far as to consider driving out to his house. But she didn't.

One evening Gwen came to sit on Jackie's bed for a little nighttime girl talk. She filed and shaped her nails, as Jackie sat cross-legged on the floor, sorting negatives in envelopes and dating them.

"I spoke to Spence today," Gwen began absently.

"Did you?" Jackie murmured, squinting over a negative as she tried to remember the name of the town where it was taken.

"He says he's been very busy the last few months."

"Ummm . . ." Jackie uttered, wiping another negative with a lint-free cloth.

"I told him the same thing I told you. Too much work isn't good for you. He said it hasn't been all work. Anyway, I told him I had someone I wanted him to meet."

Jackie's eyes flew open, stricken. "Gwen! You didn't!" she groaned.

"Why not? I've been trying to get you two together forever!"

"Then why don't you give up?"

Gwen sighed, tilting her head to examine her nails. "I guess I'll have to. Spence has been seeing someone special for weeks. He says she's the one he wants to marry." She slanted a heavy-lidded look at her friend. But Jackie didn't rise to the bait.

Jackie relaxed. "Ohhh. I've very happy for him," she said with real relief and went back to her work.

"I don't know," Gwen continued, frowning. "He didn't sound very happy about it. Just determined. I think there's still hope for you, though. You two really should get together."

"Gwen!" Jackie wailed in exasperation. "The man is practically married! Can't you see that?"

"But you two were meant for each other!"

Jackie grimaced. "I don't want to meet Spence."

"But why not! What harm could it do?"

"Because . . . because . . ." Jackie stopped, her mouth open but unable to say the words which suddenly rose instantly, naturally to her lips. The realization of what she was about to confess stunned her. It rose so easily, so naturally within her. And she didn't try to deny it.

"Well?" Gwen prompted, reaching for a bottle of nail polish.

"I . . . I just can't, that's all."

"Dumb reason, hon, if you don't mind my saying so. Unless . . . Oh my God! Jackie, don't tell me. Are you . . . is there someone else?"

Jackie didn't answer. Gwen climbed down from the bed and sat next to her on the floor. "Jackie?" Gwen shook her arm gently.

"Yes. No. Oh, I don't know, Gwen!" she ended in a strange voice.

"But who is it?" Gwen asked excitedly.

"You won't believe it," Jackie said cautiously.

"Try me!"

Jackie braced herself for ridicule. She took a deep breath. "The man who's been my guide since I got here."

Gwen quickly hid her smile from Jackie. "Your *guide*? But wasn't he a . . . a farmer or something?"

"Well, what's wrong with a farmer?" Jackie asked indignantly. "Anyway, he's a painter," Jackie admitted softly. When there was no response from Gwen she looked up to find a sympathetic and gentle smile on her friend's face.

"He really got to you, didn't he?"

Jackie nodded. There was another moment of silence and then Gwen squealed, "Jackie, I'm happy for you. When do I meet him?"

"Maybe never," she responded miserably.

"What?"

"Oh, we had this dumb disagreement. I haven't heard from him all week. He probably can't be bothered with me anymore."

"Oh," Gwen commented, a look of speculation on her face. She gnawed on a tapered nail. Suddenly she smiled rather wickedly at Jackie. "I think there's hope for Spence after all!"

Jackie threw a pillow at her.

CHAPTER EIGHT

The colors seemed oddly blue-gray, a characteristic of slate and granite. The humid thick air dropped a gauzy film over everything and the colors seemed even more false. In irritation, Jackie pushed her damp hands over her brown cheeks that were shiny with perspiration, over her temples, and swept back the limp side curls over her head. She put her hands on her hips and the curls dropped loosely back into place. She wanted one definitive picture that spoke for all the sea islands, that would also serve for promotion, and possibly the cover of the book. But the weather was not cooperating, and it wasn't working out the way Jackie wanted.

Out of the corner of her eye, Jackie caught a motion and a change of light. She looked to see a darkening in the western sky, a change that was rapidly sweeping east, toward her and the coastline. It looked like rain, which had been badly needed for several days now. But Jackie frowned. It was more than rain. It looked like the makings of a real summer storm.

Letting out a sigh of relief she gratefully accepted the decision made by the weather—to give up for the day and head back to Charleston. She was a way down the coast and had at least two hours on the road to look forward to.

A sudden dusty hot wind picked up, tearing gently at the curls on her head. Molding her denim skirt to the back of her thighs and pressing her thin white blouse to her torso. Bits and pieces of debris and sand pricked against the skin of her bare legs and arms as the wind picked up in intensity and the sky grew into purple darkness. Far off, still in the west, came the first clap of thunder, cracking through the air in warning.

The wind became less gentle and Jackie squinted against it as she made her way to the car. She merely dropped everything on the passenger side as she climbed into the quiet safety of her car. She was on the road a half hour when the first fat spatterings of rain began to hit her windshield and the darkening sky swirled in shades of blue and gray. She passed a break in the trees and caught sight of the Atlantic, still calm and blue and sunny, further east. It was there in that quick glimpse that she saw the picture she'd been looking for all morning. Jackie found a roadway to the coast again, and took both cameras off the seat next to her. It was beginning to rain in earnest now. She put her sweater over the cameras for some protection and quickly scampered out of the car again. Her legs and feet quickly got wet and her curls hung totally limp, but she didn't really notice. She positioned herself on a boulder and shot along the coastline south, effectively catching the difference in sea and land colors. She turned her back to the ocean and shot the craggy broken land with its inlets and bays under a rainy sky. Another clap of thunder sounded, and in fright, she gave up and headed back to the car.

Jackie was uncomfortably damp now, her clothes clinging to her skin. Then she was on the road again, with the rain coming down in torrents, beating against the car windows viciously, blinding her to the road and its markings. The sky got so dark she was forced to use her headlights and slow her speed. She strained with the effort of driving under these awful conditions, her hands and legs so tense she got a cramp.

Jackie was just past Meggett when she hit a deep puddle. After a quarter of a mile more the car sputtered, slowed, and as she pulled it over to the side of the road, the car died. She cursed under her breath, but knew the motor was flooded and there was nothing she could do for a while. She sat for a moment trying to think. It occurred to her that she was probably no more than half a mile from the cutoff leading to Eric's house. She could just sit in the car until the rain stopped and the motor had a chance to dry out, but that could be hours yet. Besides she was cold and clammy in her damp clothing. Jackie recognized in a moment of excitement that nature had conveniently supplied her with a reason to return to Eric's house, that her own insecurities hadn't allowed before. Suddenly, she looked forward to the muddy uncomfortable walk that would take her back to him so she could tell him how wrong she'd been.

Jackie used her sweater for whatever protection it could offer, but within minutes she was completely soaked. There was almost no traffic and no one stopped to come to her assistance. The water began to drip through the sweater onto her face, and her canvas shoes squished and bubbled water with each step. Finally, she reached the cutoff and turned onto it. The road was muddy and running with streamlets of water.

The next sound of thunder seemed to be right over her head. Jackie stopped, the noise rocking through her. She covered her ears and tried to hurry her steps. Again there was the booming noise and she squealed in fright. Lightning streaked bright as day, sending white flashes over the wet landscape. Jackie slid in the mud, once nearly falling, but she kept on doggedly. Suddenly, she felt for sure she was lost, and was just roaming aimlessly. What if this was the wrong road? What if this took her nowhere? In genuine confusion now, she moaned and hesitated.

She was at the end of her endurance, and the next crack and streak of light brought the storm to a head. She collapsed against the rough bark of a tree, hugging herself to the wood. Some sound tore itself from her throat. She was breathing hard, her heart racing in her chest. There was a sound behind her, some kind of thrashing through the foliage, getting louder, coming closer to where she stood. Jackie jumped and turned her head, trying to see. Something dark moved, swinging its enormous limbs, beating a path toward her. Pure fright paralyzed her as she wondered what animal this was. It pushed aside a branch, and it seemed to bark something at her. Gathering herself finally, Jackie turned and started to run wildly, not sure in which direction she headed. The animal grabbed her arm. She screamed and fought. The grip was painfully strong and firm, biting into her arm.

"Jackie!" The creature boomed her name. Jackie stopped struggling and opened her eyes. She didn't realize at once that it was Eric—so great was her fright—equally as wet as she, peering at her in amazement.

"Jackie . . ." he said again. "What the devil are you doing out here?"

Thunder rumbled, rolling to catch up to them from afar. Jackie couldn't believe it. Eric right in front of her. He released her arm and shook her by her shoulders as she continued to stare as though in a trance.

"I said, what are you doing here?" he shouted.

The thunder finally reached them, cracked, roared; lightning flashed. Jackie jumped. The sky opened up and yelled repeatedly, like some monster descending angrily upon them. Jackie had to get away from the noise. She pulled from Eric in a frenzy, turned and reached for the sturdy shelter of the tree. But she stumbled and fell. Something heavy fell on top of her, covering her. She struggled and turned over onto her back.

"Keep still!" Eric ordered, pinning her to the ground, his hard length matching hers as the unbelievable sounds shook the land. A branch fell across Eric's back and Jackie grabbed at his shoulders, burying her face in the soaked material of his shirt as he absorbed the shock, protecting her head and shoulders. They lay that way for long minutes, Jackie aware of every nuance of his body pressed to hers. She even imagined a warmth despite the driving cold rain. She wanted to wrap herself around him, hold him there against her. But when nothing else moved, Eric slowly raised himself away, helping her to her feet. Without a word he took her hand and began pulling her toward his house, which Jackie could not see in the failed light. She held to his hand tightly, grateful for its hard strength.

Eric took her tote from her, leaving her a hand free for balance. There was so much rain that by the time they reached the dismal looking little hut, all the mud had been washed from her legs and arms, leaving only her blouse and skirt stained. She was so happy to see the house she moaned in relief.

Eric pushed his shoulder against the door, forcing it open roughly, and pulled Jackie in behind him. He kicked the door closed on the rain and the raging storm outside. Water dripped from their bodies, spattering the floorboards.

They stood facing each other, breathing in exhaustion, though they couldn't see each other's eyes or expressions. The house was dark inside and quiet. And although the world went crazy outside, something was happening inside as well.

Jackie leaned back against the door, every part of her trembling, water running in rivulets down her face. "Eric!" she whispered, in relief at having reached him at last and having him real and solid before her now.

Eric stepped forward, his eyes the only discernible feature as he got closer, animal bright and alert. He braced his hands against the door on either side of her head. With his eyes he read every square inch of her face. His head tilted and descended and Jackie closed her eyes.

"Eric . . ."

Eric's sensuous mouth left a wet trail of caressing kisses on her face, from her forehead to her eyes, her cheeks. Jackie's lips parted as she fully anticipated his kiss, but he disappointed her, deliberately ignoring the moist curved surface to play instead at the corner.

Jackie turned her head to force the issue, but Eric apparently had no intention of complying with her sudden burning need. She pressed her hands to his chest, loving the hard surface she met as if its strength would give her strength in turn. A sigh escaped Eric as he took hold of her hands and plied them loose, moving back a little from her.

"What are you doing out here?" he asked low, in his deep voice.

Her desire for him was suddenly so great she wondered how he could not see. Only now could she fully appreciate how awful the last week had been without him. Couldn't he see she wanted him, needed him to hold her? Be with her like some steadying force? Jackie blinked rapidly at him, his cool gaze dashing her hopes.

"I . . . I was out taking pictures. I was further down the coast south of here when the storm broke."

"Where's your car?"

"It's on the main road. I . . . I think I flooded the engine." Her teeth chattered.

He seemed so remote. Was he still angry at her? Couldn't he forget what had happened between them?

"How did you know I was out there?" she asked, curiosity overtaking her chilled state.

"I was bringing my canvases inside when I thought I heard someone scream."

"Your canvases?"

"Yes. I was out painting."

Jackie began to tremble again. She crossed her arms over her chest as a chill took hold and crept over her, making her teeth snap together.

"You're cold," Eric said, frowning at her. "I'll be right back."

And he turned away to the narrow corridor leading to the back of the house.

Jackie couldn't move if she wanted to, she was suddenly so cold. She was sure she'd never be warm again. In another instant Eric reappeared with an ochre-colored terry robe over his arm. He slowly approached her, but then stopped a few feet away, looking her over. Jackie was about to reach out and take the robe when Eric placed it behind him over the back of the sofa. He looked at her, his eyes yellow.

"Come here," he said, so softly, so suggestively that a shiver shook Jackie that had nothing to do with her wet body or chattering teeth. Her eyes locked to his. A bit apprehensively but wanting to trust him, she did as he commanded. Jackie stepped within a foot of him. Eric reached out for her shoulders and pulled her yet closer.

Jackie could smell the rain on him. It loosened his after-shave lotion so that his throat, neck and face smelled sweet. His shirt smelled like wet cotton and a lingering hint of paint, permeated with his own unique male essence. His hair, still wet, glistened under the low room light. He could smell her, too, as his nostrils flared suddenly, and a muscle jerked along his jawline.

Slowly Eric's hands moved and gently uncrossed her stiff arms. Her chest was rising and falling in agitation under the thin transparent fabric of her blouse. His fingers played with the top button. Jackie held her breath, her eyes never leaving his, her mind alive now with all the possibilities.

"Eric . . ." She whispered his name.

"What?" he asked gently, smoothly. She couldn't answer.

There was barely a breath of space between them, and Jackie swayed forward, just touching him. Eric closed his eyes and put his arms around her, drawing her against him with infinite tenderness. A muscle curled down and around in Jackie's stomach. Her arms came up and around his neck, and her long fingers brushed over the soft crinkly texture of his hair. He let out a soft moan and shuddered against her. His mouth kissed along her jaw, finally reaching her mouth to kiss her deeply.

Suddenly Eric pulled back from his plundering of her soft eager mouth. He took a deep breath and rested his forehead against hers. Jackie held back a cry of disappointment at the separation.

"Ummm, Jacqueline Taylor from New York," he said in a husky emotional voice. "You are one fine lady and I'm having a tough time keeping my hands off of you!"

Jackie would have told him then and there that he didn't have to, but Eric silenced her with another deep devouring kiss, crushing her to him fully. He reached down and retrieved the robe from the floor and handed it to her.

"Go get dry. And wash out the mud from your clothes. The bathroom is in the back." Eric nodded toward the doorway, a touch of strain in his voice. Jackie looked at him with frank, open desire, but it was too dark for him to see her face in detail.

"I'll get a fire going so we can get warm," he said with a chuckle, breaking some of the tension. "But I don't think we really need it now. . . ."

Jackie continued to hesitate, so he gave her a gentle push in the direction of the bathroom. "Go on, before you catch cold."

She turned and fled.

She came back to the front room ten minutes later to find Eric squatted down coaxing the fire in the grate to larger proportions. One lamp was on near the door and the room was aglow with warm dark shadows and comfort. She was starting to become very attached to his house. Eric silently took the things from her hands and spread them out over a chair in front of the fireplace. Jackie felt a sudden embarrassment at the familiar way in which he touched and handled her intimate clothing. But Eric did not notice her reaction, nor seem to feel the same.

He handed Jackie another towel. "Here. This is for your hair." He then disappeared into the kitchen, returning with two glasses filled with a dark liquid. "And this is some brandy for your insides. It'll warm you quickly."

Jackie took the glass from him and took a hesitant sip, looking at him over the edge of the glass.

"You're not trying to get me drunk, are you?" Jackie asked with a teasing note in her voice.

Eric looked at her rather alluring form in the oversized robe exposing her neck and shoulders. There was a twinkle in his eyes. "No way. I want you aware of everything I say and do!"

The brandy was so raw and strong her eyes teared. Eric grinned, his face warm and completely relaxed. She noticed for the first time that he was bare-chested, the athletic planes of his chest wall smooth and totally hairless like some sort of broad, brown shield. Jackie was hit with the full unavoidable sense of his masculine appeal and it made her quake, her hand unsteady around the glass.

Eric saw her hand tremble and misunderstood. "Are you still cold?"

"No. I'm better now," she murmured.

She sat down on the braided rug close to the roaring fire. Vigorously, she began to rub the towel back and forth over her wet hair. Eric stood watching for a moment before lowering his tall frame to the sofa. He sat on the very edge and then leaned back until his head rested on the cushions behind him, his legs stretched out in front.

A rather satisfied smile played on Eric's features as he watched her drying her hair. It was not lost on him that a while ago she had more than willingly accepted his caresses, and went so far as to, in his mind, eagerly return them. Did that mean she was softening toward him? Or had she just needed comforting from her fright over the storm? She had not felt frightened in his arms, but rather soft and yielding, and he very much wanted to hold her again.

He was fascinated by her movements, now, in her simple chore. He watched the damp curls spring about rampant over her head.

"No Afro?" he asked softly.

"No Afro. Some people don't, you know."

"Have you done something to your hair, or are the curls yours?"

From beneath the towel came her muffled voice. "They're mine."

There was a silence for a moment. The rain still came down, but not as hard, and the thunder began to fade and disappear. The pattern of rain on the window and roof was almost soothing in its repetitiveness. And there was the log spitting and crackling in the fireplace. They were both feeling very comfortable and safe. Eric got off the sofa and dropped down next to Jackie on the floor. He knelt close behind her. Eric gently pushed her hands away and took up the toweling of her hair himself.

It surprised Jackie because she didn't know what he was up

to. But his tender massage felt good and she let herself relax against his hard thighs and chest.

"That's it," Eric crooned low, his voice husky, as she gave herself up to his ministrations. He worked quietly for a while, Jackie delighting in this intimate gesture.

"I guess you're no longer mad at me," Eric commented.

Jackie was confused. "What makes you say so?"

"You haven't called me Mr. Davidson yet. As a matter of fact, you've been pretty free with my first name all evening. I guess there's hope after all."

Jackie flinched. "I . . . I'm sorry about that last time. I didn't mean to be such a bitch. Are you annoyed with me?"

Eric chuckled, stopping the rubbing and sitting on the floor to face her.

"Not annoyed, Jackie. Just frustrated as hell. You had your guard up again and I couldn't get through to you. Just when I thought we were getting along fine." His voice was now silky, and he gently ruffled up her curls with a hand to aid in the drying before the warm fire. "Although I freely admit I wanted to shake the living daylights out of you once or twice." His fingers trailed down the side of her face to her neck, his thumb making lazy circles on the base of her throat. "Still, I'm glad it's Eric now."

They stared at one another as the air around them again became charged with the emotional current between them. The desire in Eric's eyes was just barely visible in the flickering light from the fire, so that Jackie did not know the full extent of his feelings. Instead, she broke the silence by asking him a question.

"Tell me about your art. What kind of paintings do you do?"

Eric understood at once her need to keep a controlled hand. He didn't offer resistance, thereby exerting his own will. He took the question seriously as it was intended.

"I had been doing a lot of portraits. For a couple of years now, I've been wanting to do a body of work that showed part of the character of the people and country of the Carolinas."

"But that's what I'm trying to do!"

"Um humm." He nodded in agreement, enjoying her softened teakwood skin in the flickering light.

"When you told Hannah your father was a painter, did you mean he was an artist, too?" she asked.

Eric's face grew still and a little closed. He dropped his eyes. "Yes. But not was, *is*. He still paints. And he's very good." He sounded still, almost hard about the information. Eric caught her confused look and smiled at her.

"My father was always very good. But he wasn't sure that I would be. He didn't want me to be a painter."

"But why? He should have been pleased that you wanted to be like him."

He shrugged. "It didn't matter. I think every parent wants his kid to do more—be better. He had a vision of his son, his first-born, as a starving artist in a garret somewhere. He wanted me to do something safe and sure. Like teaching!" Eric laughed in his deep voice, as though at some private joke.

"Well, you're not starving, are you? Have you been able to sell any of your work?" Jackie asked, thinking of his small house, his constant paint-stained clothing, and remembering that she herself had paid him to be a guide.

"Oh yeah, I've sold a few pieces." Eric quirked a brow at her, smiling slightly.

Jackie hesitated. "Eric, could I . . . would you mind showing me some of your work?"

Eric frowned. "Right now?"

"Yes, why not?"

"The light's not very good. And I'd hoped . . ." He stopped, speculating a moment. "Okay. I'll show you something."

He got up and took something from behind the sofa that had apparently been leaning there all the time. They were two large canvases which he set on the sofa cushions in front of Jackie so that she was eye level with the images. They were both land-scapes, deceptively simple in their execution, with light, uncom-plicated brush strokes. Upon more careful examination, a wealth of interesting details was apparent in just those few strokes. Jackie liked them very much, and was impressed and surprised. He was enormously talented.

"Why, Eric. These are wonderful!"

"Sometimes I'm not so sure," he said ruefully.

"But, you're very good. Your father should be very proud of you and encourage you even more!"

Eric came closer to her and stooped to her level, bringing his face very close to hers. The muscles rippled across his naked shoulders.

"Even if I starve and never make a cent?"

"Yes, even then. These are very good. You should do what you're good at. And"—Jackie turned back to the paintings—"I think you really love what you do. There's real love in these paintings. You shouldn't give it up."

He looked hard at her, searching her face, probing her eyes.

"You really believe that?" he asked gently, curiously.

Jackie looked back to him, his face so close she could see the amber flecks in his topaz eyes.

"Eric, it's only important that you believe it," she said seriously to him.

"But I want to know what *you* believe," Eric persisted softly, not allowing her eyes to slip from his, his will much stronger now than her own.

Jackie felt drawn to him, and oddly in that instant connected and tied to him. For once, they were exactly the same in heart and mind.

"I really believe it," she responded. Suddenly she felt overly warm, as though the fire had gotten stronger, heating her beyond endurance in the heavy terry robe. Eric knelt closer, watching her parted mouth.

"And could you love someone who might not make a lot of money?"

The heat was almost suffocating, his implications burning right through her.

"I could love someone who loved me," Jackie whispered.

"Love for love's sake is not very practical though, is it?" His voice was hoarse and deep.

"I've had practical. I can tell you from firsthand experience, it's not necessarily better."

Eric came closer and just touched her mouth lightly with his own. "Did your practical ex love you?"

"He wanted me."

He touched her mouth again. Her lips parted.

"Did you love him?"

There was a silence. Jackie watched his jaw tense.

"I needed him."

He plied another gentle kiss, their lips clinging before separating. "And now?"

"I don't need him anymore. I haven't for a very long time."

Without another word Eric kissed her hard, manipulating her mouth until he had it under his own the way he wanted. She felt as if he was trying to tell her something with his kiss. His gesture asked that she follow his lead, and she did. It was caring and tender, and that served to let her trust him with her feelings.

It was a moment or two before Jackie realized that she was slowly bending backward, supported by one of Eric's muscular arms across her back. But all of her senses were centered in his kiss. Not forceful, but expecting a full response. She readily gave it to him, enjoying the delicious texture of him, feeling herself getting lost in his embrace.

Her hands held Eric's shoulders as he lowered her to the floor. Her head was cushioned on his forearm, but only for a moment. He freed the arm so that both hands could hold her head, elbows braced on either side. Eric's body was half across Jackie's on the small rug in front of the fire.

"I . . . I think . . . we got off the track. We were talking about . . . paintings," she murmured breathlessly against his mouth.

Eric's lips brushed her cheek. "Were we?" he asked thickly. The pretense had come full circle as they wrapped their arms around one another and indulged freely in a passionate, stunning kiss. They couldn't seem to get enough of each other. A heady intoxication filled Jackie's limbs and senses, and a need for the pleasure that Eric evoked in her. She wanted to be consumed, fulfilled, and released by him, because in his arms she would know real tenderness.

One of Eric's hands slid down from the curls to her neck and throat, while his mouth and tongue continued to play havoc. His fingers trailed by the tips, sending delightful shivers through her stomach muscles. The robe, being several male sizes too big, gaped invitingly down the front but only hinted at its hidden treasures.

Her happiness with Eric was suddenly at odds with the memory of Mark, and she fought it. Mark had made her feel inadequate. Eric had proven otherwise. Amazement and discovery opened up within Jackie, and tears welled up unexpected in her eyes.

"Hey!" Eric whispered gently as she trembled anew. He comforted her, held her face buried against his shoulder. She laid her cheek flat against his chest. For a long time they lay quietly curled up together on the floor. Eric rhythmically stroked her shoulders and down her spine to the small of her back. Against her cheek Jackie could feel Eric's strong heartbeat. Then they were both aware of another silence as they realized it had stopped raining. Even the once brilliant fire had begun to die out. Jackie began to feel cold.

Eric sat up, removing his warmth from her, and she missed it instantly. He moved to stoke the fire, trying for a new life in the half-burnt log. Jackie pulled the terry robe tighter, feeling small and dissolute. She fully recognized that she'd allowed her dissatisfaction with Mark to suddenly insinuate itself into her joy with Eric. It was irrational.

Eric turned to look at her for a moment as his arms flexed and the sinews stretched with pent up energy. "I think your clothes are dry. Why don't you get dressed."

Jackie stared, trying to understand his mood now. She nodded silently, and struggling with the folds of the oversized robe, got to her feet. Eric moved to put his paintings away. His back was to her and she found the sudden silence oppressive and morbid.

"Eric . . ." she whispered his name in supplication. He turned to look at her and she couldn't think what else she wanted to say. He came toward her and she could still feel the emotions that had not totally died away in either of them. Eric reached out a finger and traced an imaginary line from her shoulder to her neck. His hand curved around the slim column of it, and his fingers rubbed the soft hair at the nape. Suddenly he bent forward and kissed her cheek. It was so chaste, so removed she could have screamed in her frustration. He took her things from the chair and giving them back to her, turned her toward his room.

"Get dressed first. Then we talk," he whispered, searching her face.

When she came cautiously back into the room, still not knowing what to expect, Eric had put back on his pale blue velour top, now dry. He was leaning against the mantelpiece, smoking and staring broodingly into the fire. He looked up at her quiet approach and stared for a long moment. He threw the unfinished cigarette into the fire and stuffed both hands in his pockets in a gesture that Jackie now found endearing, and one which she understood for the first time clearly.

"You look fine," Eric said, arching a brow and smiling lopsided at her.

But she only returned his look silently, suddenly very shy and unsure of herself. Eric reached out a hand to her. Jackie came forward and took it firmly. Eric pulled her to his side, maintaining his position against the mantle. He released her hand and put his arm around her shoulder, gently rubbing the rounded joint.

"Are you okay now?" he asked in a low even voice.

Jackie slowly nodded her head. "Eric, I just want to say . . ."

"You don't have to say anything, Jackie."

"But you don't understand!"

"I think I do. Look . . ." He stood up straight and turned Jackie to face him. He hooked his arms around her back. Jackie placed her hands on his chest. She began to smooth a nonexistent wrinkle in his shirt with her fingers.

"Suddenly you went stiff on me, and you weren't responding to me anymore. You were suddenly with your ex again, weren't you?"

Jackie's eyes flew open in horror and she gasped, about to protest strongly. Eric quickly interrupted.

"It's true and it's okay." He smiled ruefully at her, saying in a caustic voice, "It wasn't very flattering to my ego, but"—and his voice softened as a hand came up to stroke a cheek—"I also know you haven't been with anyone else since him. You're still a little scared and cautious."

His insight was a little overwhelming for Jackie. He always seemed to see so much.

"I don't care anything for Mark."

"Still, he was there in your mind. Wasn't he?"

Reluctantly Jackie nodded yes, not sure what her answer would mean to Eric. "With Mark I always felt lacking in something . . . incomplete."

"And do you still?" Eric asked her seriously, in a soft searching voice.

"Sometimes. But not recently, not with you," she said in a whisper, her eyes bright with new insight.

Eric continued to search over every facet of her expression. "Are you sure?" he questioned, squeezing her gently.

"I'm sure," Jackie answered strongly. Perhaps there was nothing she could have done about the memory of the only other man she'd ever known. But there was no longer any doubt that he no longer mattered.

Eric's jaw tensed and untensed as he thought long and hard for a moment. The color specks of his eyes were like a deep amber pool, pulling her into it as though there was some truth to be found there, and totally unavoidable. Her eyes, nevertheless, did not waver from his.

"I want you," he whispered, his desire evident in his soft gaze.

Jackie felt mesmerized. "I know that," she answered.

"And I'm very selfish. I don't want to share you with a bad memory. Now that you're here with me, I want to keep you here."

"I'd much rather be here with you."

There'd been so much longing in his words and in his eyes that Jackie's pulse began to race again. Then Eric bent to her, his firm mouth plying a feathery kiss. It was like a promise. He moved his head so that he could again see her face. He smiled fully at her, showing the furrows on his cheeks.

"You're going back to Charleston tonight!"

Jackie made a move to protest, but stopped. She was prepared to argue persuasively the benefits to her staying the night, but she sensed he had his own reasons for his decision. And she realized that she didn't want Hannah to worry. Again she nodded her head.

"Hannah will wonder what's happened to me."

Eric pulled her into his arms and squeezed her to him in a bear hug. "Next time," he said in a thick voice, "I'm not letting you go!"

"I hope not," Jackie whispered earnestly. Eric was very still for a moment and then moved back to see her face. His was a combination of surprise and wonder. "Next time I promise there will just be the two of us."

"Jackie Taylor, you are something else." He chuckled, letting out a sigh. "I think we'd better get you started for home. It's getting very warm in here again!"

Eric kissed her briefly and turned away to a storage bin next to the mantle. Opening it he took out a large heavy-duty flashlight.

Jackie stood wrapped in a warm glow, feeling happy, feeling safe. She only momentarily wondered if perhaps Eric might love her, if his feelings for her went any deeper than a sexual attraction and a desire to make love to her. She hoped it was much more, recognizing that she felt a growing love for him. It was both frightening and exciting.

He put the fire out and put a shield in front of the hearth. He took Jackie's hand and led the way from the house out into the cool damp night air. They slowly made their way along the darkened road until they reached her car. Eric got in behind the steering wheel and started the engine, fiddling with the mechanism, until he was sure the car would function with no further problem. He motioned for Jackie to get in next to him.

"I'll get off at the turnoff. Will you be okay on your own back to town?"

"Yes, I'll be fine," Jackie assured him, nonetheless disappointed that he would have to leave her so soon. They reached the break in the road in no time at all. Eric stopped the car, but left the motor running. He turned to face her before putting an arm around her shoulder to draw her nearer. Jackie didn't resist at all when he tilted her head back against his upper arm and he leaned down to quickly capture her mouth. It was as though he was firmly planting the shape, feel, and taste of his mouth to hers. And it was as though he was taking the same impression of her for himself.

Jackie placed her arm around his neck, encouraging him fully, while Eric's other hand squeezed her waist. It was all intoxicating and very unsatisfying because it was so clear that they both demanded more.

It was Eric who showed the necessary strength of purpose to separate them. His catlike eyes were warm and seductive in the dark interior of the car.

"Will you have dinner with me on Friday?" he whispered against her mouth.

"Yes."

"I want to take you someplace special, so get really dressed up for me." He looked at her another moment before moving to get out of the car. Jackie moved to the driver's seat and he closed the door on her. "I'll pick you up Friday at seven," he said, stepping back from the car. Jackie waved to him and the car moved forward. In her rearview mirror she followed a moving dot of light from his flashlight for a second before it disappeared off the road.

CHAPTER NINE

"Now don't forget . . ." Bob was informing Jackie. "The gallery is not authorized to sell any of your work. If anyone shows an interest in the pictures they'll be told to contact you personally."

Jackie drew in her breath long and sharp, clasping her hands together. "Bob, I don't believe this is happening! I've never had a show before. I thought it was much too early!"

"Well, you were wrong. It's a good thing that professor at the college saw your work and thought it was good enough."

"But what happens now?"

Bob shrugged, peering round-eyed through his thick glasses at her. "The opening is Tuesday night at six-thirty. Have you ever been to a gallery opening?" he asked her.

Jackie shook her head no.

"Well, a lot of collectors get invited. After all, the idea is to sell the work, right? There'll be press people, and maybe other artists and gallery folk." He shook his head in sudden distaste. "Some people crash and come just to be seen. But you make sure you're there! And dress to knock their socks off!"

Jackie flipped a hand in annoyance. "We're not selling me!" she retorted, remembering those long hours of being draped with someone else's clothes. "It's my work that's important!"

"You *are* your work! It comes from you," Bob pointed out.

Jackie gave in and merely nodded at him. Then she cheered. She couldn't wait to tell Eric. She wanted him to be there with her and share in the excitement and the glory. The pictures were hers, seen with her eyes and mind, imagined and captured forever on film. But it was Eric who'd shown her where to look and left her to use her camera well. In a sense, this moment was his, too. And Jackie wanted him to be pleased and proud of the results. She wanted people to know she couldn't have done as

well without his help. The results may have been as good, but
they would have been different.

"Now . . ." Bob interrupted her thoughts. From his shirt
pocket he pulled several square white cards. He passed them to
Jackie. "Here are some invitations for you. Invite some friends if
you like."

Jackie gave one back to him. "Of course you have to be there,
Bob. This wouldn't have happened without your help."

Jackie was surprised to see Bob's cheeks flush pink with both
pleasure and embarrassment. He patted his shirt pocket.

"Oh, I'll be there, all right," Bob said, smiling at her. "I know
everyone will swarm around the artist, but will you have a glass
of wine with me before you get surrounded by well-wishers?"

Jackie's mouth dropped open in surprise, then she quickly
recovered herself. "Why, Bob! I'd be delighted to have wine
with you."

"That's great," he said, clearing his throat. Jackie had never
seen him so shy and uncomfortable. She smiled to herself. Jackie
put the invitations away in her tote. She wanted to remember to
give one to Eric this evening when they went to dinner. Her
smile softened.

She was giddy with the prospect of dinner alone with him. It
seemed so intimate, as indeed it would be, to be able to talk
about what had happened between them several nights ago. A
thrill of lingering delight went through Jackie as she allowed
herself to anticipate what would happen after dinner. The idea
of being in his arms again made her almost dizzy. She shook her
head to clear the daydream.

"Well, Bob," she said with a deep sigh, "I'm almost finished in
Charleston. The gallery show is the culminating point."

"Oh, I bet you're not through with us yet! The Carolinas have
a way of sneaking into your blood. My guess is, you'll be back."

Jackie laughed. "You sound like a wise old prophet!"

Bob raised his brows. "I don't know about being old!"

Jackie laughed again.

"But I do know a thing or two. And sometimes I'm right."

"Then maybe you'll be right this time, too. I rather like it
here!" Jackie offered, knowing full well the cause of her joy in
the area. Jackie looked at her watch and gasped. "Bob, I've got to
go!"

"What's the matter? Have a heavy date tonight?" He grinned.

"As a matter of fact, yes." Jackie smiled over her shoulder as she ran out of the shop.

The outside day was cloudless, perfect, which bespoke a perfect evening in Jackie's mind. She ran her hand through her hair, already wondering how she could most attractively style it. She had a red dress she could wear, and though she looked very good in red, she wasn't sure it was appropriate. Somehow red evoked passion, raging out of control, pure unlimited feeling. She didn't need a red dress to supply her with that kind of feeling. Jackie got into her car humming. She found herself doing a lot of that lately. Both Gwen and Hannah had noticed, but only Hannah had commented on it.

Gwen had eyed her rather sagely, and raising her brows had only murmured, "Umm hum!" Hannah was more verbal. First she'd shaken all over in good humor. Clapping her hands she'd said, "Lordy, darlin', didn't I tell you it would work out?"

Jackie squirmed and Hannah only chuckled the more.

"I knew he was a man worth shedding a few tears for. 'Cause when the tears are all gone, he'll leave you with the most wonderful feeling inside!"

"Hannah!" Jackie said in a shocked voice.

"Now don't you Hannah me! I know love when I see it!" Hannah hugged herself and slipped away for a second into her own memories. She let out a short laugh and looked at Jackie with warm eyes from her dark face.

"Darlin', Alvin Curtis used to do the same thing to me!" Shaking her head with a giggle she waddled away to her kitchen.

Eric had been responsible for good feelings the night of the storm. And for Jackie there had also been hope. It frightened her to even fantasize about the future, but maybe that's what love did to people. A sense of recognition clutched at her inside. It *was* love she felt for Eric. The full weight of the thought settled on her and she knew it was true. She loved him. It was wonderful and scary all at once. In loving someone you grant them, unknowingly, a certain power and command over you. The ability to affect your feelings. Jackie didn't believe that Eric would ever knowingly hurt her in the ways Mark had. But she still had no way of knowing if he loved her. At least, she wasn't sure.

Just the night before, however, he'd called to speak to her. It was after she'd washed the dinner dishes for Hannah, and Gwen had dried them and put them away. Gwen had answered the call, and after a rather long period on the phone with Eric, had come to get Jackie from the kitchen. Gwen had smiled at her archly and in obvious amusement, enjoying the developing relationship between Jackie and her "guide." She had not mentioned Spence again, but Jackie knew Gwen had by no means given up.

Jackie had gone nervously to the phone, trepidation her operative emotion for the time being. She sat on the edge of the chair next to the phone stand and picked up the receiver.

"Hello," she said softly, hesitantly into the mouthpiece. There was a silence on the other end. Jackie frowned, about to repeat her greeting when there came an answer.

"Hello, Jackie." The voice was rich and deep. Only then did it occur to Jackie that she'd never had a real conversation with Eric over the phone, never listened to his voice disconnected from his physical form. It was an odd sensation. His voice sounded strong and commanding, and unaccountably she felt thrilled.

"Hello," she repeated, a smile in her voice. "How are you?"

"Impatient!" he said with a sigh.

"Why?"

"I don't know if I can wait until tomorrow. That's why I called. I had to hear your voice, again," he said in a low intimate tone.

"You're teasing me," Jackie responded, uncertain.

"No I'm not. Can you have dinner with me tonight? Tomorrow is too far away."

"Oh, Eric! We've already eaten. I was just finishing the dishes when you called."

"Story of my life." Eric sighed in good humor.

Jackie responded by laughing, happy with the light easy tone of the conversation.

"Tomorrow *will* come, you know."

"No it won't. With my luck the world will end at midnight and I'll never see you again!"

Jackie laughed again, but then sobered. "Will it matter?" she found herself asking. There was a pause before Eric answered, his voice again low and deep.

"Yes it will, very much. I miss you."

Jackie caught her breath. It was too much for her.

"What have you been doing?" she asked, not really paying much attention to the question, but needing to put some restraints on the turn of the conversation.

"Waiting for tomorrow!" Eric chuckled persistently. "And washing my socks."

"How totally unglamourous for a painter!" Jackie smiled.

"I agree. But totally necessary. Even painters need clean socks now and then."

"I guess."

"Want to drive out and help me?" he suggested seductively. A shiver whirled its way from Jackie's toes and ended somewhere in her stomach.

"I don't think washing your socks is what you have in mind."

Eric laughed. "Shucks! The woman is too sharp for me!" Jackie joined in the amusement.

"I'm starting to love that sound," he interrupted on a more serious note.

"What sound?"

"The sound when you laugh," he crooned. "And the sound of my name when you say it. So much nicer than Mr. Davidson."

There was another silence while Jackie, her mind in a fuzzy haze, absorbed Eric's bantering. Did he indeed miss her? And his voice was so caressing, so sincere. Still, she felt the need for control.

"I . . . I hope you've finished the work you had to do."

He chuckled in amusement, feeling her change. "If you insist on talking about my work, yes, I've gotten it all done. And while I was neck deep in paint what were you doing?"

Jackie played with the spiraling in the telephone cord, winding it around her finger. "Well, I've finished all my pictures."

"All of them?" he asked amazed.

"Yes," Jackie admitted reluctantly, aware of what that meant. She heard a sigh from Eric, hard, as if in exasperation.

"We wasted so much time!" he mumbled.

"What?"

"I said, I really want to see you." He sounded urgent.

Jackie started to answer but was distracted by Hannah walking past on her way to the stairwell.

"If that's Eric, tell him I said hello," Hannah interrupted and giggled.

"Who was that?" Eric asked.

"That was Hannah. She says hello!" Jackie told him, holding her laughter in.

Eric groaned. "I think I'm in the middle of a conspiracy."

"Why?" Jackie asked innocently.

"Hannah's kind thoughts of me are not at all like the ones I have of you!"

"I'm sure Hannah will understand and forgive you under the circumstances!"

"Not if she knew what I was thinking!"

"That sounds intriguing. Just what are you thinking?"

Eric groaned. "Don't ask!"

They both started laughing, and then the laughter died away.

"Jackie?"

"Yes."

"Come out for a while," he asked urgently.

He said it so low Jackie had to strain to catch all the words. And then they made her warm all over. Her immediate thought was to answer yes. So it was just as well that she took two seconds to consider her answer rather than one.

"I can't, Eric," she said helplessly, and tried to be very honest with him. "If I came out I'd want to stay. And I can't yet."

The sigh that Eric let out was one of relief. Some question in his mind had been finally answered in that one statement from her.

"If I haven't already said so, you're beautiful."

Jackie smiled. "Are you trying to bribe me?" she asked softly.

"I don't think that's possible. So you know I really mean it. I'll see you tomorrow . . . if it comes!"

"It will! And I'll be ready."

Eric stretched out the goodbye, letting a hollow silence on the line hold them connected.

"Until tomorrow then."

" 'Bye, Eric."

" 'Bye."

But it had not worked out that way at all. When Jackie got

home from Bob McIver's that following afternoon, she raced up to her room to begin her preparation for her dinner date with Eric. She emerged from the shower, towel wrapped turban fashion around her freshly shampooed and conditioned hair, to find Gwen seated at her vanity table experimenting with Jackie's lipstick.

"So"—she grimaced, her mouth distorted and pouting as she applied the red gloss to her lips—"you have a date with your painter, or guide, whoever he is!"

Jackie cast an impatient look to Gwen as she laid out fresh underwear and stockings. "His name is Eric, Gwen."

Gwen shrugged, but she smiled as she caught Jackie's eye in the mirror.

"Whatever . . ."

Jackie sat on the edge of the bed and began to smooth body lotion over her long smooth legs and arms. Gwen swiveled on the chair to face her.

"You had a phone call."

Jackie's head came up at once. "Was it Eric?"

"No, it wasn't. As a matter of fact, it was Mark."

"Oh, Mark," Jackie murmured, with a noticeable lack of enthusiasm.

"It doesn't matter, hon. He said he'd call back."

"Did he say what he wanted?"

"Oh, something about an unanswered question, and a fall layout. I suppose you know what he's talking about."

"I certainly do!" Jackie said, smoothing her stockings. "And he doesn't stand a chance in hell of getting the answer he wants. I must admit his business deal was interesting. I just don't like the conditions attached!"

Gwen stood up, smoothing her slacks over her narrow hips. "Well, that's between you two. Just watch out for him. Mark likes to throw curve balls."

"Yeah, I know," Jackie murmured, remembering. She looked at her friend as Gwen turned the door handle to leave. "And what are your plans for the evening?"

"Honey, you aren't the only one who can attract the good-looking men! I have a date tonight also!" She waved her jeweled hand and quietly left the room before Jackie could respond.

Jackie took her time dressing, wanting to look her very best tonight. Eric had never seen her really dressed up, and she felt the need to surprise him and to see that surprise reflected in his eyes. She applied her favorite perfume behind her ears and at her throat, and, provocatively, a dab at the start of the valley between her breasts. In the warm room air she let her hair dry naturally, and finger combed the loose curls softly over her head. Using two French hair combs, she pulled back the curls over her ears and fastened them in place.

Jackie wore her diamond ear dots, the first major purchase she'd made for herself after starting to model, and a small pendant given her by her father for her eighteenth birthday. The dress she chose to wear was a white fine-lined flowered print on a chocolate brown background. It wrapped around in front with a deep V at the throat, and modified kimono sleeves. It was curved at the bottom opening, and as she walked, the front separated just enough to show her shapely legs. She made an attractive and fashionable picture as she completed her dressing, and it was not a Jackie that Eric had ever seen before.

She was halfway down the stairs, a silk shawl and an evening clutch in her hands, when the phone rang again. Hannah was there immediately to answer, but Jackie gave no thought to the caller as she wandered to the parlor window to take a quick anxious look outside.

"Jackie, darlin'," came Hannah's whispered voice. Jackie turned to see her holding the receiver out to her, one plump hand over the mouthpiece. "It's for you."

Jackie frowned.

"It's Eric."

Jackie walked briskly to the phone, taking it from Hannah. "Eric?"

"Hello."

Gone was the seductive cadence of his voice, and the alluring resonant bass. The voice of yesterday was playful, caressing. The voice that now responded to Jackie was taut, and tired, and held some other underlying emotion.

"Is something wrong?" she asked, already knowing from the tone of his hello that the evening they'd planned was canceled. She heard a sigh.

"Not wrong, but . . . something's come up I have to see to."

"Oh."

"I'm not going to be able to make it tonight."

Jackie didn't know just how to answer. She was surprised at how overwhelming her disappointment was.

"Can I be of any help?" she asked softly, the feeling of being let down, nonetheless, unavoidable.

"Do you mean that?" Eric asked surprised.

"Yes, I do."

"Then forgive me?"

"There's nothing to forgive, Eric. If it's important, then you must see to it. We'll have dinner another time." But Jackie didn't know when. There was nothing to really keep her in Charleston beyond the end of the week. She felt suddenly very cold.

There was a strained pause on the line.

"You have no idea how much tonight meant to me!" Eric whispered in a tight voice.

Some ingrained caution did not allow Jackie to admit to the same feelings, even though they were there.

"I'm sorry," she said, sincerely, however.

He groaned ruefully. "Believe me . . . so am I! I'll call you as soon as I can. Let's see if we can pick up where we left off. Okay?"

"Okay," Jackie agreed, but not at all sure that it was possible. Eric didn't say what the problem was, and she didn't ask, but she wondered what the urgency was.

"I bet you look fantastic!" Eric said low to her.

"I do!" she managed to tease back, feeling a little hollow inside. "Eat your heart out!"

Eric chuckled. "I have to go. We'll talk later. 'Bye." And he hung up.

For almost a full minute Jackie stood holding the phone. She finally gathered her wits enough to put the receiver down. Absently she walked into the kitchen, not aware of her destination until Hannah's voice broke into her thoughts.

"Would you like some coffee, darlin'?"

Jackie finally focused her sad eyes on the short form of Hannah, and silently nodded as she sat at the kitchen table. She didn't notice when the cup of steaming coffee was placed in front of her, and it was only Hannah's voice that snapped her out of it.

"Is everything all right?"

Jackie sighed. "Well, I don't know. Something's come up and Eric . . . Eric can't make it."

"Oh, darlin'!"

"These things happen. It's no one's fault, I guess."

Hannah could only watch the disappointment in Jackie and feel for her. "I hope it's nothing serious."

"He didn't say."

"Well, maybe you'll see him later. Or he'll call you tomorrow."

"Maybe." A wariness overtook Jackie, and placing her elbows on the table she began to rub her temples. "I don't know, Hannah. I just don't know."

"And after you went and dressed so pretty, too!"

Jackie smiled wanly at Hannah's indignation. "Yeah . . . all dressed up and no place to go!"

"If you don't mind it not being the same, you can have dinner with me," Hannah said in a formal, charming voice. Jackie's eyes got watery, and she got up from her seat.

"Oh, Hannah!" She came around the table and, kneeling by Hannah's chair, put her arms around the older woman and hugged her close. "I would love to have dinner with you!"

Hannah patted Jackie's shoulder and gently smoothed over the curls. "Now it's okay. We'll have a nice dinner. And I think I even have a bottle of wine. How does that sound?"

Jackie smiled through her tears and sadness. "I think it sounds wonderful!"

"Good! Now why don't you go put on something less fancy so you don't show me up! Then you can help me finish here."

Jackie gave Hannah a bear hug. "You're a wonder, Hannah Curtis."

Hannah chuckled in embarrassment. "Now, you stop that! Go on, so we can eat."

Feeling at least revived, Jackie did as she was ordered. They were nearly finished with dinner when the phone rang again. Jackie's stomach knotted. Hannah nodded her head and grinned knowingly.

"I told you he'd call back."

Jackie tried to walk calmly to the phone but she couldn't. And anyway, Hannah was wrong. It was Mark Bennett on the line.

"Oh, Mark. It's you," Jackie said with disappointment.

"Don't sound so happy to hear from me," he said sarcastically.

"I wasn't expecting it to be you," she explained impatiently.

"Didn't Gwen tell you I called?"

"Yes, she did, but . . . oh, never mind." Jackie sighed. "I suppose you called back about your offer?"

"Of course!"

Jackie frowned. "Well, I've given it a lot of thought. I admit it's a nice project and you should do very well with it. The theme is catchy and all."

"But?" Mark asked, sensing her hesitation.

Jackie grimaced on her end. "Mark, I'm just not interested. I really don't want to model anymore. And I'm not sure that tying your theme for fashion in with mine for a book is a good idea."

"Why not?" Mark persisted.

"Because the book idea was Gwen's and has nothing to do with you—" She stopped.

"And, therefore, you owe me nothing and don't want to be obligated to me for seeing it through?" Mark supplied shrewdly.

"That's right," Jackie agreed.

He laughed sardonically. "You don't trust me at all, do you?"

"You could say that," Jackie said lightly, but then sobered. "Look, we've split the blankets and gone our separate ways. Let's just leave it at that. Okay?"

"Okay, so you're not interested in the fall layout. And you'll find your own publisher. But I was there from the very beginning, remember? Can't we get together for a drink or something like old friends?"

Jackie gave a short incredulous laugh. "We were never friends."

There was a long pause on the line. "Did I really hurt you so badly, Jackie?" he asked in a soft voice. It sounded sincere. Jackie shifted in her chair uncomfortably.

"Look. Let's forget it. It's over."

"Is it?"

"Yes."

"Then you shouldn't mind having a drink with me to say goodbye."

"Mark, really."

"Come on, Jackie. What do you think I'll do to you in a public place!"

Jackie thought, and finally sighed in resignation. "All right. When?"

"Why don't I pick you up in, say, thirty minutes. There's a place Gwen told me about downtown. Everyone gets together there to drink or just talk. Or there's my hotel. . . ."

"Forget it!" Jackie said emphatically.

He laughed again. "Okay, okay, I get the message. See you in half an hour."

Hannah was none too happy with the idea, but she didn't say so. It was Jackie's decision, and she could only hope that Jackie knew what she was doing. And she hoped that Mark Bennett could be trusted. Suddenly Hannah felt something akin to rage at Eric Davidson for letting this happen. If he'd been able to take Jackie out to dinner, as they'd planned, Mark would never have had a chance to get next to her. Hannah didn't want to see her young houseguest hurt or disappointed anymore. This concern and affection now made her unreasonable.

She told Jackie to be careful, as Jackie gave her a kiss on the cheek and went to answer the door bell a little while later. Hannah sighed and threw up her hands in surrender.

"Lord have mercy!" she murmured to herself, shaking her head at the complicated dynamics of being young these days.

The waitress placed the Tom Collins in front of Jackie and, with an extra sideways smile for Mark, sauntered away with her tray. Jackie took a mere sip of the drink and looked at Mark, only to find his eyes still following the attractive young woman who'd just served them. Jackie raised her brows ruefully. She had been right all along. Despite his best efforts, Mark had not changed at all. But what Jackie did notice at once was, she truly did not care, either. Whatever lingering feelings she may have had toward Mark when she'd arrived here a month ago had been resolved and swept away. He was totally free to chase whomever he wished. Mark Bennett was a handsome, accomplished man. Well-heeled and well turned out. And Jackie pitied anyone who got seriously involved with him. It would not be possible to be equal in a relationship with him.

"You're still one of the most beautiful women I've ever

known," Mark crooned, as he slid a thin finger up the wet surface of his glass. Jackie merely looked at him, not flattered, and not warming particularly toward him. His dark brown eyes looked her over suggestively. "You have more style and class than anyone."

"Please, Mark," Jackie said sarcastically in a low voice, "that never made a bit of difference to you. If *any* girl was willing, so were you!"

For once, Mark had the grace to look uncomfortable and embarrassed. He shrugged. "Okay. So I may have made a mistake, been a little indiscreet."

"*May* have!" Jackie said in amazement. She shook her head. "You made me feel like . . . like some inexperienced little girl. Then you made me feel guilty—*guilty*, Mark—for not understanding your infidelity. You held me up to ridicule!"

Mark just sat and watched her and listened. Not showing much remorse, and certainly not apologizing for his behavior. Jackie wasn't sure what she'd expected him to show or say to her. But in that moment she fully realized that Mark cared more for himself than for anyone else. He only meant to fulfill his own needs. She felt sad for him.

"You never should have married me. You really don't need anyone, you know." She searched his face, seeing now the real Mark. Jackie laughed softly. "We were both very foolish, and I guess I was very young." She took another sip of her drink.

"You may be right, Jackie. I realize now, however, I was very foolish to let you go."

"You didn't let me go. I left!" she corrected.

Mark ignored her words, leaned across the table toward her. She became fascinated by the texture of his mustache. It made his face look very mature. "Look, I want you to think again about modeling for me. Just this once, if you like. Afterward, if you really want to quit, I won't try to change your mind. And you have everything to gain!"

Jackie searched his face again. It was true she had lots to gain, but the thing she wanted most she wasn't sure she could have. The thing she had most to lose was herself.

Eric thought she was pretty, but he wasn't impressed by it. He'd said to her that she had talents elsewhere—in photography. He believed in that, and had helped her in that. Jackie

realized that in doing what Mark now wanted her to do she
would be taking a step backward, losing all that she'd gained for
herself.

"Why are you so anxious to use me? There are lots of models
available who'd love this chance. Why not use Gwen!"

"You would be better."

She narrowed her eyes at him in speculation. "I don't believe
that. Why can't you tell me the truth?" Suddenly Jackie remembered the rest of Mark's offer and she sat straight and alert.
Jackie's pretty brown features went stiff, but her voice was soft
and steady.

"You can forget it, Mark. I have no intention of going back to
you. I don't love you anyway!"

Mark sat back in his chair and smiled at Jackie. He caught the
waitress's attention and ordered himself another drink. "You
really know how to put a man in his place, you know that?"

"I had a very good teacher," Jackie responded, lifting one
brow at him. "You should never have expected anything else. It
just goes to show how little thought you gave to me."

He leaned forward again, frowning earnestly at her. "I can't
make you change your mind?"

Jackie slowly shook her head, looking him directly in the eyes.

Mark let out a sigh. "So, I guess this is it."

"I guess so."

"I want you to know, Jackie, and I'm serious about this. If I
could do it all over again, I'd be different."

Never had Jackie heard such a confession from Mark, and
even as his voice sounded sincere, she knew better. But in the
end she let herself relax and smiled at him. "It's nice of you to
say so."

Mark shook the ice around in his glass. "I suppose there's
someone else in your life, now?"

Jackie frowned, not sure how to answer the question. There
was Eric, but their relationship had not been clearly defined yet.
"There is someone I care very much for," she hedged.

Mark tilted his head to one side. "Do you love him?" he asked
boldly.

Jackie lowered her eyes. "Yes, I do."

"Then I guess that says everything."

They drank in companionable silence for a minute or so, as

the buzz of other conversations floated around them. The bar of the restaurant was crowded but not noisy. Inwardly Jackie sighed at the missed opportunity of a purely intimate social occasion with Eric. A couple seated at the bar had their name called, indicating that a table was ready for them for dinner. As they moved away, Jackie caught a glimpse of a man and woman seated in a booth on the other side of the room. People coming and going blocked her view, but she could almost swear it was. . . . No. She had to be wrong.

She turned back to Mark and smiled at him as he started his second drink.

"How long will you stay in Charleston?" he asked her.

She shrugged. "Probably another week." But nothing was settled. She couldn't help herself. She turned her head again in the direction of the booth. The man was turned three-quarters away from her, but the shape of the head, the width of the shoulders were so like Eric's. Except, this man was with a very attractive woman, somewhat shorter than Jackie and at the moment in animated conversation with a worried, frowning expression on her face. The man opposite her was doing more listening than anything else.

Something touched Jackie's arm. She jumped and swung her eyes to Mark.

"Did . . . did you say something?"

"I said, who do you see? Is it someone you know?"

"No. I . . . I was daydreaming. Sorry."

Mark chuckled. "That doesn't speak much for me as company!"

"Oh, it wasn't you, Mark. I just had a thought."

"Would you like another drink?"

"No thanks. I'll just finish this and then I'd like to go."

He shrugged. "If you want."

Again her eyes drifted to the booth. A knot of terrible fear was forming in Jackie's insides. Her heart began to pound and she felt a little dizzy. She just had an awful feeling of something terribly wrong. She finished her drink in a gulp.

"I'm ready. I'd like to go now."

"Hey! Take it easy! Do you mind if I finish mine?" Mark asked, puzzled by her sudden haste to leave.

Jackie laughed nervously. "I'm sorry." She forced herself to sit still, forced herself not to look again, her heart raced, she felt almost faint. She fidgeted in her chair. Against her will, her head turned.

At that moment, the man turned also to signal the waitress for the check. Jackie's heart nearly stopped. It was Eric. The waitress came toward him, and he looked up and past her catching Jackie's stunned wide-eyed stare. An icy cold wave of horror washed over her, leaving her stiff and cold. She felt as if her cheeks had sunk in from shock. Indeed, her entire body seemed to collapse back into itself as she sat staring. She closed her eyes and gripped the edge of the table, her knuckles practically popping up through the skin. A moan of real pain escaped her.

"Jackie?" Mark questioned, leaning toward her and taking her elbow.

"Take me home. Please, Mark, take me home, now!"

"What's the matter? Are you sick?"

Jackie couldn't answer as she grabbed for her purse and light jacket and swung her legs from the booth. She had to get out of there or she would be sick. Sick with disappointment and despair. She was too overwhelmed to cry, but it was not very far behind. It would catch up to her.

"Jackie?" Someone called her name again. It was filled with surprise and underlined with doubt. This time it was Eric's voice and not Mark's that reached her.

Slowly Jackie raised her eyes, brought her head up until she looked straight into the puzzled intense light eyes of Eric. At least a dozen emotions traversed both their faces in a matter of seconds. Pain, doubt, fear, hurt—anger . . .

"Hello, Eric," Jackie said and she was proud of how steady and even her voice was. "What a nice surprise!" she couldn't help adding, a bit of her old feistiness asserting itself.

Eric held on to the arm of the woman next to him. Jackie sharply caught her breath as it became obvious that the woman was very pregnant. Jackie raised her eyes reluctantly to the face of the pretty woman, who in that moment was looking at Eric with a frown.

Oh God! Jackie moaned inside herself. I don't believe this is happening.

Mark was also looking from her to Eric and back again. Once

more Jackie caught Eric's eyes. They were now settled into being stony and cold as he continued to stare at her.

"Eric, this . . . this is Mark Bennett. Mark, this is Eric Davidson."

The two men turned to face one another, unknowing adversaries. Jackie, standing somewhat off to the side, was able to observe them both. Mark was taller by a few inches, but appeared gaunt and too thin next to Eric. Jackie had to admit that Eric appeared even more virile with his broad shoulders and narrow hips. He wore a pair of black trousers and a white cotton knit shirt that contrasted sharply with his rich brown skin in a most pleasing way. But at the moment Jackie was feeling less than pleased. Eric didn't look too happy either.

The two men assessed each other silently for just an instant before Eric finally put out his hand to Mark.

"Mark," he said, nodding, and shaking Mark's hand.

Jackie looked once more at the woman whose arm Eric still held so protectively. Jackie was surprised to find herself being looked over with curiosity. When the woman's eye caught her own, the other smiled. Jackie was not prepared for such friendliness and dropped her eyes, bewildered. Eric introduced Jackie to the woman, and Jackie found herself waiting anxiously to hear who she was.

"This is Elaine Cameron, my sister," Eric said with a hard emphasis that Jackie knew was directed toward her.

"Would you care to join us?" Mark asked.

Eric hesitated, glancing briefly at Jackie. She didn't know what to say and her expression maintained its shocked expression. She had no doubt that Eric had seen her stiff attitude and correctly read her thoughts as they concerned his sister. She'd misjudged him again, and that was a mistake. She'd never seen him as angry as he was at the moment with her, and her doubting of him.

"I don't think so," Eric finally answered stiffly. "Elaine shouldn't be standing too long, and I want to get her home."

Jackie stole a look at the lovely Elaine and found her smiling in a friendly and sympathetic fashion at her. It made Jackie feel even more wretched. Elaine seemed so calm, totally unlike Jackie who felt as though a Mixmaster blade had been run through her body. She knew she couldn't continue to stand there and not say anything.

"Did you—did you settle your problem?" she asked Eric.

He looked at her carefully, his eyes hard and cold, his mouth a grim uncompromising line. "Some things, yes."

"I didn't know you knew anyone in South Carolina, Jackie," Mark said, obviously fishing for information as to her relationship to Eric Davidson.

"Eric, Mr. Davidson helped me quite a lot with my book while I was here," Jackie admitted, looking quickly at Eric's cold expression, and away again.

"Are you writing the book, Jackie?"

Jackie's head came up. She was fascinated at hearing Elaine Cameron speak, and intrigued by her familiar use of Jackie's name.

"I'm not a writer. I'm a photographer. Someone else is writing the book."

"That sounds like fun." The woman smiled. Jackie couldn't seem to stop herself. She smiled back.

"I think we should be going," Eric said to his sister Elaine, steering her toward the door. All offered goodbyes, and without looking at her anymore, Eric and Elaine left.

Jackie's tear-filled eyes followed them out the door. Mark was watching her carefully, and she forced herself to speak calmly.

"Have you finished your drink?"

"Yes, I have," Mark answered, a little confused by her attitude.

"Then, please, let's go," she said wearily.

Mark could not get another word out of her on the short drive back to Hannah's. He finally pulled up in front of the green door and Jackie turned to get out of the car. Mark put a hand on her arm to stop her.

"I'm leaving in the morning. I'm headed back to New York."

"Oh," Jackie responded absently.

"I don't think I'll see you again."

She finally understood what he was saying. Jackie focused her eyes on him. "No, Mark. I don't suppose you will."

"There's no chance, is there?" he asked, totally out of character.

She only shook her head, feeling very tired suddenly. To her surprise, Mark laughed softly, stroking her arm once.

"I think I really blew it!"

There was nothing for Jackie to say. Nothing she wanted to say.

"How about a kiss goodbye? The last one?"

Jackie stared before finally leaning forward to allow his mouth to press to hers. But it was all wrong. It was too hard, and not caressing. With a strangled cry Jackie twisted away, seeing only Eric's generous, sensuous mouth. She quickly got out of the car, ignoring Mark's calling her. She slammed the door and ran up the stairs and into the house.

The house was strangely quiet, and she only wondered for a second where Hannah and Gwen might be. With only a hallway light to guide her, Jackie made her way to the parlor and sat heavily on the love seat. Over and over she repeated in her head the whole scene from the restaurant. After witnessing Eric's anger, she was no longer sure she'd had any right to be suspicious of him. She could never forget the hard steeliness of his eyes as they looked deeply into hers, searching out and finding her mistrust.

Jackie was too numb to cry, and she wasn't sure it would have helped. She had no idea how long she sat there before there was a strong knock on the front door. She started almost violently, her heart lurching against her chest. With an almost melodramatic feeling of doom, Jackie got up and slowly went to open the door, somehow not surprised to find a still glowering Eric standing ominously in front of her.

"I want to talk to you!" he said without preamble, brushing coldly past her into the foyer of the house. Jackie's reactions were slow. She watched him as he stiffly stood under the hall light. She closed the door finally, and reluctantly moved toward him.

Eric reached out a hand and taking her firmly by the elbow, moved away from the hall and into the parlor. His voice was for her ears only, and she winced at the hard pressure of his fingers on her arm.

"You're not very trusting, are you?" he said through tightly clenched teeth.

"I'm sorry." Jackie swallowed. And having said it, straightened her back and spine proudly.

"Are you?" Eric asked mockingly in disbelief.

"I . . . I didn't know."

"And you didn't wait to find out, either. Didn't you believe me when I said how much I was looking forward to having dinner with you?"

"Yes, but . . ." she began and then stopped.

"Well?" he persisted, his anger making his eyes snap amber flashes of fire.

Jackie raised her chin defiantly. "When I saw you in the restaurant with Elaine . . ." How could she adequately explain her fear and uncertainties? Seeing Eric tonight had stripped her of the confidence she'd gained that she was important to him. It left her feeling much too vulnerable for comfort.

"You thought that I'd lied to you. You thought the 'something' I had to see to was another woman. Well, in a sense you were right. But there's a hell of a lot more you don't know about!"

"But you don't understand—" Jackie began clearly, but was interrupted.

"But I do understand, dammit! I just thought that with me you'd gotten beyond all of your barriers. I was foolish enough to think my word would be enough for you."

He didn't shout, didn't raise his voice, and that made it worse. She could think of no more to say in her own behalf, and that was probably just as well. There were no more excuses to use, nothing to fall back on. She'd have to deal with the situation openly, and with Eric honestly and completely in the present. Eric released her elbow and thrust his hands into the pockets of his pants, and his jaw continued to tense furiously.

"Okay . . ." Eric breathed out. "Let's get this out in the open. I want you to ask me all those questions running through your head."

Jackie sat down on the love seat and clasped her hands together. "Eric, I know I was wrong. I don't have to ask."

"Yes you do, Jackie," he said grimly. "If we don't get this over with, we may never."

She looked at him and saw that he was very serious. "Why did you have to cancel dinner?" she asked softly.

"I said to you something came up. It wasn't even all that

important. My dad has to go into the hospital for some minor eye surgery—cataracts. My sister was concerned and thought one of us should be in Delaware with our folks just in case. Well, you saw Elaine. She's in no condition to travel anywhere. That left me. There wasn't any choice."

"No. Of course not," Jackie agreed, barely audible, looking down at her twisting hands.

"When I leave here I'm headed for Delaware." Eric walked to stand directly in front of Jackie, and she had to tilt her head way back to look into his face. She stood up, not wanting to cower before him. "Elaine's husband suggested I get her out of the house and away from the kids for an hour or so to calm her down, to talk privately to her. That's why we were in the restaurant. She had caffeine-free coffee and I had a beer," he added on a soft sarcastic note.

Jackie's face felt flushed with the warm blood of embarrassment that coursed through her.

"What else do you want to know?" he continued, unrelenting.

She looked at him squarely. "Are there any other women in your life?"

Eric arched a brow and almost looked amused. "Yes," he answered at once. "My mother and my sister."

Jackie felt miserable. She tried to move around Eric and away, but he grabbed her arms and held her still.

"Jackie, I can't begin to tell you how much I wanted to see you tonight, what I'd hoped for afterward," Eric crooned in a now low, seductive voice, his desire momentarily overcoming his anger.

"Me too," she admitted urgently in a whisper.

"But none of it's ever going to mean a thing if we can't trust one another. I know you've been hurt. But we have to start somewhere." His eyes searched her face. Having said that much in understanding, he released her, and his voice was once again caustic. "And might I ask who your, er, escort was? You didn't exactly sit home crushed with disappointment either, did you?"

The sarcasm in his voice stung her. Gwen had been so right about how easy it was to jump to the wrong conclusions.

"That . . . that was my ex-husband."

"I see," he bit out mysteriously, and Jackie knew full well he didn't see at all. But then, neither had she.

Eric waited for her to continue. Suddenly Jackie knew she was being served with a strong dose of her own medicine. It had a very bitter taste. Nonetheless, she met his gaze and didn't back down. "It wasn't my idea. He . . . he arrived unexpectedly. He had a business deal to offer me."

The expression on Eric's face remained skeptical and he raised one brow in doubt. Jackie's teeth clamped down tightly. "But I refused!" she said with emphasis. "I wasn't interested. He just took me out for a goodbye drink." But as much as she tried to be as aloof as Eric appeared, she couldn't. She wanted him to believe her so much. "That's all there was to it," she finished softly. Eric continued to look at her closely, searching over her features.

"Once explained it sounds so simple and reasonable"—he paused—"doesn't it?" His voice was very low. Jackie raised beseeching eyes to his.

For a long silent moment they stared at one another. Jackie was afraid to make the first move and wasn't sure if Eric would. And then Eric turned away. Jackie stood paralyzed, unable to even call his name, as Eric quietly left the house.

Luckily there was still no one around when she reached her room. She dissolved into instant tears, her body sobbing itself into exhaustion. Jackie felt as if she'd lost something very dear, which she wasn't even sure had been hers to lose in the first place. She didn't know how she could ever begin to make things right again. And would he still want her anyway?

She didn't hear the door open and close, but she felt the weight of someone sitting next to her on the bed. A slender hand gently shook her. It was Gwen.

"You sure don't sound like someone in love," she said low, and Jackie only cried harder. "Hey! Come on. It can't be that bad!"

"Oh God, Gwen, it's worse!"

"Come on, tell me what happened."

Tearfully, gulping for air, and sniffling between words, Jackie related the evening. When she finished Gwen merely sighed.

"Did he tell you who Elaine was?"

"Yes, but . . ."

"So why did you think the very worst thing? Why didn't you trust him?"

"But, Gwen, he could have told me everything when he called."

"Why? Maybe he felt he shouldn't have to explain to you. And what do you suppose he thought seeing you there with Mark?"

Jackie gasped, her mouth dropping open. "But there was nothing to think! I was just having a goodbye drink with Mark!"

"Do you expect him to know that? And how do you think he'd feel finding out you're having drinks with a man you used to be married to, and who you've said treated you so poorly?"

Jackie hadn't thought of that. "Oh, Gwen!" she wailed and indulged in a fresh fit of weeping.

"Just hang in there, hon," Gwen advised. "You know, they say the course of true love never runs smoothly."

"I don't know if I can stand any more ups and downs!"

"Yes you can," Gwen said prophetically. "In the end it will be worth it!"

CHAPTER TEN

Jackie sat in her room, a room that would not be hers for much longer, and prepared to attend the gallery opening for her photographs. It should have been a joyous climax to her stay in Charleston. Instead, it was a glaring reminder, to be survived after she was gone, of every moment spent in Eric Davidson's company.

Jackie moved and silently walked to the bed and reached for the summer white slacks that lay ready for her to pull on with the deep violet camisole top. Gwen quickly got up from her chair by the window and reached the bed before Jackie.

"You're not wearing that," she said firmly, snatching the pants out of Jackie's limp hands.

Jackie looked at her with bewildered glazed eyes, but offered no resistance.

"What do you mean, I'm not wearing that? Why not?"

"This is a special night, hon. And you should wear something special."

"What difference does it make, Gwen?" Jackie asked listlessly. "I just want to get this over with. And then I want to go home."

Gwen was patient. "One thing at a time. First you have to get dressed—but not in this!"

She went to the open suitcase sitting on the floor at the foot of the bed, and proceeded to rifle through it.

Jackie had started packing several days before, against everyone's objections. But it was a halfhearted, absentminded task. She'd fold a few things and put them away, and then seem to grow weary of the chore, and walk away. A half hour or an hour later, she'd be back at it. Three days later it was still only half done.

Gwen came up with a white dress that had a softly flared skirt, a top with short dolman sleeves and a boat neckline. There was a wide, apple-red belt to go with it. Gwen put the pants and camisole into the case and stood up with the dress in hand.

"Here. I think this is much better!"

"I don't really care."

"Well, one of us has to!" Gwen said with feeling. "Now you do something with your hair while I go press this. And if you haven't by the time I come back, then *I* will!"

Gwen walked to the door and pulled it open. Jackie blinked at her as if clearing her eyes, as if seeing something that hadn't occurred to her before.

"Gwen!" she said urgently. Gwen turned in the doorway to look at her, scowling in exasperation. "Gwen . . ." Jackie began helplessly, holding out a hand. "I don't mean to give you a hard time. I know you're trying to help."

Gwen's frown faded and was replaced by a softer look of concern and affection. She came back to stand in front of Jackie. "And I don't mean to bully you. But I don't want you to just give up. *Believe* me, hon. It's not as bad as you think!"

Jackie sighed and rubbed her throat and neck. "Maybe you know something that I don't. I don't know what I think," she said in a vague voice. "I just know how I feel. . . ." She turned to sit back warily on the vanity chair. "And I just don't know what to do anymore."

"That's okay," Gwen assured her. "But when you're not sure, then don't do anything! It'll work itself out."

Jackie said nothing as she began to finger and play with the curls over her forehead. She shook her head from side to side slowly and looked at Gwen. "But I've been doing nothing for days!"

Gwen gnawed her bottom lip, thinking hard. She started to say something but thought better of it and stopped.

"And I can't wait for it to work out. I'm not convinced it ever will!"

Gwen stood a moment longer in some kind of indecision. "Well, let's just wait a bit longer and see." With that she left the room, not sure that any of her words had penetrated any better now than they had in the last three days.

Jackie had been trying to reason and be calm for days, no matter what Gwen or Hannah thought. She'd tried to remember that Eric had never promised anything, had never admitted to anything, other than the obvious desire to make love to her. He had made no declarations, and offered no commitments. It was not his fault, then, that she had fallen in love with him. She had somehow come to that all by herself. But love also requires trust if it is to hold together, and she'd been guilty of not giving that to Eric. She began to push and pull at her hair, pinning and unpinning, combing, brushing, fluffing, in an effort to be interested in her appearance. She put the brush down impatiently and turned away.

Gwen was going to force her to wear the white dress, so she at least dug out a slip and red sandals that tied daintily around the ankle and that matched her belt. As she pulled the slip over her head, there came a tap on the door.

"Come on in, Gwen," she muttered. She heard the door open and close.

"It's not Gwen, darlin'. It's Hannah."

"Oh, come in, Hannah." She got the slip in place and lifted her head to face Hannah. "Oh, Hannah! You look just lovely!"

Hannah fidgeted in embarrassment, her plump little hands smoothing down the material of her navy blue dress with its white collar and belt. She wore a pair of pearl ear buttons, and a pearl choker around her neck. And for the first time, she wore a touch of lipstick.

"Oh, this is such an old dress!"

"It's a beautiful dress. And you look perfect in it!"

"Thank you, Jackie," Hannah breathed, delighted despite herself. Then she pulled herself up straight, her generous bosom heaving up. Hannah clutched her hands together, and Jackie wondered at her nervousness.

"But I really came because I had to talk to you!"

"Of course," Jackie responded, curiosity getting the better of her former lethargic state. She moved her robe from the vanity chair.

"Here, sit down."

"Thank you," Hannah said primly and sat stiffly on the edge of the small chair. Jackie frowned, but sat quietly on the side of her bed and waited. She watched as Hannah struggled with her words.

"Now, darlin', I don't want you to think I'm being an old busybody, interfering in your affairs and all, but I've grown

very, very fond of you. And I think of you like you were my
own daughter."

Jackie's eyes widened.

"Well, I mean if I had a daughter I'd want her to be like you!
You're smart and pretty, and clever, and a lovely girl."

Hannah stopped. She glanced quickly at Jackie and away
again. She took a deep breath.

"So I'm going to talk to you as if you were my own."

Jackie held her breath, curious beyond endurance as to what
Hannah would say. Hannah cleared her throat.

"Now I've sat and watched you for the last week while you
worked yourself up into a positive state over Eric Davidson."

Jackie gestured to interrupt, but Hannah spoke up first.

"Now just you wait until I've had my say. Then you can tell
me to mind my business." She gathered a breath again into herself and continued. She had Jackie's full attention now. "Now I
don't know what's happened between you two, but it's not
worth you going into a decline over! I can hear you crying at
night . . ."

"Oh, Hannah . . ."

"And it breaks my heart! And then I want to come and shake
you good and tell you to stop that! Stop feeling sorry for yourself. You have no cause to!"

Tears welled up in Jackie's eyes. Her arms circled the bedpost
and she bit down hard on her lip.

"Now I think you're a wonderful person, and any man in his
right mind would be lucky to have you. Of course, I'm a bit
prejudiced, but still it's the truth, and the truth don't change."

Jackie smiled wanly, despite her inner turmoil of emotions.

"When Alvin Curtis and I was courtin' he wasn't even sure he
wanted to get married. And I came right out and told him he
was a fool if he let me slip away from him. I guess in the end he
agreed. We were married more than thirty years! And if Eric
Davidson is too blind to see what's waiting for him, loving him
with all her heart—then he's a fool too. Even if I do like the
man!"

Jackie was crying, but she was laughing, too. She wasn't sure
she deserved the care and concern that Hannah and Gwen gave
her, but in this moment it felt wonderful having these two people worry about her.

"I believe that things always manage to work out for the best. They always come around in time!"

Jackie looked at Hannah. It sounded so familiar. Hadn't Eric told her once that his grandmother used to say so? All good things in their time.

Hannah stood up. "Now I've talked enough." She wagged a finger at Jackie and bent her fist to her hip in the manner of a parent scolding a child. "You are going to get dressed in something pretty, and we are going to go to the gallery and really give those folks something to talk about."

Jackie sprang up and wrapped her arms around Hannah, leaving the shorter woman's forehead wet with tears. "Thank you, Hannah."

Hannah softened at once, hugging Jackie to her. "Oh, darlin', I hope you're not mad at me."

"Never, Hannah. I'm very lucky to have you on my side."

"There now, you go finish getting dressed." She patted Jackie's arm and gently pushed her away. Her own eyes were misted over.

The door opened and Gwen came in, the white dress ironed into gentle folds, and placed on a hanger. Gwen looked from one to the other in puzzlement at the sniffling, and the wet eyes, and the hugging.

"What's going on?" she asked.

Jackie smiled a watery smile and wiped her face with the heel of her hand. Hannah turned from Jackie and headed through the door past Gwen, grabbing the doorknob behind her. "We were just having a heart to heart talk, that's all. Mother to daughter!"

Jackie tried her very best. If Hannah and Gwen could be lighthearted and cheerful, then she would not be the odd man out. She wore the white dress, which was the perfect contrast and foil to her smooth brown features. She pinned her hair up in back, and let Gwen talk her into wearing a flower behind her ear. It was a little corny but visually very effective. And if her spirits were still somewhat sore and bruised, at least she looked like summer brightness.

The gallery was a medium space on one of Charleston's main streets. The name, *ARTIST'S EYES*, was graphically lettered horizontally along the bottom pane of the glass, and there was a small window showcase used to preview what was to be shown on a larger scale inside. As the three women approached the storefront from Jackie's parked car, an enlarged black and white picture taken of a fisherman off the Johns Island coast was visible in the showcase window on an easel. Its position faced inward toward a painting displayed the same way.

Jackie frowned. She had not been told she would be sharing the gallery space. Or had she just forgotten all that Bob McIver had told her? When they entered the gallery, Jackie's excitement rose despite herself. An elegantly dressed middle-aged woman approached them. The woman's chestnut hair was worn in a gentle knot at the neck, and her green eyes were bright behind an oversized pair of tortoiseshell glasses. She smiled and introduced herself as Carol Winters, owner of the gallery. When she heard Jackie's name she raised her brows in surprise.

"Oh, you're the photographer! It's nice to meet you at last. I've heard quite a lot about you since I saw your first pictures." She looked at Gwen and Hannah standing alertly nearby and spoke to them. "As you can see you're the first to arrive. Would you mind if I took Jacqueline away for a moment? Business first!"

Hannah smiled and nodded. Gwen spoke for them both. "We'll just take a quiet look around." And she and Hannah turned away.

"Come. Let's sit over there," Carol Winters said, indicating a French Provincial desk in the back of the gallery, discreetly hidden by a room divider. She sat behind the desk and Jackie sat in the other chair at its side.

"I'm surprised not to have met you before this. I thought you'd want to participate in the selection of your work and help in the hanging arrangements," Carol said, clasping her hands on top of her desk and smiling doubtfully at Jackie.

Jackie felt a bit confused. "I did have some say in the picture selection, but Bob, that is, Mr. McIver, the owner of the lab where I took my work, said everything would be arranged."

"I see," Carol responded. "The work came in all framed and everything about a week ago. I was told you were very busy every day."

"I never really knew how it all came about. You see, I'm not from South Carolina. I'm just here to work on a book. I'll probably be leaving soon to go back to New York. That's why this show is so much of a surprise."

"Yes, I was told most of that. But I agreed with Mr. McIver and Dr. Davidson that the work was excellent and should be shown."

Something clicked inside Jackie at the mention of the name Davidson. An immediate pulse of emotion vibrated through her. Her hand pressed to her stomach.

"D . . . Dr. Davidson?" Jackie asked in a strange voice.

"Yes. He's from the art department of the local college. It was he who first brought the pictures to my attention. He'd purchased several from Mr. McIver. You really have him to thank for this." She gestured around the open space with its track lighting illuminating each framed piece of work. The photographs occupied one part of the gallery along one wall, and the remaining wall space and dividers were hung with paintings.

Carol Winters caught Jackie's attention again. "We call the show 'Two Views of the Sea Islands.'" She looked at Jackie. "You did know you were sharing the gallery space, didn't you?"

"No. I . . . ." Jackie stopped as Carol Winters's eyes shifted to someone behind Jackie.

"Oh, you're here!" Carol smiled and stood up, coming around from her seat and extending her hand.

Jackie turned to look over her shoulder at the newcomer, and her heart jumped to her throat in surprise. Extending his hand to Carol Winters was Eric Davidson. At least Jackie was almost positive it was Eric. A little behind him came Bob McIver, and Jackie's surprise doubled. Bob was dressed in a light blue suit with a navy tie on his white shirt. But Jackie's eyes swung back in disbelief to the tall form of Eric, also dressed formally, for the first time since she'd known him.

"I'm glad you arrived early," Carol was saying to Eric as he shook hands with her. He hadn't looked at Jackie yet, and all she could do was stare.

Carol turned to Jackie. "Ms. Taylor arrived just moments ago. Of course, you two know each other." She beamed and turned to greet Bob McIver.

Eric's jaw tensed, and his eyes narrowed as he looked at her. Jackie wasn't sure what she saw. Curiosity, surprise, and something that might have been anger. But as his eyes swept over her slender form dressed in white, there was also, undeniably, desire. "But we don't, do we Jackie?" he questioned her in a low voice.

Jackie felt a hopelessness settle on her. She knew she was on the verge of some new discoveries and they would indeed make him a stranger to her. She shook her head sadly, agreeing with him. "No, we don't."

"And do you suppose we ever will?" he asked oddly.

Her eyes flew up to his face, searching his meaning. "I . . . I . . ." she floundered, not sure how to answer. Was there hope in his voice?

Several people had begun to wander into the gallery and turned their heads to Eric and Jackie, and their curious low, intense conversation. There could be no mistaking the subtle emotions flying between them. Eric took the time to pull back his broad shoulders and let out a long, tensely held breath. The lines and muscles around his mouth began to relax, but his eyes remained remote. He put his hands into his pockets, the fingers playing nervously with the loose change and keys, creating a jingle of sound.

Carol Winters caught Eric's attention again, and he was forced to turn away from Jackie. She felt as if a door had been closed on her.

"Well." She recognized Bob's voice. "This is the big night, isn't it?"

Jackie took a deep breath and turned to smile at Bob. "Yes, it is! How are you tonight, Bob?"

"Still waiting to have that glass of wine with you."

Jackie laughed lightly, and Eric turned to the sound, but Jackie ignored him. She hooked her arm to Bob's. "That sounds like a wonderful idea. I could use a glass of wine," she said shakily, causing Bob to notice the tremor in her voice.

"Are you okay? Having opening night jitters?"

"Yes, a little, I guess."

"Come on. The wine will take care of that."

And Jackie quickly had two glasses at the little reception table that had been set up for that.

People were slowly beginning to arrive now, and Jackie shortly lost sight of Hannah and Gwen. She and Bob slowly walked around the gallery examining the photographs and the paintings. She was pleased with the way Bob had framed her work, and also thought the paintings hung were lovely and looked somewhat familiar to her. But still, half her mind and all of her heart remained with Eric as he continued in deep conversation with Carol Winters. She was more confused than ever. Was Carol Winters's Dr. Davidson, Eric? She was now dismally aware of how little time she'd taken to really know this man she was in love with.

Jackie took a private moment to watch him. He was formally dressed tonight in black trousers and black slip-on loafers. He wore a white shirt under his gray summer sports jacket, and the tie was black and gray diagonal stripes. The jacket hugged to his broad shoulders, the slacks fitted well to his legs. Jackie held her breath. She had come to love the raw animal magnetism of him in his usual casual wear. But she had to admit that at this moment he looked magnificent. Here stood a man who knew what he was about in life.

Eric's eyes swung to hers, locking for an instant. Jackie was still not sure what it was he saw or what he looked for, but being unsure, she quickly turned away, a deeper misery taking hold than she'd previously known. She wandered through the crowd absently, accepting congratulations and praise. She got herself absorbed in examining the paintings again, trying to decide why they looked so familiar. They captured, wonderfully, brightly, the black people of the region, and the many aspects of their lives in South Carolina, past, present, and perhaps said something about the future.

"Well, what do you think?"

Jackie swung around to find Eric behind her, a glass of wine in one hand, the other hidden in his pants pocket. That gesture alone made her begin to weaken. He looked so supremely masculine. So tall and sure of himself. As if reading some of her thoughts, he suddenly raised a brow at her and a smile began to curve his mouth.

"I think they're very good." She hesitated, still unsure of him.

"Only very good?" he mocked.

"These are yours, aren't they?"

He continued to look at her as though not having heard her words.

"And you teach in the art department at the local college?" she asked in a tone bordering on accusation. Eric grimaced. "I'm on sabbatical from the college for a year. I guess I got a little tired of being an administrator," he said with a rueful laugh. "I wanted to get back to doing my own thing. I figured a year should be enough time to do a body of work and have a show."

"And that's what you were doing when we met?"

"Yes. As a matter of fact, I was in back of the house when you arrived. I didn't hear the car, but I saw you nearly sink in the mud near the pond."

"And you didn't even offer to help me?" she said indignantly.

"You did okay on your own. And besides, I don't think you would have wanted my help."

Jackie frowned and gnawed on the inside of her bottom lip, keeping her eyes on Eric. "And are you also *Dr.* Davidson?"

For the first time ever, Jackie watched as Eric seemed to squirm under the question.

"I'm not really a doctor, of course. It's just an Ed.D. in education."

Jackie raised her brows and gave him a skeptical look. "*Just* an Ed.D. That's quite enough. Was that appeasement to your dad, so you wouldn't starve to death?" she asked.

Eric shrugged. "I guess, but I did enjoy teaching for a while. The college made me head of the department three years ago. But I missed painting very much. That's why I took the sabbatical. I needed perspective. I wanted to see if I'd forgotten how to paint."

Jackie looked for a moment at one painting, and finally back to Eric who watched her movements almost in anticipation. Jackie suddenly felt anger building up in her because Eric had been less than totally honest with her. She stood straight, and raised her chin stubbornly.

"I hope you enjoyed making a fool of me!" she said with a hurt tremor she couldn't disguise.

"That wasn't my intention, Jackie. . . ." Eric responded very low.

"Nonetheless, you've succeeded. I guess it's just revenge for the way I behaved earlier."

"Jackie . . ."

"If you'll excuse me . . ." and she made to move quickly around Eric and into the crowd. But suddenly Gwen appeared out of nowhere blocking her escape.

"Where on earth have you been?" Gwen asked urgently.

"Oh, Gwen . . . I was looking at the exhibit." She hid her tear-filled eyes.

Gwen sucked her teeth. "Girl, you can do that later. I've been looking all over for you! There's someone I want you to meet finally!"

Jackie looked with pleading eyes at her friend. "Oh, Gwen! You didn't! I couldn't. Not now," she wailed, glancing quickly at Eric, who stood with a smile playing around his mouth.

Gwen smiled almost wickedly. "Oh yes you can! And you're going to meet Spence if I have to sit on you to hold you still!"

"Gwen, why are you doing this to me? I can never feel anything for Spence!"

"How do you know until you've tried?" Gwen said without compromise. Taking a firm hold of Jackie's arm, she swung her firmly around until she was face to face with Eric. Just beyond Eric Jackie saw his sister Elaine moving slowly in their direction. She finally stopped next to Eric, smiling warmly at Jackie and, looking radiant and very pregnant. Jackie was trying to avoid looking at Eric and what appeared to be amusement in his topaz eyes.

Jackie stiffened and pulled her arm out of Gwen's grasp. "This isn't funny!" she said in a shaky voice, and started to turn away.

"Oh no you don't!" Gwen said, recapturing her arm and laughing. Obviously Gwen did find this whole thing amusing. "Jackie, I want you to meet Spence. Spence, here she is, and she's all yours!" And with that, Gwen released her, and stood looking very satisfied.

"What do you mean, she's all yours! I'm beginning to think you're all crazy!" Jackie responded angrily.

She felt a large strong hand grab hers and thread its fingers with her own, making it impossible to pull away now.

"Eric, stop teasing her!" Elaine said softly, pulling on Eric's sleeve.

"Thank you, Gwen," Eric said, pulling Jackie to his side.

"This is absolutely the last time I ever do you a favor and you better not forget!" Gwen threatened.

Jackie looked from Gwen to Eric, from Eric to Elaine, and back to Gwen again in total bewilderment. "Will someone tell me what's going on?" Jackie asked. Again she looked from a beaming Gwen to Eric—or Spence, whomever, with a slight smile of amusement on his face.

"Someone will," Gwen said, winking at Jackie as she moved away. "I have to go find Hannah and tell her everything's okay at last." She turned to Elaine. "And I want a boy this time!" With that, Gwen waved her hand and walked away.

Jackie refused to look at Eric, and she gave up trying to free her hand from his.

"Jackie . . ." he coaxed seductively, his soft voice working on her susceptible system. She felt herself giving in. She cast a sideways glance at him, to find him looking at her with what could only be described as tenderness. "Everything *is* going to be okay," he said, confirming Gwen's statement.

Elaine cleared her throat and smiled winsomely at Jackie. She seemed to be the only one who was calm. Eric looked briefly in her direction.

"Jackie, I'm sure you remember my sister." Eric quirked a brow at her. Jackie blinked rapidly, painfully reminded of her previous thoughts. Elaine's smile grew. Jackie smiled in return, as Elaine reached behind her and pulled on the arm of a man of medium build and height who had his back to the group. Feeling the tugging on his arm, he turned. "And this is my husband, Ross. This is Jackie. You remember my telling you about her?"

It was clear that the bespectacled Ross did not. But he politely smiled and nodded to Jackie.

Jackie was feeling like she'd walked into the middle of a badly written comedy routine in which all the actors knew each other —and the punch line to the joke. She still was not clear on what was going on. Eric's fingers squeezed her own reassuringly, and she looked at him, wanting to understand.

"Ross, do you think you could find me a chair?" Elaine said as she rested a hand on her protruding stomach. She smiled ruefully at Jackie. "I can't stand very long these days. But I do hope we'll get a chance to talk soon, Jackie."

"I think we'll all be too busy for a while," Eric told his sister knowingly as she was gently led away by her husband.

Eric and Jackie looked at one another. Eric started to speak, and then became aware of their surroundings.

"Come with me," he said, moving toward the gallery entrance. Jackie had no choice but to follow since he had her hand so fast in his. He got her outside and it was suddenly quiet, and much cooler, the night air smelling of fragrant flowers. Eric pulled her halfway down the block until they were in the shadows of a building and they couldn't hear the noise from the gallery they'd just left. Jackie had to hurry to keep up with him. He stopped suddenly and put her back against the side of the building, and grabbed her by the shoulders.

"We can't stay out here very long."

"Eric . . ."

"I have only one question to ask you," he interrupted urgently.

Jackie stared, confused at him.

"Do you love me?"

Her stomach dropped away as they confronted each other. She was afraid to be honest with him. Afraid to tell him the truth as she had known it for weeks. Afraid that he would nevertheless see. Eric shook her impatiently.

"Well?"

"Y . . . yes. Yes, I love you." She sounded breathless. It was said.

Eric's brow cleared; his jaw stopped tensing. He released her shoulders and stepped closer to cup her face in both hands. Jackie's eyes filled with tears and the image of Eric began to swim before her.

"There's no need to cry. Don't you realize that I love you, too?" he said hoarsely, bending down to kiss her lightly, like a promise. Their lips separated and Eric gathered her gently into his embrace. Jackie finally came back to life, and melted into his arms with a small sob, holding on to him.

"Eric, I still don't understand!" Jackie cried. She could feel Eric chuckle deep in his chest. It had the sound of relief in it.

"What? That I love you or that you love me?" he whispered, kissing her ear.

"No, everything else."

Eric pulled back to look at her. "I promise I'll explain everything later. Will you wait until after the opening?" He searched
her face, his fingers brushing gently over the smooth skin.

"Yes."

"Good! Now if I recall correctly, there are at least two editors
inside looking for a book to print. Have you met them yet?"

"No. I didn't know any had been invited," she said, dazed.

"That was Carol Winters's doing, but I hinted it might be a
good idea. You *do* still want to get your book published?"

"Of course!" she said strongly, pulling herself together.

"Fine. Now let's go back inside and enjoy this thing. It's for
both of us, you know!" His look made her smile happily at him,
her eyes sparkling brightly.

Eric reached and took the flower from her hair and put it into
his buttonhole. Again taking her hand he pulled her back to the
gallery and inside. From that point on, Jackie recovered her
spirit and peace of mind. If Eric really meant that he loved her
then she could bear anything.

At some point during the festivities a photographer from a
local paper took pictures of Eric and Jackie together. He commented on what a handsome pair they made. Jackie stole a
glance at Eric only to find him smiling and winking at her.

"Yes, I think so too," he said to her quietly before they were
again separated.

Carol Winters introduced her to one of the editors, a schol-
arly-looking black man in his early sixties, and the other, a
vampish young woman from a local university press, introduced
herself later. Gwen was also introduced as the author, and a
business arrangement of some kind looked promising.

Continually during the evening, Eric caught her eye to smile,
or just look with contentment at her. He found an excuse once
or twice to brush past her and touch an arm or a shoulder. They
wanted to be alone together, and the unfolding evening became
one of subtle torment and sweet promises.

Jackie found Hannah sometime later seated in a corner, flirt-
ing outrageously with the scholarly editor, who seemed overwhelmed but fascinated by her. Jackie left Hannah with her
audience, smiling to herself as she walked away. She and Gwen
literally bumped into each other at the wine table and Jackie
grabbed her arm before she could escape.

"You are a rat, Gwen, for doing that to me. You knew all along who Eric was!"

"That's not true!" Gwen defended herself with a laugh. "I only figured it out after I got here and spoke to Spence."

Jackie frowned. "Why do you insist on calling him Spence? Who in the world is Spence?"

"Spence is Eric," Gwen said simplistically, teasing. Jackie pinched her arm.

"Ouch! After all I've done for you!"

"You've given me a headache, that's what you've done!"

Gwen shook her head sadly, rubbing her bruised arm. "People in love get so mean. I swear! Okay, I'll talk. He's Eric Spencer Davidson. Spencer is his mother's maiden name!"

Jackie continued to frown. "So?"

"Well, as I told you, Spence was my brother's best friend at college, but they both had the same first name! We took to calling Spence Spence—I mean Eric Spence—you know what I mean—when my brother first started bringing him home. He's always been Spence to us. I forget half the time that his real name is Eric."

"When I got here and you started talking about your guide I admit I was curious. But when I finally spoke to Spence and he told me all about this fantastic lady he was in love with, I really got suspicious. I put two and two together and asked him about you. It turned out I was right, but he made me promise not to tell you anything. He said he had his reasons."

"But what were they?"

Gwen hesitated, her smile softening on her friend. "Jackie, one of the things you learned the hard way through modeling was that people didn't always see who you really are. They get all caught up in the glossy cover and forget all the other stuff underneath. You said as much to Eric. But then you turned around and did the same thing to him!"

Jackie immediately recognized the truth in that, and she was shocked that she'd been so insensitive. She hugged herself and briefly closed her eyes.

"You took him at face value instead of giving him a chance to show you all he really was," Gwen added.

"Gwen," Jackie said, "I was so scared."

"I know, hon. Spence saw that but he wanted you to find out

all by yourself how wrong you were about him. He wanted you to see how it was possible for anyone to be wrong, make mistakes. You made a mistake with Mark, but you should have learned something from that beyond just being defensive!"

Jackie grimaced, "I know, I know!" she moaned. "I'm so sorry."

"You don't need to apologize to me. Look, when I saw how confused you were I begged Spence to let me tell you everything, but he said no. And you know what? Even though it might have made it easier for you both at first, I think his way was best.

"And I was right. I told you you'd like him!"

Jackie's smile lit up her whole face. "Yes, you were right. I do think he's wonderful!"

By the end of the evening a little more than half of Jackie's pictures were committed to sales, a little red dot placed in the corner of the frame to indicate that. She was aglow with joy. Eric turned from a conversation with Carol Winters just as Hannah came over with a pained expression on her face. She looked at Jackie.

"Lord, darlin', I don't mind telling you my feet are killing me! But it was a beautiful show. I'm proud of you!"

"Thank you, Hannah," Jackie responded, taking Hannah's plump hand in hers. "I guess you're ready to go home?"

"That sounds lovely!" Hannah admitted with a tired sigh.

Eric put an arm possessively around Jackie's waist and squeezed. "Let me have your car keys," he said softly to her.

Jackie frowned, but took them out of her purse and put them into Eric's outstretched hand. Eric then passed the keys to Gwen.

"You can see to it that Hannah gets home. Jackie is coming with me. And don't wait up for her!"

He didn't wait for reaction or response as, his hand on Jackie's waist, he guided her out the gallery door. Behind her Jackie could hear Hannah's soft amused laughter.

The special meal, delayed by several nerve-wracking days, was wonderful and well worth the wait. Under the intimate glow of the restaurant's candlelight Jackie felt mellow, sated—and in love. She and Eric wrapped themselves in a cocoon of privacy with eyes and thoughts only for each other. The amused maitre d' kept the interruptions at their table to a minimum, all in the cause of love.

They were through with the elaborate French meal before the conversation came back to the events of the last month or so. Eric lit a cigarette and with his free hand reached out for one of Jackie's, his thumb stroking gently over the soft skin.

"I guess the whole explanation goes back to the very beginning. What was it you thought of me when we first met?" he asked with a slight curious smile, mocking her in his familiar way.

"You told me you were a painter," Jackie said uncomfortably.

"That's not what I mean," Eric said softly, squeezing her hand. "And you actually thought much less than that." He waited for her to speak.

"I thought you seemed aimless. I thought you had no goals or purposes in your life. And I thought you were arrogant and pompous. . . ."

"Don't forget orthopedic and dull!" Eric chuckled, blowing out smoke.

"Oh my God! Did Gwen really tell I said that?"

"That and a few other things. Like how you didn't want to meet me. And she told me a few things about you."

"Like what?" She was curious.

Eric inhaled from his cigarette and shook the ash from the end. He watched her face, the planes of his own looking strong and clearly defined under the light. "Like you'd been badly hurt and confused, and not to hurt you anymore. As a matter of fact she threatened me with bodily harm if I did."

"How?" Jackie asked, astounded by such protectiveness from Gwen.

Eric quirked a brow, chuckling in his chest in amusement. "She said she'd get her brother after me!"

Jackie laughed with him.

"But I had no intentions of hurting you," Eric continued seriously.

"Just what were your intentions?" she asked archly.

"Strictly honorable," he crooned low, the sound suggestive and private.

"You confused me," Jackie admitted, examining their clasped

hands. "You seemed so tuned in to me. Too aware—" She stopped.

"For someone who was a mere painter?" Eric added.

Reluctantly she nodded. "I'm very ashamed of the way I felt at first. You weren't like anyone I'd ever met."

"I hope not." He smiled, searching her pretty face.

"You made me feel so hostile, so defenseless and open. And you always seemed to know what I was feeling. It was scary. I didn't know if I could trust you, and I was afraid to."

"I know." Eric frowned, signaled the waiter for the check. "I could see right away I'd have to go slow with you."

Jackie looked at Eric in surprise. "But how could you tell?"

"Jackie . . ." he said softly, for her ears only, "your vulnerability was hanging out all over the place. There was an invisible sign across your forehead stamped 'Damaged heart. Do not approach. Do not pass Go'!

"You were very cautious and protective of yourself. It showed in the way you held yourself physically aloof, and in your conversation. I wanted to get next to you the moment I saw you. But I knew from our first conversation I had to give you time to trust me, to let down your defenses long enough to see that hurting or using you was the last thing on my mind."

Jackie looked at him amazed, seeing the truth of his words in his serious expression.

"I don't know what I would have done if you hadn't agreed to letting me guide you around the coast. Probably kidnap you, or park myself on your doorstep!"

Jackie smiled at that. "Somehow I can't imagine you parked on anybody's doorstep."

"That's right!" Eric confirmed. "But that's how much I wanted to see you again and get to know you. Believe me, you didn't make it easy!"

"So you've said," Jackie murmured, hypnotized by his loving look.

"I also once told you I'd figure out why you gave up modeling."

"And have you?" she asked, curious herself to know the answer.

"Umm hum," he said, smiling at her gently, as if the answer he'd found explained everything. "Modeling is a superficial occupation. People only get to know you on the top layer—your hair, your figure, how you dress. They never take the time to find out how you work inside, what makes you happy or sad. Or what you might want to do with your life, maybe—five years from now."

Jackie pulled her hand away from his, suddenly feeling transparent. Eric recaptured it.

"You wanted to be taken seriously, for the person you are inside . . . and so did I," he finished softly.

Jackie drew in a sharp breath.

"But I didn't."

"Not at first," he agreed, "but I could see the change."

"When?"

He slowly smiled at her, his brows lifting upward. "The first time you let me kiss you. I knew then even though you wouldn't admit it. I also think you were surprised and frightened of how I made you feel. Weren't you?" he finished on a soft note. "If you weren't beginning to feel something for me you never would have allowed it."

Jackie looked at him, her lips barely parted, her eyes staring into his, and Eric had the answer he wanted. Eric paid the check and looked at her. Her rampant curls were combed from the neck up to the top of her head, a cascade of loose ones falling over her forehead. Her cheeks were tinged just now with a natural color, and her eyes were soft and questioning. Eric watched her mouth. Involuntarily her tongue nervously moistened the surface. Eric looked back to her eyes.

"Let's get out of here," he suggested. Jackie nodded silently and gathered her things. Once outside the restaurant, she felt unsure. She turned to him.

"I guess you'll take me home now?" she asked, on a sigh.

"Yes." He smiled lopsided. "You're coming home with me. We have a few things to discuss in private. Don't worry, Hannah knows where you'll be and she understands."

Jackie nodded happily as they walked to Eric's car. Jackie didn't remember having seen it before, and Eric explained that he'd left it with his sister to cut down on the temptation to do other things besides painting. On the front seat Eric possessively reached out a hand to bring her close to him again.

The ride seemed so short, as Jackie wondered what to expect

now. She couldn't help her heart racing a little in anticipation, but she wouldn't let her feelings take anything for granted either.

Eric pulled the car off the road at the familiar break and the car curved its way down the last stretch to the small house on the pond. Eric turned off the motor and turned to her in the black darkness of the car, unable to really see her, but knowing exactly every feature of her by heart.

Jackie suddenly felt the need to say something, to make the first overture to him so that he'd be sure of how she felt. "I love you. . . ." she whispered, finally overcoming her insecurities. It was all she was able to say as Eric responded by turning his head to capture her mouth, stifling any further flow of words. All she could think of was how foolish she'd been and how close she'd come to losing Eric.

"Let's go inside," he said thickly, reaching past her to open the car door.

In the small house Eric removed his jacket and tie, and quickly got a fire going against the cool night air. Jackie quietly watched him, her breathing shallow and irregular as she anticipated his next move. Eric stood up and walked slowly toward her, the firelight playing games on his face. He settled his arms around the small of her back and contemplated her lovingly.

"I wasn't sure I'd ever see you here again." He curved the lower part of her body into his, and brushed her temple with his lips.

She closed her eyes dreamily against his gentle assault on her senses.

"Were you really taking a break from painting, or was that just an excuse to spend time with me?"

"Both. I'd been at it pretty hard, and I needed a break. I only had a few more canvases to do and I figured they could wait a few days while I went in hot pursuit of the elusive Jacqueline Taylor from New York.

"Then the show deadline was right on top of me and I had to get those paintings done. Believe me, it was hell having to tell you I had other things to do." His mouth nuzzled her cheek again, and he tightened his hold.

Jackie sighed, absentmindedly twisting loose a button on Eric's shirt. "It was hell having to hear it. It made me feel insecure and defensive again. I thought you'd just decided not to be bothered."

Eric chuckled. "Oh, I was bothered all right! Shall I tell you about all the cold showers I've taken?"

Jackie shook her head in embarrassment. She hadn't realized it hadn't been easy for him either.

"What happens now?" she asked, barely audible.

Eric's face for a quick second showed surprise, delight, and warm love. He put his hands closer around her and lightly pressed kisses to her throat.

"I've got two important questions to ask you, my love," he whispered in her ear.

Jackie closed her eyes, her whole body relaxed against Eric's. She felt safe and protected.

"The first thing I want to know, Jackie, is have I answered all your questions?"

"Yes," she breathed. She couldn't have asked another question if her life depended on it.

"Are you sure?"

"I'm sure."

"Positive?"

"Eric . . ."

"Then *I* have one more question."

"Yes?"

"Will you marry me?"

Jackie went very still. She was almost totally surrounded by Eric's warmth, and in that moment of her silence, he tried to pull her even closer. He felt the goose bumps on her flesh and frowned.

"Jackie?" he asked, puzzled. He pulled his arm free and turned her face to him, seeing a doubtful, almost shy look on her face. He felt uncertain himself, not understanding right away her emotion.

"Jackie, I love you," he said to her, one hand cupping the side of her face, his thumb under her chin.

For weeks she'd fenced with him, keeping him at a distance, being strong and independent and indeed proving she could manage on her own. Until finally she'd relented enough to let him show her love. What did it mean now that she'd hesitate because he wanted to marry her?

"Jackie? Don't you want to?" he asked, the possibility too strong to be ignored. After all, she'd been that way once before.

She nodded, her eyes closed tightly against him. "Yes, I do, but . . ."

"But what?" he asked gently, trying hard to understand.

"Oh, Eric . . . I . . ."

Eric looked at her, dumbfounded. Then he relaxed with a smile of relief, putting her face against his shoulder. "Jackie," he began, "I don't believe your first marriage had very much to do with you. It was the wrong time, and the wrong person, and for the wrong reasons. I love you. And I want to marry you because I love you." His voice was shaky with emotion. "Let me try and make you happy!"

"But you do!" she said with strong feeling. "I just didn't think you'd want to."

"I *want* to! And I don't care where as long as it's soon!" he said with a tremor in his voice. He smiled as he bent to kiss her eyelids until they fluttered open for her to peer with uncertainty at him.

"My grandmother was right," he whispered. "And we've waited long enough. Our time is now, and I want you."

Jackie's frown slowly smoothed away until she offered a tentative smile and said, "Oh, Eric, I've found myself, and through doing that, I've found you. I guess Hannah was right when she told me good things come to those who wait."

"And, my love, the waiting is over for the both of us," he whispered as he gently kissed her and felt her surrender to the promise of their love.